BAD LIAR

USA Today and International Bestselling Author

Lauren Rowe

Books by Lauren Rowe

The Reed Rivers Trilogy (to be read in order)
Bad Liar
Beautiful Liar
Beloved Liar

The Club Trilogy (to be read in order)
The Club: Obsession
The Club: Reclamation
The Club: Redemption
The Club: Culmination (A Full-Length Epilogue Book)

The Josh and Kat Trilogy (to be read in order)
Infatuation
Revelation
Consummation

The Morgan Brothers (a series of related standalones):
Hero
Captain
Ball Peen Hammer
Mister Bodyguard
ROCKSTAR

The Misadventures Series (a series of unrelated standalones):
Misadventures on the Night Shift
Misadventures of a College Girl
Misadventures on the Rebound

Standalone Psychological Thriller/Dark Comedy
Countdown to Killing Kurtis

Music Playlist for *Bad Liar*

"Had a Dad"—Jane's Addiction
"Father of Mine"—Everclear
"Hustle"—Pink
"Bad Guy"—Billie Eilish
"Truth Hurts"—Lizzo
"Bad Liar"—Selena Gomez

Chapter 1
Reed

Fifteen years ago

As the sorority girl in the purple wig kneels before me, her mouth working enthusiastically on me, I lean back in my armchair and try to clear my mind. I don't want to think about my father's lifeless body dangling in his prison cell while this girl is sucking me off. Actually, I don't want to think about that under any circumstances, obviously. But after getting that horrible call this morning, I can't stop imagining the grisly scene. I thought getting this pretty girl onto her knees would distract me from the images ravaging my mind.

Apparently not.

I should probably pull her off me. Pay her the usual fifty bucks and explain I'm just not feeling it tonight. But my dick is rock hard in her mouth, despite the chaos swirling inside my mind... So, fuck it. I sit back, close my eyes, and will her talented mouth to coax my racing mind into a temporary state of amnesia.

This girl isn't a professional, despite appearances, even though she's presently sucking my cock for cash. She's a student here at UCLA, the same as me—a fresh-faced sorority girl I met at a costume party at my fraternity house a month ago. The theme of the party was "Hookers and Pimps," and she was dressed like *Pretty Woman*. So, naturally, there was no shortage of raunchy jokes throughout the night... all of

1

which ultimately led to her following me to my room upstairs and giving me head like a pro.

When the girl finished her task that night, I patted her head, congratulated her on a job well done, and handed her a fifty. I was joking, of course. Being an ass. Acting like a john. But damned if this pretty woman didn't surprise me by taking my fifty with gusto, stuffing it into her push-up bra, and purring, "Call me whenever you've got another fifty to spend." And I've been paying her for sex ever since. Fifty bucks for a blowjob and a hundred to fuck her. Plus, twenty bucks to eat her out—that last item being completely backwards and stupid, I know. This girl should be paying *me* to lick her into a frenzy, especially considering how well I do it. How hard I make her come, each and every time. But it's okay. I figure I've spent far more than twenty bucks on far stupider things in my nineteen years than making a pretty girl come like a freight train.

I gotta say, this whole *Pretty Woman* experience has taught me something interesting about myself. Something I didn't know before. Namely, that I get off paying for sex. It doesn't matter which of us is having the orgasm, or what particular sex act we're doing. I've realized I like paying for it because it makes things uncomplicated. We both know what we're getting, and what we're not. Specifically, we know feelings aren't involved. I'm not her Prince Charming, and she knows it, which, in turn, immunizes me from hearing any of the usual deal-breakers women say to me around the one-month mark. The stuff that sends me running for the hills. *Let down your guard, Reed. I want you to let me in, Reed. Am I your girlfriend or not, Reed?* And, of course, the biggest deal-breaker of them all: *I think I'm falling in love with you, Reed.*

I touch my fake whore's purple hair as she continues her enthusiastic work, trying in vain to clear my tortured mind. But it's no use. Even with her working on me, I can't stop imagining my father's lifeless body dangling in his prison cell.

Why'd he do it?

I understand what *specifically* triggered him to wrap that cord around his neck this morning: the feds tracking down the last of his secret offshore accounts. I'm just having a hard time comprehending how *that* particular event finally pushed my father over the edge, after everything that's happened over the past ten years.

I mean, shit, my father didn't kill himself during my parents' bitter divorce and custody battle. Or, right after that, when Mom suffered a catastrophic mental breakdown and had to be institutionalized. Dad didn't off himself six years ago, after the jury sent him to prison for financial fraud. Or when Dad's photo was splashed across the news as the poster boy for "corporate greed." If my father was going to hang himself, why not do it during any of that? Or, at least, during those first few years of his incarceration, when he was forced to sit back and watch his thirteen-year-old getting passed around from one distant relative to another before finally landing in a home for teenage rejects at age fourteen. Honestly, if Dad was going to end it all, I would have preferred he'd have done it then, when his son got shipped off to that horrible hell of a group home. At least, that way, I would have felt like Dad actually gave a shit about me, more than his stolen fortune.

But, no. Apparently, being an incarcerated felon with an ex-wife in the loony bin and a fourteen-year-old basket-case of a son in foster care was perfectly survivable to Terrence Rivers. Just as long as he still had his secret pot of gold. But, God forbid, the man was stripped of his last illicit penny, and, suddenly, his life just wasn't worth living anymore. Asshole.

Well, news flash, Dad: you're not the only one who went flat broke today. Thanks to the purportedly "untraceable" trust fund you set aside for me, the one that was supposed to transfer to me on my twenty-first birthday, I'm now as poor as the poorest guy in my fraternity house. But am I going to kill myself over today's reversal of fortune? No. Because unlike you, Dad, I know that no matter what life throws at me—which, by the way, has been a fucking lot in my nineteen years—I'll always come out on top in the end. Despite what I've been through these past ten years, despite what I've had to steel myself against, to fight against, to overcome, I've never lost sight of my future destiny—the one I've seen in my dreams—and I won't let anyone keep me from achieving it. *Not even you.*

Thanks to you, people hear my last name and think things like "liar" and "thief" and "fraud." But one day, after I've built my empire from nothing but my blood, sweat, and tears and relentlessness, people will hear the name Rivers and think words like "mogul" and "winner" and "self-made man." And if not any of those things, then, at least, they'll think "Hey, there's that asshole who's living the life of my dreams." Because if I can't earn the world's respect, thanks to your name, then I'll settle for earning their *envy.*

At that last thought, I grip my fake whore's fake hair, shove myself even farther down her supple throat, and release with a loud groan. A moment later, as I pull out of her, I'm trembling—but not from physical exertion. No, in this moment, I'm quaking from the resolve flooding my veins.

"I don't need him," I grit out through clenched teeth. And, by God, for the first time in my life, I'm positive it's the truth. In fact, I don't need anyone. At my comment, the sorority girl looks up at me quizzically. But before she says a word, I pull a fifty from my wallet and toss it onto the brown carpet at her knees. "Well done, Pretty Woman. Now run along. I've got something important to do."

She looks surprised. "*Now?* It's midnight."

"And I'm running late."

She makes a face that lets me know she's offended—and for a split-second, I think she's going to tell me to fuck off, as she should. But, nope. The spineless sorority girl who so desperately wants to be liked rises and slides into my lap.

4

"What's wrong with you tonight? You've been acting weird all night."

I've got no interest in baring my soul to this girl. Or to anyone, for that matter. I say nothing.

Sighing, she puts her arms around my neck and presses her nose against mine. "Let's not play Pretty Woman anymore. I'm tired of that game. It was fun at first, but not anymore."

Shit. I have a feeling a deal-breaker will be coming my way, any minute now.

"Tell me what's wrong," she coos, stroking my cheek. "You look so sad—like you could cry. Come on, Reed. Tell me what's going on. Let me in."

And there it is. Right on cue. *Let me in*. With a deep exhale, I grab her wrist to stop her from caressing my cheek. "You're reading me all wrong, Audrey. That BJ was just so damned good, it almost brought me to tears."

She holds my gaze for a moment, her blue eyes telling me she's not buying my bullshit. But does she push back? No. Of course not. Because she's a doormat. With a deep sigh, she stands, slides off her purple wig, revealing her blonde tresses underneath, and drags her tight little ass toward the door. "Call me tomorrow?" she asks, her hand on the knob.

A puff of scorn escapes my nose. I won't be calling this girl tomorrow, or ever again. Not now that I know she wants more than I'm willing to give her. But seeing as how I've got bigger fish to fry than setting a pretty girl straight about her foolish, unrequited crush on me, I reply, "Not knowing what tomorrow will bring is one of life's greatest pleasures."

She scoffs, and a part of me hopes she'll finally grow a pair and tell me to fuck off. But, no. Passive little Audrey Meisner rolls her eyes, blows me a kiss, and slips quietly out the door, never to return to my room again, unbeknownst to her.

When the girl is gone, I shove earbuds into my ears and

blast my current obsession—an indie band I stumbled across on YouTube. I swear, if these guys would only market themselves properly, they'd be the biggest thing going. Music blaring, I grab a whiskey bottle and a joint and flop back into my chair, determined to get shitfaced and stupid until I pass out cold.

But after only a couple swigs of whiskey, before I've even lit up the joint, I suddenly remember something a fraternity brother said a couple months ago during a poker game at the house—a comment that suddenly makes me want to add him to the guest list for my solo pity party.

Josh Faraday.

He's the richest guy in my fraternity house. Maybe even at UCLA, thanks to a massive inheritance he got last year, split down the middle with his fraternal twin. But money isn't why I'm suddenly thinking about calling Josh. It's the shocking thing he said.

I was sitting next to Josh at the rowdy poker table when another fraternity brother, a hard-partier named Alonso, stumbled through the front door, looking like a drunken hobo in a back alley. So, of course, everyone started slinging insults at Alonso. Telling him he looked like roadkill, etcetera. It was all the usual stuff—except for what Josh said. "Damn, Alonso," Josh threw out. "You look as fucked-up as my father did the last time I saw him... and he'd just blown his brains out."

I was shocked by Josh's comment. Before then, I'd known Josh's dad had passed away right before Josh had started UCLA, but I'd assumed, like everyone else, that Josh's dad had died of natural causes. And also that Josh, understandably heartbroken about his loss, didn't want to talk about it. Not that I would have asked Josh about his father's death, regardless. I never ask anyone questions about their parents, lest they get the bright idea to ask me about mine. But, now, sitting here in my fraternity room with nobody but my buddies Jack and Mary Juana, I'm suddenly hell-bent on asking Josh a thousand questions about the shocking thing he said while sitting next to me at the poker table that night.

My heart clanging, I rip my earbuds out and grab my mobile.

"Are you at the house?" I ask Josh, interrupting his greeting.

"No, I'm in my car, about fifteen minutes away. What's up?"

I swallow hard. "Don't mention this to anyone, but my dad's been in prison the past six years, and, today, I found out he hanged himself. I'm hoping you've got some words of wisdom about how to handle the situation."

With a heavy sigh, Josh says he's sorry to hear the bad news, and that he's turning his car around. "About that confidentiality thing, though...?" he says. "You're on speaker right now in my car, and Henn's sitting here. Sorry. I didn't think to mention it before you started talking. But don't worry. Henn's a steel trap."

Henn's voice says, "Absolutely."

"Henn's the best guy in the world to have around in any kind of shit storm, Reed. Would it be okay for me to bring him along to hang out? I think, once you get to know him, you'll be glad I did."

I pause. I've interacted now and again with Peter "Henn" Hennessy—a funny, nerdy hacker dude from our pledge class—but always in loud, boisterous groups. I'm not sure tonight is the night I want to get to know him better.

As if reading my mind, Josh says, "Other than my brother, Henn's the only person I've talked to about my dad. Honestly, I don't know what I would have done without Henny this past year. He's been the best friend a guy could ask for. My rock."

Emotion unexpectedly rises inside me, constricting my throat. I've never had a "best friend" before, let alone a "rock." But, sitting here now, I feel near-desperation to have both. I take a deep breath and push my emotion down— something I've grown accustomed to doing these past ten years. "Henn can come, as long as he's down to get shitfaced. That's the price of admission to this particular pity party."

"I'm down," Henn says. "Whatever you need, I'm in."

"That goes double for me," Josh adds. "Whatever you need, we're here for you."

"Thanks. I'll tell you exactly what I need. Three things. One, to get shitfaced and stoned out of my fucking mind tonight, until the images in my head fade to black. Two, to talk to someone before I pass out who can help me make sense of this fucked-up situation. And three, and this is the biggie: I need to figure out a Plan B."

"A Plan B? For what?"

I take a deep, steadying breath. "For conquering the world, all by myself."

Chapter 2
Georgina

Present day

As I walk past swarms of students on my way through campus, I get a call from my stepsister, Alessandra. Well, my *former* stepsister, technically. As busy as we both are—Alessandra's majoring in music in Boston while I'm majoring in journalism here at UCLA, plus, we both work part-time jobs—we still manage to talk multiple times per day.

"Are you headed to that career-thing for journalism students now?" Alessandra asks.

I press my phone into my ear to hear my stepsister's soft voice above the din of campus life around me. "I'm walking there now. But the event isn't for journalism students. It's for music students. CeeCee Rafael is the only journalist on the panel."

"Who are the other panelists?"

"Bigwigs in the music industry, I guess."

Alessandra gasps, which isn't a surprise, considering she's obsessed with music. "Who are the bigwigs?"

"I don't know. I saw CeeCee's name and looked no further. Hold on." I quickly locate the event flyer and text it to Alessandra. "I'm praying I'll be the only journalism major with the brilliant idea to crash a music school event to get a job."

"Pure genius."

"Only if it works."

I have reason to be skeptical, unfortunately, based on the countless résumés I've sent out over the past two months, to no avail. Thankfully, I've got my bartending gig to fall back on after graduation next week, and my boss, Bernie, has already said I can pick up additional shifts through the summer. It was a nice offer, and I appreciate it, but if I'm being honest, bartending with my degree in hand would be soul crushing. Plus, working at the bar throughout the summer would be a tough commute if I have to move back to my dad's house in the Valley after graduation, which I'm planning to do.

"CeeCee won't care about your grades once she meets you," Alessandra assures me. "Just come right out and explain why your grades tanked last year. She's known for being really active with cancer charities. Oh my God! Georgie! I'm looking at the event flyer, and it says—"

Bam.

After turning a corner, I walk smack into the broad chest of the one person I have no desire to see: UCLA football god, Bryce McKellar. I first met Bryce months ago, while waiting in line for coffee on-campus, and sparks instantly flew. He wasn't just physically gorgeous, but charismatic and cocky, too. Best of all, he had a bit of a dark edge to him. A dick-vibe. Which, unfortunately, is my thing, I'm not proud to say. But since I stupidly thought my relationship with Shawn, the biggest dick of them all, was still intact, I took off after getting my coffee and didn't stick around to flirt with Bryce.

Of course, once I found out Shawn was a lying, cheating dirt-bag dick, I kept an eye out for Mr. Football, hoping to bump into him again. But, unfortunately, I never did... until a few days ago... which was when, out of the blue, like manna from heaven, I spotted Bryce standing outside Royce Hall, looking even hotter than he had at the coffee place months before. And, to my thrill, when Bryce's eyes landed on mine, they lit up, every bit as much as they had during our first encounter at the coffee place.

Immediately, Bryce jogged over to me that day on-campus, and we made flirty small talk. "I've actually been keeping an eye out for you," Bryce told me, flashing me his dazzling smile. But since we were both in a rush—Bryce to get to class and me to get to the campus gym to teach a spin class—he quickly got my number and promised he'd text me "really soon." Which he did. Ten minutes later, as a matter of fact. And then again that same afternoon. And, again, later that night. But each time Bryce texted, he'd caught me at a bad time, and I could never text with him for long. "Damn, you're even busier than I am," Bryce texted. To which I replied, "Hustle beats talent, when talent doesn't hustle, baby."

We agreed to touch base the next day with an actual phone call, so we could compare our busy schedules and find a time to "connect"... which I prayed was code for "find a good time to have sex." Because, Lordy, I'm ready to have some good, fun sex with a smoking hot guy. No strings attached. I haven't had sex since Shawn, and I think I'm suffering from physical withdrawals. But since the last thing I want is another relationship right now, especially with another athlete, "no strings fun" is the only thing on my menu.

Unfortunately, though, things didn't go according to my big plans. When Bryce and I finally had that phone conversation the following day—for a full hour, in fact—it quickly became apparent we weren't on the same page. Not at all. As it turned out, Mr. Football wasn't the sexy, cocky, bad boy I'd been projecting onto him. In fact, much to my dismay, he made it clear during our call he's been raised by his God-fearing momma to be a one-woman kind of guy. To always, *always* look for a girl who, get this, is "wife material."

And it only got worse from there. As I sat there silently

freaking out on my end of the line, Bryce went on to proclaim he's not looking for an "easy" woman, like all the girls who throw themselves at him, day in and out, but, instead, wants a faithful, loyal girl who'll "support him religiously" through the NFL draft and beyond. Someone he can trust. Someone he can lean on. Someone who'll love him, unconditionally, and not care about all the money and fame coming his way. All of which I thought was a bit much to say during our first phone conversation. I mean, come on, is it really so wrong for a young, horny girl to want a smoking hot guy for nothing but his dazzling smile and hot body?

But Bryce had more bombs to drop during that crazy-ass phone call. As I sat in stunned silence, thinking maybe I was being punked, he asked, "Do you believe in love at first sight, Georgie?

"Uh, no," I replied honestly, my insides knotting at how badly I'd misjudged him. "Why? Do you?" Obviously, I shouldn't have said that last part. Indeed, the moment my question left my lips, I knew I'd messed up.

"Not before I met you," Bryce replied. And I swear I threw up, just a little bit, into my mouth. Just like that, the lady-boner I'd had for Bryce McKellar at the coffee place sagged to my knees, and I couldn't get off the call fast enough.

I knew in that moment I'd have to come clean with Bryce and confess I'm not the future wife he thinks I am. That, in fact, at this particular stage of my life, I'm probably closer to the "easy women" who throw themselves at him, thanks to the past couple of years that have left me emotionally drained and determined to fly solo for a while. But right then, I was too stunned to make that particular speech to Bryce. And so, I got off the phone without saying any of it—and also without confirming any plans to "connect" with him any time soon.

But now, Bryce is here. Holding my shoulders so I don't crumple to the ground after bouncing off his hard chest. And, this time, I can't simply hang up my phone to avoid him.

"Bryce," I gasp out, teetering in his firm grasp.

"Are you okay?" he replies, chuckling.

"Yeah. Sorry. I was running."

"I could see that." He grins. "I was just about to text you, actually."

"Oh, yeah? Wow. Hang on." I pick my phone up off the ground—noting, thankfully, that the screen didn't crack upon impact—and breathlessly tell my stepsister I've got to call her back.

"Did you say *Bryce?*" Alessandra says.

"I did."

"As in, Mr. Football?"

"Correct."

"Only pretend to hang up. I want to listen in."

"Okay, bye."

As instructed, I pretend to disconnect the call, and return to Bryce, my stomach churning and my mind racing.

Bryce says, "I was going to text and ask what you're doing tonight."

"Sorry, I'm working at the bar until about two thirty."

"Hey, that works for me," he says. "I'm a night owl."

Shit. Fuck. "I can't. I've got class on Friday mornings, so I always race home after my Thursday-night shift to catch a few hours of sleep." I look at my watch. "Shoot. I'm running late for an event in North Campus. Gotta go!" And off I go, resolved to call Bryce tomorrow to tell him the truth: *I'm not looking for a relationship. I'm not looking to support any guy's dreams "religiously" or otherwise at this particular time. In summary, I'm just not feeling it.*

The moment I'm out of earshot of Bryce, I bring my phone to my ear. "Ally?"

Alessandra laughs. "*Coward.*"

"I know. I'll call him tomorrow and set him straight."

"You realize you're the only girl at UCLA who'd ever turn that boy down, right?"

"Dude, he's looking for a freaking wife."

"Running away all the time, you're only going to make him want you more. I'm sure he's used to girls throwing themselves at him."

"Oh, he is. And they can have him. He's way too big a momma's boy for me."

"Oh, the horror. A genuinely nice guy."

"You know what I mean. I'm still in my bad-boy phase, as I should be. It's what's going to make me ready for Mr. Right whenever he finally comes along in six point five years."

"I'm shocked you don't want to give Bryce a quick test drive before you cut him loose. Even if he's a Cling-On, why not at least hit that hard body *hard* before turning him away? He's panty-melting, Georgie. I looked him up after you told me about him, and almost had a stroke at his hotness."

"I know. If only he'd played it the least bit cool with me, the way he did at the coffee place that first time, I would have been hitting that hard body *hard* as early as this week. As it is, I can't run away fast enough." I sigh audibly at the heartbreaking situation. "Now, what were we talking about before I bumped into Mr. Love at First Sight?"

"Reed Rivers. I was freaking out he's listed as one of the panelists."

"I didn't hear any of that. Who's Reed Rivers?"

"The founder of River Records—the record label."

"Never heard of it."

"Well, you've sure as hell heard of their bands and artists. Hang on. I'll consult the mighty Google." Alessandra pauses briefly. And then, "Holy shit. The River Records roster is insanity. They've got *both* Red Card Riot *and* 22 Goats. Plus, Danger Doctor Jones, Laila Fitzgerald, 2Real, Aloha Carmichael, Fugitive Summer, Watch Party... "

"Holy crap."

"Right? The list goes on and on. That's only the top tier

of the roster, but the next tier down is still pretty damned impressive."

"Those are all my favorites."

"Those are all *everyone's* favorites. It's why every student at my school would sell their soul to get signed by River Records."

"Including you?"

"Dude, I'd sell my soul, kidneys, and freaking virginity to get signed."

I cringe. "Please, don't joke about selling your virginity. I took a class on sex trafficking this quarter that was horrifying."

"I was kidding. Obviously."

"I know. But that would be a disgusting way to lose your virginity—to some pervy old guy you don't even *like*. Also, careful what you put out into the universe. From what I've heard, the music industry is full of predators, every bit as much as the movie business. Creeps who'd happily promise a sweet little virgin like you the sun and moon, just to get into your pants."

Alessandra laughs. "Interesting your momma bear comes out to protect my virginity, but not my soul and kidneys."

"Only one scenario seems like a real-world possibility."

If I know Alessandra, she's rolling her eyes at me right now. But smiling, too. "Okay, Georgie," she says. "I promise I won't sell my virginity to anyone, okay? Well, except to Reed Rivers. I can't make the same promise when it comes to him. That man can have anything he wants."

"Stop."

She giggles. "Google him, and you'll see what I mean. Honestly, Reed wouldn't need to promise me the sun and moon in exchange for my V-card. Just an Uber ride home. Actually, not even that. I'd demand nothing from him. Take my virginity, Reed Rivers! Please!"

I can't help giggling with her. "How old is he?"

"Mid-thirties, I think. No older than forty."

Oh, my sweet Alessandra. The girl's got daddy issues, that's for sure, every bit as much as I've got mommy issues. When our parents got together, Alessandra had just lost her father in a hit and run, and I'd just lost my mother in a car accident. And both our parents wrongly thought they could find comfort and solace and a fresh start in marrying another grieving person.

Unfortunately, they quickly found out that was a bad idea. That marriage in the midst of deep grief, especially to a person with whom they had nothing in common, actually made both of them feel ten times worse in their times of need. But, whatever. As confusing and chaotic, and short-lived, as the marriage of my father and Alessandra's mother turned out to be, I wouldn't undo it, even if I could. Because it brought me my beloved sister, Alessandra.

By the time I reach the lecture hall for the music event, my breathing is slightly elevated from jogging across campus, so I take a nearby seat on a bench to finish my phone call. "So, which three songs of yours do you want me to load onto a flash drive to give to the record label guy? I'm going to get you signed to River Records, baby. Absolutely no selling your virginity required."

Alessandra sighs. "Oh, Georgie. You're so sweet. But getting me signed to River Records, especially at an event like this, would be like hitting a golf ball on Earth and landing a hole-in-one on the moon. Last year, the most amazing singer-songwriter at my school won a contest where the grand prize was having Reed personally listen to her music. And guess what? He listened and turned her down."

"That's because she's not *you*."

"She's better than me."

"Impossible. But for the sake of argument, let's say she's *as good as* you, then the reason she got turned down was she didn't have a hype-woman, like me, singing her praises."

"The odds are miniscule you'll get the chance to talk to him at all. And, if you do, it'll be four seconds where you won't have the chance to dazzle him with your patented Georgina Ricci magic. If the situation were different—if you were going to be meeting him one-on-one, I'd put money on you being able to charm him, like you do everyone else. It's a well-known fact he loves beautiful women, so I'm positive you'd be able to grab his attention. But, as it is, this event is going to be packed with hundreds of music students, all of them toting flash drives in their pockets."

My shoulders droop. "Maybe, but there's no harm in me at least trying, right?"

"*Wrong.* I don't want you speeding through a conversation with CeeCee because you're preoccupied with trying to talk to Reed for me. I've got two *years* before graduation. You've got a week. Just this once, kick my dreams to the curb and look out for number one, girl."

I watch a group of students enter the lecture hall and glance at my watch. "Ally, I hear what you're saying. But I can't be in the same building as a man who could *literally* make your dreams come true, and not—"

"Stop," Alessandra says firmly. "You need a good-paying journalism job, Georgie. Not just for yourself, but for your dad, too. Now, stop arguing with me about this and go in there and get CeeCee Rafael to take your writing samples and make all your dreams come true."

17

Chapter 3
Reed

As I park my car in a structure at UCLA, I continue grumbling on the phone to my longtime attorney, Leonard. The entire drive here, we've been talking about the latest batch of frivolous lawsuits and settlement demands leveled against my various businesses—my record label, real estate holdings, nightclubs, and more—and I'm beyond annoyed.

"It's the way of the world when you've got extra-deep pockets," Leonard says. "These plaintiffs' attorneys are hoping you'll settle their bogus claims quickly for a nominal sum, rather than paying me quadruple the amount to fight them."

"Well, they can suck my dick. I don't settle meritless claims, Leonard."

"Yes, I know. And as your attorney, may I say it's the thing I like best about you."

"Not my sparkling personality?"

"That's a distant second." I hear papers rustling on Leonard's end of the call. "Okay, let's talk about that copyright infringement suit against Red Card Riot for a second. Also bullshit?"

"Total and complete. That same chord progression can be found in everything from Mozart to Bruno Mars."

"Well, then, it should be easy to get the case dismissed on a motion. I'll just need to attach a declaration by a musicologist, explaining what you just said. Know anyone?"

"Angela McGavin. She's the head of UCLA's music

school. Coincidentally, I'll be seeing her at an event on-campus in about a half-hour. I'll chat with her about it then."

"Perfect. Lemme know. What's the event?"

"I'll be speaking on a panel, telling wide-eyed music students about the business side of the industry."

"Look at you, giving back to the college kiddies who are hoping to follow in your illustrious footsteps."

"I'm not doing it out of the goodness of my heart. I got roped into it by CeeCee."

Leonard chuckles. "Ah, the indomitable CeeCee Rafael. I find it hard to say no to that woman, myself."

"*Hard*? Try *impossible*, thanks to all the publicity she's given my up-and-comers over the years. The feature she wrote about RCR in time for their debut release is what bought me my first house." My phone buzzes and I look down. "I've got to take another call, Len. Don't forget to text me how many tickets your daughter wants for the RCR concert. I'll make sure she and her friends get backstage to meet the band."

"Wow! Thank you. You're going to win me Father of the Year with this birthday present."

"Show me some mercy on my next bill, and we'll call it even." I disconnect the call and pick up with Isabel. "Well, if it isn't 'America's Sweetheart.'"

Isabel giggles. "Oh, you saw that interview, did you? Wasn't it amazing?"

"I wouldn't call the interview 'amazing,' no. The *headline* was amazing. That's the kind of nickname that'll stick. But the interview itself was only okay. You laid on the 'relatability' factor a bit thick. The photo spread was smokin' hot and on-brand, however, although I'd have told them to lay off the photoshop, especially on your face. You're not twenty-two anymore, but why would you want to be? Overall, though, I'd say the piece was a win. It was certainly well timed, considering the studio's big announcement last week. Congratulations on that, by the way. I've always said you've got superpowers, haven't I? And now, it's official."

"Holy fuck, Reed. A simple 'Yes, Isabel, the interview was amazing' would have sufficed."

"You want me to lie to you?"

"Absolutely."

I scoff. "Don't ask for my opinion if you don't want to hear it." I check my watch. "Why are you calling me? Aren't you filming pick-ups in Toronto?"

"I've got a few days off, so I flew into LA for a meeting with the studio head. Unfortunately, though, he had a family emergency while I was in the air and needed to reschedule. Which means, lucky you, I've just landed in LA with zero plans for the next thirty-six hours. Let's fuck like rabbits! I'm a horny bunny."

"Sorry, I'm booked solid between now and the break of dawn, when I'll be boarding a flight to The Big Apple."

"Break all your silly plans. It's been way too long and I miss you."

"I would if I could." I'm not sure that's a true statement, actually.

Isabel's voice turns stiff. "You've got a hot date?"

I look at my watch again. Shit. I need to end this call in exactly four minutes to make it to the stupid panel on time. "No, I don't have a hot date—not that it'd be any of your business, if I did. I've got an event at UCLA in a few minutes, and then I'm meeting a couple friends for dinner and drinks."

Isabel sighs with relief. "Perfect. Yes, I'll join you for dinner. Thanks for asking."

"Not this time."

"Oh, come on. Whoever your friends are, they'd be thrilled to break bread with 'America's Sweetheart.'"

"Nope. It's a Boy's Night Out. Maybe next time."

"Who are the friends?"

"Josh Faraday and another guy from college you don't know."

"Josh Faraday! He'd *love* to see me! Remember how much fun you, me, Jen, and Josh—"

"That's ancient history. Josh is happily married these days."

She gasps. "*Josh Faraday is married?*"

I look at my watch again. "Yup. He's married with children and living in Seattle. And I've got to hang up in three minutes to make my event."

"Wow, I thought for sure Josh would die a bachelor, the same as you."

"So did Josh. But the minute he met his crazy wife and her even crazier family, all he wanted to do was build a white picket fence with her. He's got two babies and another on the way and says he wants to fill a minivan. Josh is so happy these days, I'd hate him if I didn't love him so much."

Isabel scoffs, and I know she's aggravated to hear me use the word "love" in relation to Josh, when I've never once said it in relation to her. "Come see me after you're done with your friends," she says. "Whatever time it is. I don't care how late you come, as long as you do." She snickers. "And then make *me* come."

My stomach tightens. If I didn't know it before this call, I know it now: I've got no desire to hook up with Isabel again. And not just because I'm busy tonight. If I were as free as a bird tonight, I'd still say no. "If you're horny, call some aspiring model or actor," I say. "Fulfill your Mrs. Robinson fantasies."

Isabel scoffs. "I'm not horny for just anyone, Reed. I want *you*." Her tone becomes vulnerable. "I miss you."

Fuck. How did I let myself get into this situation with this woman, *again*? Drunkenly fucking her at that party in the Hamptons was a felony stupid thing to do, no matter how much she swore she could handle a no-strings arrangement.

I look at my watch again. "I have to go, or I'm gonna be late. Travel safe back to the land of Maple Syrup. And congrats again on the franchise deal. I love being able to say, 'I knew her when.'"

21

"*Wait*," Isabel says sharply. "I need to see you, if only for an hour. I won't take no for an answer, Reed."

I clench my jaw. Oh, how I hate that expression. If I want to say no to a request, then I'll say no. Unless, of course, the person asking me for something is my mother, sister, CeeCee, Josh, or Henn. Also, my housekeeper, Amalia. That woman can have anything she wants from me, too—although she'd never ask, so it's a moot point. Clearly, it's time to cut the cord, once and for all. "Isabel," I say calmly. "It's obvious this 'whenever we happen to be in the same city' arrangement isn't working out as well for you as you promised it would."

"I'm not allowed to miss you?"

"You're not, actually. I certainly don't miss you."

She inhales sharply. "Don't be mean."

"I'm not. I'm being honest. I have no ill will toward you. No desire to hurt you. But the truth is I don't think about you when I'm not in your presence. Which, literally, means I don't miss you. And, clearly, being missed is something you want and need."

"Yeah, I'm such a weirdo. Do you enjoy hurting me? Is that it? You get sick pleasure from being mean to me?"

"How am I being mean? You're literally *begging* me to fuck you. If you had an ounce of self-respect, you wouldn't be telling me you 'won't take no for an answer.' You'd be telling me to fuck off."

Isabel says nothing to that. But I can tell by her stilted breathing she's holding back tears.

I soften. "I'm not good for you, Isabel. Never have been. Let's walk away, once and for all, before you get hurt again, okay?"

"You want me to walk away before I get hurt?" she spits out. "Yeah, it's a bit too late for that, Reed."

I sigh. "I've got to go. Congrats on becoming a superhero."

"Are you getting back at me for hurting you? That was a

million years ago, and we weren't even dating exclusively at the time."

"You didn't hurt me. Don't conflate my passionate desire to seek revenge against a punk-ass ingrate with a passionate desire for *you*."

She draws in a shocked breath.

"You're obviously looking for more than a sexual fling with me," I continue. "And that's not something that interests me. Not with you, not with anyone. It's nothing personal."

"Nothing personal?" she shouts. "Reed, I'm in love with you! I'm sorry if that's an inconvenient truth, but I can't help what I feel."

For a long moment, I look out the window of my sports car at the cement walls of the parking structure, feeling angry with myself for opening myself up to this drama again. And for what? Some drunken, nostalgic pussy at a party. "I can't fathom you're actually in love with me, like you're claiming. But if you are, then that's your misfortune, I guess."

"What the fuck is wrong with you?" Isabel whispers.

I can't help smiling at the question—the same one I've been asked by women my whole life. Shit, I've even asked it of myself plenty of times, too. Most memorably, when I stood next to Josh on a beach in Maui and watched him exchange marriage vows. And then again, when I stood next to Henny on my patio in the Hollywood Hills and watched him do the same. When I stood on a beach in the Bahamas and watched my baby sister say "I do." And, most recently, when I sat in a castle in France and watched CeeCee exchange marriage vows with a French billionaire, certain her third time down the aisle would be the charm, even though she and her new husband weren't even planning to reside on the same continent after the nuptials. All those times, and others, too, as I've watched the people I care about promising their eternal love to one person, I've found myself wondering, if only fleetingly... *What the fuck is wrong with me?*

"This isn't goodbye," I say, my heart softening at the sound of Isabel's sniffling. "If you need a date to a red-carpet event and you can't find anyone who looks as good in a tux as I do, then call me. And it should go without saying, your secrets will always be safe with me. We started this climb together as kids, and I'll always have your back. But if you're genuinely in love with me, like you say, then it's time for you to move on. There's no happily ever after I can offer you, sweetheart. No ending to this story where I'm the prince and you're my pretty princess, and we ride off together into the sunset on a white horse."

Isabel sniffles. "You're selling yourself short. You could be the prince, if you'd let yourself."

"I've gotta go. It's time for me to 'give back' to some college kiddies, all of whom are almost certainly plotting to ambush me with their music demos afterwards."

"*Reed.*"

"I'm sure I'll see you at all the parties during awards season. And when I do, don't worry, I'll always make sure everyone thinks you're my 'one that got away.' Not the other way around."

"Reed. *Stop.* Please. You can't just—"

Click.

Oh, yes I can.

Chapter 4
Reed

Ten years ago

I pick up my cell phone... and then immediately put it back down on my desk, my pulse pounding. I look around my garage, at the large cardboard boxes stacked against the walls, all of them filled with merch samples for RCR's upcoming debut tour. All of them requiring my approval by tomorrow. And all of them reminding me I'm going to be up shit creek if this massive gamble doesn't pan out.

I glance at the notepad on my desk, its pages covered with the furious editing notes I've scrawled for the director of RCR's debut music video. I glance at the documents stacked on my desk—licensing deals I've been chasing down for all three of my bands for the past four months. But, mostly, for Red Card Riot, the band I'm betting the farm will put my fledgling label on the map when their album debuts in two months.

Yeah, I've got to make this call. *Go big, or go home.*

"Majestic Maids," a female voice says, answering my call.

My heart pounds even harder. "Is this Francesca?"

"Yes. How may I help you?"

"I'd like to book an escort for later this month—for an important event."

"We're a cleaning service, sir. Not an escort service."

25

I tell her the name of the guy who referred me, a star midfielder for the LA Galaxy whom I met last month at one of Josh's raging parties, and the woman quickly changes her tune.

"To whom am I speaking?" she asks, her voice suddenly light and bright.

"Reed."

"Your last name, please?"

I pause, nerves tightening my belly. Am I being reckless here? It's technically illegal. But, oh well. I've come this far. Stolen from Peter to pay Paul for months now. I'm so close now, I can taste it. Which means now isn't the time to start playing it safe. I mean, come on. If a star soccer player and his teammates, plus a whole bunch of his famous friends, can trust this woman to be discreet, then I can, too.

"Rivers," I say, my tone surprisingly calm, despite the thundering of my heart.

"Hello, Mr. Rivers. I'm glad you called. When and where is your event?"

"The twenty-first, at Greystone Mansion in Beverly Hills. It's a black-tie event, so my date will need to rock a designer gown. Something that makes her look like ten million bucks."

"Not a problem. Tell me about the kind of woman you're envisioning. What type are you most attracted to?"

"Curvy brunettes always turn my head the most," I admit. "Even more than that, though, it's women with lots of confidence and sass. Actually, though, in this instance, sass maybe wouldn't be such a good idea. I don't think what personally attracts me is relevant here. For this event, the woman needs to be what *other* people covet. Someone who looks like she could walk a Victoria's Secret runway. You know, the kind of woman who looks like she could get any man she wants."

"And yet, she's chosen *you*. And what about later that

night, after the event? Would you like to spend time with her, in private—perhaps enjoy some intimate, one-on-one time? It would be a good idea to choose someone you're personally attracted to, in case you'd like to leave yourself that option."

I lean back in my leather chair and gaze up at the ceiling of my garage. At my surfboards and snowboards and kayak resting above the wooden rafters. If everything goes according to plan on the twenty-first, if I find a way to meet CeeCee Rafael at that party and pique her interest in RCR enough to secure a well-timed mention in *Rock 'n' Roll*, it'll be a whole new ballgame for me. I'll finally be able to move my operations into an actual office space—hopefully, that amazing one on Sunset Boulevard. I'll be able to hire a couple full-time staffers. Maybe even buy myself a condo, if I catch a few other lucky breaks. Yeah, if I hit a grand slam at the party, then I'll surely be in the mood to celebrate with at least a BJ from my smoking hot escort. On the other hand, though, if things *don't* turn out the way I'm hoping, if I leave that mansion on the twenty-first in the same position I'm in now—crossing my fingers and toes I've done enough to squeak RCR onto the bottom rung of the fucking alternative rock chart, then I'll surely want to be alone after the party.

"I'll play it by ear on hiring my date for 'intimate services' after the party," I reply. "I want to be certain there's sufficient chemistry between us to move forward on that."

The woman snorts, like there being a lack of sexual chemistry is a ridiculous notion.

"Look, I'm not calling because I can't get laid," I say, annoyance flashing through me. "I can. And by exceptionally beautiful women. I'm calling because this is going to be a critical work event for me, possibly life-changing, and I won't have the time or bandwidth to deal with a date who's pissed at me for God knows what. For not paying enough attention to her. For not introducing her around or trying to help her career. I want someone on my arm who understands I'm building a fucking empire here—a *brand*. And that means I need to communicate my place in the hierarchy the second I walk through the fucking door."

"I understand, Mr. Rivers," she says soothingly. "I think you're brilliant to realize an exceptionally beautiful woman on your arm is a must-have status symbol in this town. But how about I tell you the pricing on intimate services, just in case?"

Without waiting for my reply, she quotes me a number for "unlimited services." It's a number I consider to be ludicrous, and tell her so. So, she offers to take twenty percent off her price, if I book now.

"That's still too high a price for something I can get for free on my own," I say. But the truth is, I simply can't afford that price tag, whether it's reasonable or not. Not now, I can't, before I know if I've secured a feature in *Rock 'n' Roll* for RCR.

"Mr. Rivers," Francesca says, like she's talking to a moron. "You want a girl who looks like she could walk a runway? Well, my girls actually *do* walk runways. Indeed, they're signed to the best modeling agencies in the world. And as far as you getting it 'for free' on your own... we both know that's not true. Nothing comes for free. One way or another, a man always pays for it. With my girls, however, the only thing you pay is what's been agreed upon in advance. There's simplicity in that, don't you think? Freedom. Honesty, in a way. Far more so than having to wine and dine a woman to get to the same result."

She's speaking my language now. But since I'm cash-poor, whether I agree with her philosophy or not, I reply, "I'll decide that night, once I know for sure if we've got chemistry."

"Suit yourself. I was just trying to save you twenty percent."

"Let's talk next steps," I say, switching gears. "I want to be able to hand-pick my date from *unedited* photos. Headshots *and* body shots. Absolutely no photoshop."

"Not a problem. Wire me a deposit, and I'll send you a link to a gallery."

"Is the deposit refundable, if I'm not happy with any of the options?"

"Of course. But, trust me, you'll be happy."

"Make sure my date knows she's not allowed to network for herself that night. There are going to be lots of influential people at this party—household-name celebrities and power brokers—and I don't want her trying to hustle for herself."

"When I call the girls to ask about their availability, I'll be clear about that."

"My date can say she's a model with such and such agency, if she's asked about her career. In fact, if all goes well, I'm sure some of the power brokers at the party will seek her out afterwards, for music videos and whatever. And that would be great. I genuinely hope she cashes in. Just not that night. That night, she's there for *me*."

"Of course. What's the event, if you don't mind me asking?"

"A birthday bash for the founder of *Rock 'n' Roll*."

"Oh, wow. Sounds like fun."

"A 'who's who' of the music industry will be there. It's going to be the party of the year in my industry. Even more so than Grammys after-parties."

"So, you're the 'Reed Rivers' of River Records, then? I've been googling you as we've been talking."

"Yeah, that's me."

"Do you look anything like the photo on your website?"

"Yeah. It's unedited. Taken two months ago."

She chuckles softly. "Well, then, I can see why you have no trouble attracting beautiful women on your own. You're a very handsome man, Mr. Rivers."

"Unfortunately, I attract beautiful women who have no idea what it takes to build a fucking empire from scratch. Beautiful women who require way more attention than I can possibly give them at this point in my life."

"Well, Mr. Rivers, you've come to the right place. I can assure you that whatever girl you choose will have no trouble understanding what you're trying to accomplish here—and enthusiastically playing her part to assist you. Indeed, after seeing your photo, I'm quite certain your date, whoever she is, will have no problem staring at you at the party, all night long, like you're the handsomest, most powerful man in the world, a sex god who just got finished fucking her with his huge dick minutes before you two walked through the door."

I chuckle. "Francesca, has anyone ever told you you're damned good at your job?"

"I've been doing this a long time, Mr. Rivers."

"I'll send you the deposit right away. I'm looking forward to seeing those photos."

Chapter 5
Georgina

Present day

After settling into a third-row seat of the packed lecture hall, I pull out my laptop and do the exact thing Alessandra commanded me *not* to do: I load a flash drive with her three best songs. Obviously, I'm going to focus the majority of my energy on charming CeeCee Rafael. But there's no way in hell I'm *not* going to have my stepsister's music at the ready for the record label guy, just in case.

After stuffing the loaded drive into my purse, I pull out my phone and google Reed Rivers, as Alessandra suggested. And, lo and behold, the photo that pops up on my phone makes my jaw clank to the floor. *Hot damn.* My stepsister made Reed sound like a chick magnet, and now I can see why. He isn't only a young, rich, powerful music mogul—all of which would be catnip enough for virtually any woman—he's also scorching hot by any standard of male beauty. The kind of sexy that makes even the smartest women turn as stupid as a box of rocks.

Reed's chocolate eyes are piercing and intense. His dark hair is stylishly mussed. And, damn, his cheekbones look like Michelangelo himself chiseled them from a hunk of perfectly tanned marble. Surely, if the music thing hadn't panned out for this hunk of gorgeousness, he could have made his living starring in cologne commercials. He's just that beautifully crafted.

I flip to the images option on my browser, thirsty to see more photos of this insanely hot creature, and quickly discover Reed's tattooed, muscled body is every bit as jaw-dropping as his face. Add "swimsuit model" to the list of potential careers for him in a parallel universe. Holy crap. From top to bottom, Reed Rivers is more than a chick magnet—he's a Taser gun. A crossbow. Even if he were a pauper without an ounce of power or clout, any red-blooded woman would tumble into this man's bed without a second thought, if only to experience one delicious, reckless night with a god among men.

My heart rate increasing, I click onto Reed's Wikipedia page and devour the basics. His record label, River Records, burst onto the music scene with Red Card Riot's debut album ten years ago. And ever since, it's churned out hit after hit, with an ever-increasing roster of top-notch bands and artists.

Along the way, smart man that he is, Reed's parlayed his success in music into other successful investments and businesses, as well—in real estate, tequila, nightclubs, restaurants, and more. The man has even successfully invested in some hit independent films. Apparently, whatever he touches turns to gold. Which, of course, is why he's earned the nickname "The Man with the Midas Touch."

I come to the "personal information" section of Reed's Wiki page and find out Reed is thirty-four years old, six-foot-three, and an exercise enthusiast. No surprise on that last thing, given his sculpted frame. Snowboarding, triathlons, jumping out of airplanes, surfing, scuba-diving, rock climbing, cycling, beach volleyball, basketball, kayaking... If it gets Reed's body moving and his heart pumping, he's all over it. And, lucky for the world, there are plenty of hot photos online of him doing it all. *Damn.*

Back on Reed's Wiki page, I learn he's never been married and has no children. And that, apparently, he likes it that way. "I'm not a married-with-kids kind of guy," Reed has been quoted as saying. "Being Uncle Reed to my baby sister's and best friends' kids is perfect for me."

I keep reading and discover a bit of shocking news: Reed's father, now deceased, was a renowned white-collar criminal who hanged himself in prison fifteen years ago. His surviving family consists of his mother, a paternal aunt, and a much-younger sister. No details supplied on any of them.

I glance at the empty stage to make sure I'm not missing CeeCee's grand entrance, and then eagerly return to my phone. I click on the "romantic relationships" tab of Reed's page, and discover he's been linked to a smattering of high-profile women, some of them instantly recognizable actresses and models. It seems the highly likeable model-turned-actress, Isabel Randolph, is in more photos with Reed than anyone else. Did adorable Isabel manage to tie Reed's hunky, playboy ass down longer than anybody else?

I google to find out, and immediately discover my hunch is right: Reed and Isabel had a two-year relationship that ended about six years ago. I search their names in the images tab and a cache of sexy photos of the pair pops up. In some of them, Reed and Isabel are dressed to kill for a night on the town. In others, they're dressed casually, or in ski clothes, or swim suits, always looking perfect.

In one particularly gorgeous shot, they're both tanned and dressed in white, walking through what looks like a small village in some oceanside paradise. And that's all my brain needs to conjure images of the sexy pair going at it *hard* in some beachfront vacation villa, the aquamarine ocean their backdrop as they fuck each other's brains out...

Suddenly, Isabel in my hot fantasy becomes *me*. Out of nowhere, I'm the lucky woman who's sweaty and moaning and getting fucked hard by Reed on some Greek island. I'm the one on my hands and knees, growling as he invades my body with his, over and over again...

Oh, holy hell. I'm seriously losing it. These days, I think

about sex as much as magazine articles always say the average male thinks about it. Gah. Why'd Bryce have to turn out to be such a Cling-On? If only he'd played his cards right, if only he'd been the cocky football star I'd thought, it's fifty-fifty I would have been having hot, sweaty sex with him this week. Not on a Greek island, with an aquamarine ocean as our backdrop, but I'd take it, just the same.

Applause erupts around me, jerking me from my reverie. Quickly, I drop my phone into my lap and direct my attention to the stage, just in time to see my idol striding across it in a sleek pantsuit, right alongside Mr. Hottie himself, Reed Rivers. Who, by the way, looks even more tantalizing in person than in his hunky photos. *Wow.*

CeeCee and Reed and the other panelists take seats onstage as a woman with a lovely smile approaches a lectern. Our host for the event welcomes the audience, introduces herself as the head of UCLA's music department, and proceeds to introduce each panelist. We meet a renowned songwriter, a composer for movies, a singer who apparently had a huge hit in the '90s, and a music supervisor who selects songs for TV and film. Finally, the moderator introduces CeeCee, and I whoop and clap far more vigorously than anyone around me.

"Maybe some of you have heard of CeeCee's little magazine?" the moderator says with a sly smile. "It's called... *Rock 'n' Roll?*" Everyone, including me, laughs and applauds. "And last but not least," the moderator says, beaming a huge smile at Mr. Panty-Melter on the far end. "Help me welcome a gentleman known in the music industry as 'The Man with the Midas Touch.' He's one of this university's most esteemed alums. The founder of River Records. *Reed Rivers.*"

The crowd cheers wildly, much more enthusiastically than they did for anyone else. And, in a flash, I know Alessandra was right: everyone here has a music demo in their pockets they're hoping to slip to Reed after the event.

The moderator says, "Reed founded his label eleven years ago, at the age of twenty-three, right after he'd obtained both a BA in business *and* an MBA from this fine university."

The crowd cheers at the mention of our beloved school.

"In an early interview, Reed said he founded River Records with two goals in mind: one, bringing 'stellar' music into the world, and, two, making a 'shit-ton of money' while accomplishing goal number one."

The room explodes with laughter and applause.

Chuckling with the crowd, the moderator adds, "I think it's fair to say 'mission accomplished' on both counts. Would you agree, Reed?"

Reed smiles. "So far, so good. But, to be clear, I'm not even close to done with either of my stated goals yet."

The moderator looks like she's swooning at that response, but after taking a few deep breaths, she manages to return to the audience with a professional demeanor. "Let's get started. I'll begin with you, Reed. Your label is known for being particularly selective about the artists you sign. Correct?"

"Correct."

"Why is that?"

"Because we don't stockpile our artists, the way other labels do. If River Records signs you, it means we're committed to putting our full faith and resources behind you. Most labels sign a hundred acts, hoping one will have a hit, almost by chance. But while they play the odds like bean counters, we shoot for the stars, each and every time. But, of course, the flipside of that philosophy is that we need to be highly selective at the front end."

"Have you ever experienced a miss, despite your best efforts?"

"We've had disappointments, sure. But a complete miss? No, not yet. Knock on wood."

He raps his knuckles against the side of his head, a move he's obviously not inventing—and, yet, every student in the audience laughs and swoons like they're seeing the maneuver for the first time. And I can't help thinking, *Poor Isabel didn't stand a chance.*

As the moderator asks Reed some follow-up questions, I take a surreptitious photo of him, and quickly shoot it off to Alessandra. And, of course, within seconds, my stepsister sends me a gif of a nuclear explosion, with the caption: "MY OVARIES," making me chuckle out loud.

After putting my phone in my lap again, I return to the discussion, just in time to hear the moderator say, "Thank you so much, Reed. I think you've shown us all why every aspiring artist I know would give their left kidney to get signed by your label."

Reed leans back in his chair, the king of all he surveys. "Actually, our contracts require new artists to give their *right* kidney. I keep them in mason jars in my office and nibble on them whenever I'm low on protein bars."

Again, everyone in the room, including me, laughs and swoons at Reed's wit and charm.

"I stand corrected," the moderator says, her face aglow. She clears her throat. "Moving on."

And away we go. Question. Answer. Rinse and repeat. Sometimes, the moderator addresses the full panel. Other times, she talks to a specific panelist, like she did with Reed. But, through it all, nobody holds my attention like CeeCee and Reed. But mostly Reed, if I'm being honest, except for when CeeCee is the one speaking. And even then, I can't help sneaking peeks at Reed to see how he's reacting to whatever CeeCee is saying.

After about twenty minutes, while the moderator chats with the music composer, I find myself sneaking yet another peek at Reed—and then jolting like I've been electrocuted when I discover his dark, piercing eyes fixed firmly on me. My heart lurches as our gazes mingle, and then stampedes when he doesn't look away.

Am I imagining this staring contest? Am I nothing but a horny woman projecting her fantasies onto an incredibly successful and sexy man? Surely, a man of Reed's stature wouldn't notice some random nobody in a crowded lecture hall... Yeah, I decide, Reed must be staring blankly, letting his mind wander, perhaps to the woman he banged last night, and I happen to be in what *appears* to be his sightline.

And yet... it really seems like he's actively, and quite flirtatiously, checking me out. But how could that be? Yes, men frequently check me out. It's part of the reason I became a bartender—because I realized I could channel some of that male attention into tips. That, and my father would kill me if I became a stripper. But, still, I think I'm being ridiculous to think a man who dates supermodels and actresses and *literally* parties with rock stars would notice *me* in this situation.

Deciding to find out, once and for all, I drag my teeth suggestively over my lower lip, smile brightly, and then... *wink* at Reed. And, to my shock, Reed Rivers *immediately* winks back. In reply, my flirtatious smile morphs into a full, beaming, goofy one, which Reed returns in kind. Although, to be sure, Reed's full smile is anything but goofy.

Still smiling broadly at me, he dips his chin, as if to say, *Hello.*

So, I return his gesture. *Hello, Handsome.* I waggle my eyebrows, just to triple-check I'm not imagining this. And, to my sizzling delight, Reed sends me a return eyebrow waggle that makes me giggle. How is it possible his eyebrow waggle is actually sexy? So sexy, in fact, it sends arousal pooling between my legs.

"What do you think about that?" the moderator says. "Reed?"

Reed abruptly swivels his head.

"What advice would you give anyone dreaming of a career in music, Reed?"

"Oh. Uh." Reed clears his throat. "Yes. Well, to begin

37

with, I'd say 'fake it 'til you make it.' Not original, I know, but still good advice. People in this industry don't want to be the *first* or the *last* to jump on a bandwagon. So, your job is to convince them they've personally discovered the next big thing—someone only the coolest of cool kids know about at the moment." He launches into explaining his point further, and I force myself to look away—at CeeCee, the moderator, the other panelists... until, finally, I allow myself another quick peek at him. And, to my thrill, he's staring at me again. This time, when our eyes meet, Reed leans forward and says, "My last piece of advice would be this. When opportunity knocks, say *yes*." He flashes me a naughty smile. "Actually, say yes, yes, yes, without apology or hesitation. You might only get one shot. No regrets."

Arousal zings through my body, reddening my cheeks and hardening my nipples. Without meaning to do it, I nod slowly, letting Reed know I've heard him loud and clear. That I'm ready to say yes, yes, yes to him, any time, any place. All he needs to do is ask.

Reed smirks at me one last time, before turning to look at the moderator. "And that's pretty much it, Angela."

As everyone applauds, the moderator thanks Reed for his comments, which she calls insightful, inspiring, and "oddly arousing." And then, with a laugh, she announces we've reached the end of the presentation and asks the panelists to hang around to answer students' questions. And through it all, Reed and I can't stop eyeball-fucking each other from across the lecture hall like our lives depend on it.

Suddenly, I become aware students around me have risen from their chairs and are working their way toward the aisles.

"Did you see Reed flirting with me?" a blonde in front of me says excitedly to her friend.

"With *you*?" her friend says. "He was looking at *me*."

Shit. Does every woman in this building, including me, think Reed has been flirting with them for the past hour? My heart in my throat, I jockey through the slow-moving crowd and make my way toward CeeCee, who's standing on the opposite side of the hall from Reed. When I reach the back of CeeCee's short line, which, thankfully, is only a few students deep, I peek at Reed's massive line... and then at him... and discover, to my thrill, his eyes are on mine *again*.

Without hesitation, Reed sends me a sexy little wink, followed by an eyebrow waggle. And I can't help smiling broadly at the gesture. Of course, I give him as good as he just gave to me, making him smile... and just that fast, I know we're both thinking the same thing: whenever he gets through his long line, he's going to come over here to talk to me. And whatever that man suggests, whatever he asks, wherever he suggests we go, I'm going to follow his explicit directions and say, without a moment's hesitation or apology: yes... yes... *yes*.

Chapter 6
Georgina

G eorgie!" a female voice says, and when I peel my eyes off Reed's white-hot smolder at the far end of the lecture hall, my favorite professor—the one who taught two of my investigative journalism classes this year—is standing before me.

"Professor Schiff!" I say brightly. "What are you doing here?"

"I came to say hello to CeeCee. We went to school together." She indicates CeeCee's line, now only four students deep in front of me. "You're here to meet her?"

I nod. "I'm hoping to charm her into reading a couple of my writing samples."

"Brilliant! Are you hoping to write for *Rock 'n' Roll*?"

"I'd love that, of course. But my dream job would be writing for *Dig a Little Deeper*. It's CeeCee's newest magazine, devoted to investigative journalism and in-depth interviews."

"I know it well. You'd be perfect for that, Georgie."

My heart leaps. "Thank you so much. I don't have high hopes, unfortunately, thanks to my overall GPA being less than stellar. But a girl can try."

"But you're a gifted writer. You aced both my classes."

"Thank you. Yes, thankfully, my grades bounced back this past year. But the first years of college were a bit rough on me, personally. Especially last year. And my grades suffered, unfortunately."

My professor's features contort with concern. "Do you mind me asking what happened?"

I pause, and then decide there's no choice but to tell her. "My dad was battling cancer the past couple of years. Last year, I was the one who took care of him, while still juggling a full-time course load and two part-time jobs."

"Oh, my gosh. I'm so sorry. Helping him was all on your shoulders?"

I nod. "He has some neighbors who've been great. But it was mostly me. It's just my dad and me. My mom passed away when I was nine, going on ten." I look down at my blue toenails, peeking out of my flip flops. "I probably should have taken last year off, or at least dropped down to a part-time course load—but we'd already paid my full-time tuition and housing, so... " I look up, forcing a smile. "The good news is, he's doing great now. And his sister recently moved in with him, to help out. So, it's all good."

"Aw, Georgie. I'm so sorry." She puts her hand on her heart. "I'm so glad he's doing well now."

"Thank you. Me, too. We're both super excited for me to graduate and move full steam ahead on my job search, if only I can convince potential employers to look past my mediocre GPA."

My professor looks thoughtful. "Have you considered applying for an unpaid internship? I know it'd be tough at first, what with student loans and all. But lots of companies, including CeeCee's, use unpaid internships as their initial proving ground for new hires."

My spirit sinks. "I'd love to be able to do that, but I can't afford it. I need a good paying job, not just for my own expenses and student loans, but to help my dad afford some expensive medicine he still needs to take."

My professor looks downright distraught. "You know what, Georgie? Wait here. I'm going to personally introduce you to CeeCee."

My heart leaps. "Really? Thank you!" But as she turns to leave, my heart lurches into my mouth. "Professor?"

She turns around.

"Please, don't tell CeeCee what I told you about my father. I want to get a shot at a job because of my writing abilities, not for sympathy."

My professor smiles kindly. "Of course. I'll tell her only that you're one of the brightest, loveliest, most talented, and passionate journalism students I've ever had the pleasure, and honor, of teaching. All of which will be true."

A lump rises in my throat. "Thank you."

With a little wink, my professor turns on her heel and strides to CeeCee's line. My skin buzzing with excitement, I watch her apologize to two students at the front before exuberantly hugging her old friend. The two women talk for quite some time. Long enough that I find myself glancing at Reed after a bit, to make sure he's still there.

When I spot Reed across the room, he's talking to a female student. A pretty redhead who's got her hand outstretched, like she's offering him something. Is that a music demo in her palm? I bet it is, just like Alessandra predicted. Whatever it is, Reed's clearly not interested in taking it from her—also, exactly as Alessandra predicted. God, I was so naïve.

"Georgina," my professor says, drawing my attention.

Oh my God. *It's CeeCee.* She's standing before me. Looking like the legend she is.

Brief introductions are made, after which I begin babbling like the fangirl I am. I tell CeeCee about my admiration for her, for her magazines and fashion sense and philanthropy and business acumen. About my love for investigative journalism and her latest magazine, especially. And when I'm done rambling, CeeCee looks charmed, not annoyed. So much so, she invites me to join her and Professor Schiff for coffee at the nearby campus place—the one where I first met Bryce, actually.

But just before our threesome reaches the double doors at the front of the hall, I can't help glancing over my shoulder once last time at Mr. Music Mogul. To my thrill, he's watching me intently. A lion tracking a gazelle. Or, rather, a rich, powerful man watching the nobody he assumed he was going to fuck, just because he felt like it, walking straight out the door without even saying hello to him.

With a wistful smile, I flash Reed a wink, letting him know I'm as disappointed as he is not to get to experience whatever deliciousness might have transpired between us. And then, I straighten up and march out the doors behind CeeCee and my professor, feeling enthralled I'm getting this amazing opportunity... but also, if I'm being honest, a little disappointed I'll never get the chance to say the words "yes, yes, yes!" to the man who instructed me to say them, whenever opportunity came knocking for me.

Chapter 7
Reed

"Honey, I'm home!" Josh hollers as we enter the crowded bar, and Henn and I laugh.

All three of us have fond memories of this place, but especially Josh, since he's the one who tended bar here in college, albeit briefly. Just long enough for Josh to realize he loved tending bar, but hated punching a clock. A few months into his first-ever stint as an hourly wage worker, Josh struck a deal with the bar owner: Josh could tend bar whenever he wanted, without notice, provided he paid for whatever drinks he poured—using only expensive top-shelf liquor—and generously tipped whichever bartender he'd screwed out of tips by showing up unannounced.

Some of the guys in our fraternity house razzed Josh for essentially paying to work. But I totally understood: Josh wanted the same thing I'd wanted when I'd paid that sorority girl to eat her pussy a few years before—all the pleasures of a job he thoroughly enjoyed, without any of the associated hassles or commitments. As far as I was concerned, Josh was a genius for striking that deal with the bar owner, Bernie. In fact, he was my fucking hero.

I nudge Josh's shoulder and motion to the pool table. "You and Henn get next game while I get our drinks."

"You bought dinner," Josh says. "I'm buying drinks."

"Fuck off, Faraday," I reply, already walking away. "I could buy dinner and drinks for three lifetimes, and still not repay you for everything you bankrolled in college."

When I arrive at the crowded bar, I elbow my way to an open spot at the far end... and promptly lose my shit. *It's her.* The sultry, sassy brunette from the music school event this afternoon. *She's the bartender.* And she's every bit as boner-inducing as she was this afternoon. More so, actually, now that she's dressed to maximize her curves—and, surely, her tips—in a low-cut tank top, push-up bra, and skin-tight jeans.

She's standing in profile to me at the moment, taking orders from a rowdy group of frat boys, all of whom plainly think she's as big a knockout as I do. And who wouldn't? She's a bombshell, this girl. A bodacious siren plucked straight out of a Fellini flick. Thick, dark hair. Full, tempting lips in the perfect shape of a bow. Eyes that blaze with confidence. Sass. *Charisma.* Her skin is olive. Her limbs long. And those curves! Jesus Christ. They're enough to make a careful man do some seriously reckless shit.

When she left the lecture hall with CeeCee without saying a word to me, despite all the winks and smiles and heated smolders we'd exchanged for a full hour, I was shocked. Also, impressed. But, mostly, *intrigued.* Was she a wannabe pop star playing a master game of chess by ditching me—gambling I'd track her down through CeeCee? Or had I pegged the girl all wrong, and she was merely CeeCee's new personal assistant or niece?

The latter scenario seemed like a long shot, given the nature of the event and the girl's pop-star good looks—not to mention her brazen flirting with me. Nobody her age would ever flirt *that* aggressively with me, just because. They always want something. But I had to know for sure. Hence, my decision to do the very thing she was most likely counting on: I resolved to call CeeCee tomorrow to track the bombshell down, even if it turned out she was a music student wannabe pop star who was decidedly off-limits to me.

It's funny. Dumbshit guys at parties always assume I fuck aspiring artists, the same way I snack on kale chips. All the time. Without a second thought. But that couldn't be further from the truth. In actuality, I don't touch anyone who's hoping to further her career by fucking or blowing me, no matter how attractive she might be. It's the same whether she's an aspiring artist, an artist I've already signed, or one of my employees. They're all off-limits to me. No exceptions.

See, what I've learned, after a few unfortunate missteps early on, is that even the hottest sex isn't worth risking the possible fall-out—the risk that the same woman who throws herself at me on Tuesday will claim I've used my power and influence inappropriately with her on Wednesday, once it's clear I'm not going to give her what she wants.

I mean, sure, I'll fuck models or actresses who want to use me *indirectly* to boost their clout or Instagram following or finagle an introduction to a powerful friend. That's the way of the world. But fucking a woman who thinks giving me a BJ will *directly* advance her career—whether that's getting her signed to my label, or assigned to a headlining slot on a tour, or getting a promotion at one of my companies? Nope. I won't touch that woman with a ten-foot pole. Ever.

Well, until today, apparently, when I saw this bartender and immediately started flirting with her, without knowing for sure if she was free and clear or not. And then, to top off my recklessness, started telling myself all sorts of things I never tell myself. Stuff like, *Rules are made to be broken.* And, *Maybe it wouldn't be the end of the world if I fucked a wannabe, just once...* All the same things I'm telling myself now, yet again, as I watch this siren mesmerize that pack of fraternity boys into handing over all their cash.

Holy shit, she's mouth-watering. If I were casting her in a music video, I'd make it a tribute to old, black-and-white Italian flicks. The video would take place on a vineyard. She'd be The Vineyard Owner's Daughter in a peasant dress with a low neckline. The sultry virgin bursting out of her dress, who comes out of her villa with a jug of water and a basket of grapes, just as a group of soldiers shows up demanding lodging...

"Can I get you something?"

I peel my eyes off the siren to find a male bartender standing before me, his eyes narrowed. He looks like a younger version of Henn. A wouldn't-hurt-a-fly kind of guy with a goatee, the same as my sweet best friend—although, unlike Henny, this dude has forearm tattoos. Clearly, the ink is his attempt at "edging up" his classic nerd-vibe. It's not a bad look for him, actually.

"I'll wait to order from her," I say, motioning to the object of my lust at the other end of the bar. "We met today on-campus. I'd like to say hello."

The guy flashes me a look of disdain that says, *You and every guy in this bar, douchebag.* But all he says is, "I'll let Georgina know."

Georgina. It's the perfect name for her—a name I'll enjoy growling into her ear as I fuck her raw, without mercy...

No, Reed.

Stop.

You're almost certainly not going to fuck this little college kiddie, with or without mercy, because she's almost certainly an off-limits wannabe. Not to mention, quite possibly, a fucking teenager. Although, come to think of it, if she works behind the bar, she's got to be at least twenty-one...

It doesn't matter, my brain says. *She was at an event for music students. Walk away.*

But I want her, my dick replies, rather forcefully.

Well, tough shit, my brain replies. *You can find out why she left with CeeCee today, simply to satisfy your curiosity, but that's it. After that, you're going to walk away and shoot pool with your best friends, and forget this gloriously endowed goddess with the most kissable lips you've ever seen exists.*

My dick laughs heartily at that. And so, I laugh, too. Out loud. Like a fucking lunatic.

The bartender whispers something into sultry Georgina's ear that makes her turn around. And when she spots me, a wide smile spreads across her sensuous mouth.

Returning her smile, I put my arms up like, *I guess it's fate, huh?*

She saunters over to me like she owns the joint, places her elbows onto the bar, and leans over, giving me a much-appreciated view of her pushed-up tits in her tank. "Well, well, well," she says. "Look what the cat dragged in. Did you follow me here, Mr. Rivers?"

Up close, she's mesmerizing. Irresistible. I swear, if this supernatural girl can sing a note, and maybe even if she can't, I'm going to launch her to the top of the pop charts, even if I have to buy stock in Auto-Tune to do it. "I wish I could take credit for this happy reunion," I say. "But this is pure coincidence..." I look down at Georgina's nametag, just for appearance's sake. "*Georgina.* Or should I call you Miss... ?"

"Ricci. But, no. Call me Georgina or Georgie." She extends her hand with full confidence, and when I slide my palm in hers, my skin ignites at the point of contact. *Lust.* It's palpable. Undeniable. Sending my heart rate skyrocketing and my dick tingling.

I want her, my dick shouts, deftly muting out my brain's objections.

"Hello, Georgina," I say, shaking her hand. "Georgie. And, please, call me... *Mr. Rivers.*"

She laughs. "Well, that hardly seems fair."

"Life isn't fair." I lean forward, a wide smile etched onto my face. "Although, sometimes, it can be pretty fucking awesome, when you least expect it."

She returns my smile, a gleam in her hazel eyes. "This truly is a coincidence?"

"I'm smart, but not clairvoyant. I was at dinner with friends, and then happened to stop in here. How could I possibly have known you work here?"

"You could have followed me. Or had me followed."

"Pretty sure that's what's known as stalking, sweetheart. Way beneath my pay grade."

"You sure about that? I'm getting a serious stalker vibe from you."

"Okay, full disclosure, I was going to call CeeCee tomorrow to gather intel about you, in order to track you down. So, maybe stalking isn't beneath me so much as your accusation is a day premature."

She giggles. "What would you have asked CeeCee about me?"

"Your name, to start with. Your age. I definitely would have asked if you're a music student."

She shakes her head. "Journalism. I'm graduating next week."

My dick cautiously jumps for joy. *She's not off-limits.* "Congratulations. Are you a musician on the side, maybe? A singer?"

"Nope. Just a writer. My passion is investigative journalism."

I'm losing my mind with relief. Euphoria. Lust. Even as the business side of my brain is slightly disappointed I won't have the chance to make her a star. "How old are you, if you don't mind me asking?"

"I'm turning twenty-two next month."

She just keeps getting better and better. "I'm relieved to know you're not a teenager," I admit. "The thought occurred to me at the panel, as I was flirting with you, that your age could very well end in the word 'teen.' Once I realized that, I was pretty disgusted with myself for continuing to flirt."

"Not disgusted enough to stop, apparently."

I chuckle. "True."

"So if I'd turned out to be nineteen, you would have hung up with CeeCee tomorrow, and not tracked me down?"

I pause, unsure. Hearing her say that out loud, it doesn't

ring true to me, even though before today, I would have sworn I'd never be caught dead pursuing a teenager. But, come on, I saw Georgina today and brazenly came on to her for a full hour, even though I knew there was a good chance she was eighteen or nineteen... So can I honestly say I wouldn't have pursued her if it had turned out she wasn't old enough to order a beer?

But, still. There's no reason to say any of that out loud, and come off as a dirty old man. And so, I say, "If CeeCee had told me you were a teenager, then I'm pretty sure I wouldn't have tracked you down."

She laughs. "*Liar*. If I'd been nineteen, you'd have told yourself 'Hey, she's legal,' and then done exactly what you're doing right now. Whatever that is."

"*Whatever that is?* Oh, God. I've got to step up my game, if you don't know. Georgina, sweetheart, I'm hitting on you. With all my might."

She bites her luscious lower lip. "*Oh?* Good to know." She smiles. "I think it's interesting you think nineteen is too young for you, but twenty-one isn't. Explain that one to me."

"Oh, twenty-one is too young for me, too."

We both laugh.

"Actually, before this moment, I would have sworn I'd never hit on a twenty-one-year-old. Never say never, I guess."

She adjusts her elbows on the bar. "To what do you attribute this astonishing reversal of yours, Mr. Rivers?"

I motion to her, like the answer is self-explanatory, and then add, "It's easy for a man to draw imaginary lines in the sand before he knows Georgina Ricci exists in the world."

She blushes. "Aw, well. Don't beat yourself up too much about being a creeper. Age is just a number, anyway."

"I think you have to get to your late twenties to be able to say that with a straight face. Before then, you come off as naïve."

"Oh, I'm not naïve. Not in the slightest."

My dick tingles at the possible subtext of that statement. Does she mean that as code for something naughty? Is she trying to tell me she's a freak in the sheets? "I didn't mean to insult you. I just meant there's a lot of highly formative life experience a person acquires between the ages of eighteen and twenty-five."

"There's a lot of highly formative life experience a person acquires between the ages of zero to a hundred."

"Well, that's true."

"Speaking for myself, I've acquired an ocean of 'highly formative' life experience between the ages of ten and twenty—too much of it, to be honest. But that's life. If we're doing it right, then we're constantly learning and growing."

"True, again."

"Except when it comes to you, I guess. You're so smart, so much smarter than the rest of us, you're all done learning and growing, now that you're the wise old age of thirty-five."

Holy motherfuck. Just this fast, this sassy girl's got me tied and trussed like a pig over a spit. And I'm loving it. I lean forward, smiling. "First off, I'm only thirty-four. Don't rush me. And, believe me, just like everyone else, I'm still figuring plenty of stuff out."

"Which proves my point. *Age is just a number.*" She lays her cheek in her palm. "You've honestly *never* dated someone my age?"

"Not since my early twenties. And, to be clear, I don't plan to date you, Georgina. Just *seduce* you."

Her eyebrows rise at my brazen comment, though she seems more amused by it than offended. "Points for honesty. Damn."

"I'm a big fan of honesty."

"When it suits you, apparently." She smirks. "I'm pretty sure you've already lied to me at least a couple times."

I shrug. "Things may come to those who wait, but only the things left by those who hustle."

"Ah, so you admit you're a hustler?"

"I do. Proudly."

She drags her teeth over her sensuous lower lip. "So, tell me, Mr. Wise Old Rivers, why don't you date—or, sorry, *seduce*—much younger women? Is it some sort of firm rule for you, or has it just sort of happened that way?"

Good God, she's relentless. And I fucking love it. "I haven't given it much thought. I don't tend to be in situations where I meet women your age, other than in a business context, which means they're not a good idea for me to pursue, no matter their age. And, also, if I'm being honest, I'm a sucker for a confident woman—and genuine confidence, in my experience, as opposed to youthful cockiness, or play-acting confidence in mommy's heels, usually takes a bit of time to develop."

Oh, I've pissed her off now. "'Play-acting in mommy's heels'? How condescending."

I chuckle. "You asked me a question, and I answered it honestly. You don't like honesty?"

"I like honesty. Just not *assholery*."

I laugh heartily. I think she might very well be perfect.

"Just a tip?" she says, twirling a lock of dark hair around her finger. "Don't look down your nose at me and treat me like I'm a stupid child, which I'm not, if you want to have any shot at 'seducing' me. I've got a bit of an allergy to assholes, I should warn you, and also a bit of a temper. And I don't tend to respond well in the face of condescension or assholery."

My breathing hitches at the blaze in her eyes. The flush in her cheeks. She's the sexiest little creature I've ever beheld. "Duly noted. I apologize. Condescending to you wasn't my intention."

"Well, shit, I hope not. If it was, that would make you absolutely terrible at seduction."

I can't help laughing my ass off. She's unleashing the kraken on me in a way that's making me smile from ear to ear.

"You want to know a secret, Mr. Rivers?" she says conspiratorially. "I truthfully can't wait to see you take your best shot at seducing me. Don't get me wrong; I haven't yet decided if I'm going to let you be successful. But I'm certainly up for watching you try."

Okay, who's the liar now? Georgina's red-hot desire to get absolutely desecrated by me has been written all over her face from the minute she winked at me in the lecture hall.

I lean forward, matching her posture. "Aw, Georgina. Don't bullshit a bullshitter. I'm going to be wildly successful at seducing you, and we both know it. In fact, when the time is right tonight, I'm going to invite you to come to my house. And we both know what you're going to say in reply when I do."

She flashes me a snarky look. "I have no idea what I'd say to an invitation like that. Maybe if I had more highly formative life experiences, it'd be a different story. But as it is, I'm too busy play-acting confidence in my mommy's heels to know what I think or feel or want."

She flashes me a spicy little look that says, *Take that, you condescending prick*, and I'm suddenly dizzy with my desire for her.

I bite my lip. "So, it's gonna be like that, huh?"

"You bet your ass it's gonna be like that."

A palpable current of electricity passes between us. Sexual desire that shoots straight into my cock. "All right, beautiful. We'll go around and around for a while before I extend my invitation. We'll play a pointless, but highly entertaining, game of cat and mouse, just for the fun of it. But, I promise you, when the game ends, you're gonna say yes to me."

She shrugs. "Who knows what I'll say?" She winks. "But I can't wait to find out."

I return her wink. "*Let the seduction begin.*"

Chapter 8
Reed

"Georgie!" the male bartender shouts from the other end of the bar, making her jerk backwards from our sexy conversation. "You need help over there?"

"No, I'm good!" She returns to me. "You've got to order something, or I'm gonna get in trouble."

I throw down a hundred, order a beer for me, Scotch for Josh, and a gin martini for Henn. "Keep the change, as long as you take your sweet time making that martini."

"You got it." She gets to work.

"You're not even going to *pretend* to check my ID?" I say teasingly. "Way to make a guy feel old, bartender."

She slides my beer across the bar. "You already told me you're thirty-four. Are you saying you're a liar?"

"I'm saying I *could* have been lying."

"Yeah, well, the woman at the panel said you graduated from UCLA a decade ago. So unless you're one of those baby-geniuses who graduates medical school at age ten, I'm thinking it's safe to assume you were telling the truth. Also, Wikipedia says you're thirty-four. And we all know Wikipedia is never wrong."

A stool opens up in front of where Georgina is currently pouring Josh's Scotch and I quickly snag it. "Ah, you googled me."

"I did. No shame in that. While I was sitting in the lecture hall, waiting for the start of the program. I'd heard

54

your name for the first time while walking to the event, so I figured it would heighten my experience if I knew a little something about you in advance. I also devoured every photo of you I could find."

I chuckle. "Did you google all the panelists to 'heighten your experience,' or just me?"

"Just you. I'd heard you're smoking hot, and I wanted to see for myself."

"And?"

She slides Josh's Scotch toward me. "And you didn't disappoint."

I take a sip of my beer to hide my wide smile. This girl could teach a master class in sexy flirting. "After all the photos you 'devoured,' the real-life version of me didn't disappoint?"

"The real-life version of you made my ovaries vibrate."

Holy fuck. I can't believe it, but I feel myself blushing. When was the last time that happened to me? "If I haven't made it clear enough, I find you smoking hot, too. Seriously, you're absolutely stunning, Georgina."

She bats her eyelashes. "Thank you."

"If I'd seen you while waiting for the panel to start, and somehow knew your name, I would have sat there googling the shit out of you, too, including devouring every photo of you in existence online."

"Sorry to say, you would have been disappointed. I'm boring online. Not a single scandalous photo out there."

"No? Come on. There's got to be *something* scandalous out there. Maybe some naughty photos with a male stripper at a drunken twenty-first birthday party?"

She grabs a shaker for Henn's martini. "Nope. Your online presence is way more scandalous and naughty than mine."

"Uh oh. What photos of me did you see?" I gasp in mock horror. "You saw my crown jewels, didn't you?"

She freezes mid-shake on the shaker. "You're telling me there's a photo of your crown jewels out there, and I missed it? Shit on a shingle! I'm embarrassed to call myself an aspiring investigative journalist."

I chuckle. "No, no. I have no idea if anything like that exists. I'm just saying it *could.* I've jumped fully naked off more than a couple yachts and diving cliffs in my day. Gone surfing and kayaking and waterskiing buck naked while shitfaced. I even went snowboarding naked down a private bunny slope once, after losing a bet at a party. Almost froze my ass, dick, and nuts clean off."

She giggles.

"It wasn't a laughing matter at the time. Unfortunately, the shrinkage factor was off the charts."

She laughs even harder.

"After all the crazy stuff I've done," I say, "God only knows what photos of me could be out there. I haven't googled myself in a long time to find out, so I really don't know."

She slides Henn's martini onto the bar. "Why haven't you googled yourself in a while? Shouldn't a guy like you keep up with what the world is saying about you?"

I take a long swig of my beer. "I used to keep up with that stuff, back when I was first coming up. I considered myself a student of the fame industrial complex. The cult of celebrity. I was ahead of my time, well aware the secret to my success was positioning myself as an 'influencer.' But once I got to the top of the heap, I realized keeping up to date on what people think of me—or, rather, of the online avatar they *think* is me—is a colossal waste of time. I'm not real to them, so who gives a shit what they think?"

She bends over to grab something behind the bar, and, as she does, I peek at her outrageous cleavage. Goddamn, I can't wait to suck those incredible tits. That's the first thing I'm gonna do when I get her to my house: peel off that shirt and absolutely devour those—

Oh. She's straightened up again and is staring at me—fully aware I just got hopelessly lost in fantasies about her tits for a minute there.

"I looked at your Instagram," she says, running a rag across the bar. "Looks like your avatar is having a pretty exciting life."

"He is."

"Sadly, though, I saw no evidence he's gone naked-snowboarding recently."

I finish off my beer and shrug. "Partying is an important part of my job."

"Poor, poor Reed has to work *so* damned hard."

I laugh. "I'm not complaining. I have fun. But make no mistake about it: I really do work hard. Very hard. You might have read on my Wikipedia page, I've got a few businesses to run?"

"Honestly, I was too focused on drooling over photos of you in your swim trunks to read too much about what you do for a living. And it's a good thing I didn't waste my time reading about all that stuff, anyway, seeing as how you're only planning to 'seduce' me. Who gives a crap what either of us does, or likes, or dreams about, or feels passionately about, when the only endgame is you getting me into your bed, right?" With that, she slides a refilled beer glass in front of me, even though I didn't order it. "A gift from me, Mr. Rivers. Because I can only imagine how thirsty seduction makes a guy. Especially when he's trying to seduce a young, stupid thing like me who's running around in her mommy's heels, play-acting confidence." With that, she turns on her heel and strides to the other end of the bar to tend to another customer.

And I've never been more determined to make a woman say yes to me in my entire fucking life.

***

"You're still sitting here?" Georgina says, sidling up to me.

"I'm still sitting here," I reply. I toss two hundred bucks onto the bar in front of her, right next to the two untouched drinks I ordered for Josh and Henn mere minutes ago. "Let's make it three martinis this time, Georgina. All of them made extra slowly. Keep the change, like before, as long as you take your sweet time making my order."

"You got it." She scoops up the cash, thanks me, and gets to work.

"Can I ask a stupid question?" she asks. "Are you famous? I can't tell. You were the biggest star on the panel. And you're all over the internet, hanging out with rock stars and celebrities. In some photos, you've even got a bodyguard or two. And yet, here you are, at Bernie's Place on a Thursday night, with no bodyguards, acting like a regular dude. Well, a very well-dressed regular dude with an extremely nice watch."

I take a sip of the Scotch originally intended for Josh. "I have what I'd call 'situational fame.' People in the music industry know who I am. At music festivals, I have to roll with at least two bodyguards, so I don't get attacked by wannabes. But just living my life in the world, like tonight, I can hang out with no problem. It's the best of both worlds."

"Meaning you wouldn't want to be more famous, if you could?"

"Hell no. I've seen massive fame close up, with some of my artists and past girlfriends, and it's not all it's cracked up to be. That's what doomed a few of my relationships, actually. The woman being too famous, or wanting to be. It's a drug for some people. And, as we all know, drugs don't lead to a happy ending."

"*Fame* is the culprit in your failed relationships? You're sure about that?"

I chuckle. "Well, that and I can sometimes turn into a colossal prick when I get bored."

"I'm shocked."

"Plus, I'm generally what you'd label 'non-committal' when it comes to relationships in the first place, so that could have contributed to the demise of a few of my relationships, as well."

She frowns. "Ah, so, you're a cheater?"

"No. If I say I'm exclusive, then I am. It's just really, *really* hard to get me to say I'm exclusive."

She nods, apparently approving of that answer. "I'm the same way."

"You turn into a colossal prick when you get bored, too?"

She giggles and winks. "Only when provoked. No, I consider myself 'non-committal' at the moment, too. For the foreseeable future, anyway. While I'm trying to launch my budding journalism career, I've decided not to focus on anything or anyone else."

"Do you have a job lined up after graduation?"

"No, unfortunately." She secures the lid on a metal shaker. "That's why I went to that event today. To try to give CeeCee a couple of my writing samples. My dream job is writing for her latest magazine, *Dig a Little Deeper*."

"I'm familiar with it. I think you'd be great at that. You're obviously good at connecting with people. Drawing them out." *And wrapping them around your pretty little finger, I'm sure.*

"Thank you. Fingers crossed."

"Was it mission accomplished with CeeCee? Did she take your writing samples?"

"She did. I got lucky and bumped into a professor after the panel who introduced us, and then CeeCee invited me to coffee. That's why I left without saying a word to you—because when opportunity came knocking, I did exactly what you told me to do: I said, 'Yes, yes, yes!'"

I chuckle. "Well, fuck. When I instructed you to say

those three magic words, I was hoping you'd be saying them to *me*—and under much more intimate circumstances."

She flushes. "What did you think when I left with CeeCee?"

"I was intrigued. I couldn't decide if you were CeeCee's new personal assistant or intern or niece, or if you were playing the world's most masterful game of chess with me."

She slides a martini in front of me. "With *you*? How could me leaving with CeeCee have anything to do with *you*?"

I shrug. "It was an event for music students, so, I assumed you had to be an aspiring pop star with a demo in your pocket, like everyone else in the building. I thought you'd seen my long line and decided you'd get far more traction out of leaving with CeeCee—and gambling on me tracking you down tomorrow—than staying and trying to compete for my attention."

She looks shocked. "Damn. That's quite a leap. When I left with CeeCee, I was sure I'd never see you again. I can't even imagine thinking two moves ahead like you've suggested."

Jesus, she's such a bullshitter. "Yeah, well, if you'd actually been a music student who wanted to use me for more than my hot body," I say, "then I guarantee you'd not only have played chess with me, you'd have been fucking Bobby Fischer."

"Who's that?"

I smile to myself. For a second there, I'd forgotten how young she is. "He's generally regarded as the best chess player who ever lived."

"Oh."

"After observing you, I've got no doubt you'd be fully capable of playing chess like him, if the need arose." I sip Josh's Scotch again. "Seriously, Georgina, you wouldn't believe the shit people do to get my attention. Nothing surprises me anymore." I take a sip of the martini she slides across the bar and suddenly realize she looks sincerely offended by something I've said. "Oh, come on. Really? Don't act like I've slandered you by calling you out, Little Miss Journalism Student Who Goes To A Music Event to Ambush CeeCee Rafael. You're a hustler, baby. Scrappy and relentless. I've seen the way you expertly hypnotize your customers, including me, into giving you big tips. Don't even try to pretend you're not fully capable of playing chess as masterfully as Bobby Fischer."

She blushes crimson, letting me know I've pegged her right.

"But it's all good, Georgie girl. I'm a chess-playing hustler, too. In fact, one of my mantras in life is 'All good things come to those who hustle.'" I raise my glass to her. "To being scrappy and relentless. To hustling and playing chess."

She slides my third martini in front of me, looking tentative. But after a moment, a delightful sort of "what the fuck" expression washes over her gorgeous features. She grabs one of the martinis and clinks my glass with it. "To playing chess." She grins. "Even more masterfully than Bobby Fischer."

Chapter 9
Georgina

Y ou about done over here?" Marcus asks, appearing out of nowhere next to me. "We're slammed, Georgie. Now isn't the time to take an extra-long break."

"Oh, I'm sorry. Mr. Rivers here just—"

"Ordered ten more drinks," Reed interjects. He pulls out his wallet, and places *another* Benjamin onto the bar—this one, for Marcus. "A little something for the extra load you've been carrying because I've monopolized Georgina's attention."

Marcus glares at the bill on the bar before returning to me. "You need help making his order?"

"No. They're all pretty simple drinks."

"And I'm in no rush," Reed supplies.

"I'll work like a bunny," I say. "Sorry I've been MIA."

"Here's another hundred for you, man," Reed says, placing another bill next to the first. "I didn't think about how me monopolizing Georgina was impacting your night. Hopefully, this will make up for it."

Marcus mutters something under his breath. But, ultimately, he scoops up the cash and shuffles away, looking thoroughly annoyed as he goes.

"Oh, God. It *killed* him to take that money from you," I say, laughing.

Reed resumes his bar stool. "And yet, he took it. Proving, once again, the accuracy of one of my favorite mantras:

'Everybody's got a price. To get what you want from someone, you just have to figure out what their price is, and bribe the shit out of them with it.'"

I scowl. "That's one of your favorite mantras? Jeez, Reed. That's dark."

"I'm wildly successful in a cut-throat industry. You expect my favorite mantras to be about rainbows and unicorns and singing 'Kumbaya'?"

I squint at him. Is it weird I'm not sure I like him, but I'm hella certain I want to fuck the living hell out of him? "Do you actually want another ten drinks, or was that just a ruse to get Marcus out of my hair?"

"Heck yeah, I want ten drinks. Let's give my buddies a magical mystery tour of beverages to choose from."

"You've got buddies here? This whole time I thought you were alone."

He turns around and directs my attention to two guys at the pool table: a hot male-model type who's cut of the same cloth as Reed, and a nerdy-hipster guy who looks like he could be his hot buddy's modeling agent. Reed returns to me, smiling. "Let's make my buddies ten of the most complicated, time-consuming assortment of drinks you can muster." He places three hundreds in front of me. "Your tip, on top of whatever the ten drinks cost, *if* it takes you at least twenty minutes to complete my order."

Whoa. That's quite a tip on top of what Reed's already paid me tonight. Thanks to him, I'm already having the best night of tips of my life, by far. And I'm grateful for it, of course, given the medical bills stacked on my father's kitchen counter. But I'm also wary. Does Reed think he's finding *my* "price" with these tips—and bribing me with it? If so, he's dead wrong about that. If I decide to go home with him tonight, or any night, it won't have anything to do with his financial generosity.

I get to work on filling Reed's ten-drink order, *slowly,*

while he settles onto his bar stool and chats me up. About ten minutes in, when I slide the fifth drink of his order across the bar, Reed finally makes his move. "Hey, do you think you could get out of here a couple hours early?" he asks. "I'd really like to spend some time alone with you tonight, but I'm flying to New York first-thing tomorrow, and I'll be gone for a week. The thought of waiting that long to get you alone is torturing me."

Holy shit. My mind is racing and my heart pounding. I want to say yes, despite all the "good girl" reasons I probably shouldn't. And not simply for the chance to give him Alessandra's music in private, but because... holy hell, I want to have sex with this sexy, arrogant man! But, unfortunately, that's a moot point because I truly can't leave my shift early.

"Sorry, I can't leave early," I say, pouting. "I wish I could."

Reed's face perks up. "Is that true—you genuinely wish you could leave early and come home with me? Or did you say that simply to be polite?"

I bite my lip, realizing I've just given up the ghost. "I wasn't being polite," I admit. "I'd genuinely love to leave early and go to your house tonight, but I truly can't. I guess we'll just have to get together after you get back from New York. It's too bad, but unavoidable. I won't get out of here until around two thirty, and it sounds like you have to get to the airport pretty early tomorrow."

Reed's jaw muscles pulse. He takes a long gulp of one of the drinks I've laid before him and shakes his head.

"What time do you have to leave for the airport?" I ask hopefully, on the off-chance we could make tonight work.

"Five, at the very latest."

I grimace. "Yeah, tonight definitely won't work, then. We wouldn't get to your place till three, and then you'd have to shove me out the door at four thirty. No, thanks. I'm up for a meaningless good time with you tonight, no strings, but, still, that's way too big a wham-bam-thank-you-ma'am for me. At least for our first time." I slide another drink across the bar and hold my breath, hoping Reed will try to convince me I'm wrong. But, no, Reed remains unusually quiet, looking deep in thought.

"Are you going to New York for business or pleasure?" I ask, simply to break the awkward silence.

He takes a sip of his drink. "Both."

I force myself not to frown at that answer. *Both.* Surely, the personal "pleasure" part of Reed's trip will involve him hooking up with a gorgeous woman. Or two or three. Probably some glamorous model or actress. *Shit.* It's suddenly dawning on me: if I don't go home with Reed tonight, due to time constraints, and he then flies off to New York to party with rock stars and fuck supermodels this entire week, he's going to forget I ever existed. And where will that leave my lady-boner? With blue balls, that's what.

But, more importantly, what would that mean for Alessandra? If I miss out on sexy times with Reed, because I wasn't willing to subject myself to a lightning-fast one-night stand, I'll cry into my pillow at the lost opportunity for a night or two. But I'll live, and eventually find myself another hottie to screw. A hottie as sizzling as Reed? Not bloody likely. But, still. I'll survive. But if I miss out on the chance to quite possibly make my stepsister's lifelong dreams come true, simply because I didn't want to rush some no-strings sex with Reed, I'd never forgive myself.

Out of nowhere, Reed lets out a tormented sigh. "Okay, look, Georgie. There's no way in hell I can wait a full week to get you alone. I respect everything you've said about not wanting to rush things tonight. In fact, I couldn't agree more. You're not a woman I want to rush anything with, believe me. I want to be able to explore every nook and crevice of your body for hours and hours."

I blush. *Whoa.*

"But I wasn't kidding: waiting a week might physically kill me." He looks at a clock on the wall, so I turn to look, too. It reads a few minutes until eleven. Reed says, "What if you could get off tonight in an hour—at midnight? That would give us over four hours together. Still, not enough, but certainly better than the alternative. What if I could arrange that, and promise you won't piss anyone off by leaving early and won't miss out on a single dollar of tips. Would you say yes to doing that tonight—to being my naughty Cinderella at the stroke of midnight?"

He's rendered me speechless. Confused. Frozen. *Turned on.*

Smiling like a shark smelling blood, Reed leans forward. "If I could arrange all that at the stroke of midnight, my sexy Cinderella, would you say yes? Would you say yes to letting me take you to my house to do every filthy fucking thing imaginable to your gorgeous body for four non-stop hours?"

Hell yes. That's what I'm thinking. *Hell to the freaking yes, Reed Rivers. Do all the filthy things to me. Bring it.* But that's not what I say. No, somehow, I manage to keep a straight face and reply, "No, I don't think I'd say yes to an offer like that." Much to my delight, Reed's face falls. Which is when I lean forward, lick my lips, and say, "You should already know me better than that by now. If given an offer like that, then I'd follow your explicit instructions from the lecture. I'd say exactly the thing you told me to say to you, whenever opportunity came knocking. I wouldn't say yes to you, Mr. Rivers." I wink. "I'd say, 'Yes... yes... *yes.*'"

Chapter 10
Reed

As Georgina walks away to process my credit card, Josh's unexpected voice at my shoulder jolts me. "What the hell happened to you?" he says. He elbows his way to an open spot at the bar next to me. "You were supposed to be getting us drinks, dumbass."

"And I did exactly that." I motion to the astonishing array of beverages before us on the bar. "Take your pick, my friend. They're all ours."

Josh laughs. "What the fuck?"

"Take a look at the bartender and all will become clear."

Josh glances to where I've indicated and immediately rolls his eyes. "I should have known."

"It was the only way I could get her to stand here talking to me for more than two minutes."

Josh surveys the concoctions in front of us. "What's what? It's like a box of chocolates."

"Yeah, you kind of have to taste them to figure it out."

He picks up a martini glass. "This looks safe."

"Since when are you 'safe'?"

"Since I've been waiting for a drink for fifty fucking years and I'm thirsty. Is this gin or vodka?"

"No idea."

He takes a sip. "Gin. And it's good." He takes several gulps. "You've seriously sat here flirting with her this whole time?"

67

"No, not this whole time. Before this stool opened up, I *stood* here flirting with her."

He glances at Georgina again. "She looks exactly like T-Rod when she first started working for me. I'm assuming that's a big part of her allure for you?"

T-Rod. It's a reference to Theresa Rodriguez, Josh's longtime personal assistant who's now a part-owner with Josh and T-Rod's husband on a chain of bars. A woman I've wanted to fuck since I first saw her ten years ago, when she was a twenty-one-year-old college grad and I was a twenty-four-year-old founder of a brand-new record label. And he's absolutely right: Georgina looks strikingly like her, although I hadn't made the connection until Josh pointed it out.

"She could be T-Rod's little sister," Josh says. "Emphasis on the word *little*. How old is she?"

"Almost twenty-two."

"Cradle-robber."

Smiling, I bring my glass to my lips. "She can vote, get a tattoo, buy cigarettes and liquor in all fifty states and weed in Washington and California. What more does a person need to be considered a full-fledged adult, other than all that?"

"Well, for starters, she could live in something other than student housing."

"If she can join the military and get permanently inked without her parents' consent, that's good enough for me. She's an adult."

"Keep telling yourself that, old man, if it helps you sleep at night."

"Weirdly enough, 'sleep' isn't the thing that keeps popping into my head whenever I look at her."

Josh drains the rest of his gin martini. "Is she a spitfire, too—just like T-Rod? How close a match is this, you fucking sicko wack job?"

"Yeah, she's a spitfire. She's already bitch-slapped me pretty good a few times. I deserved it, by the way."

"Of course, you did." He rolls his eyes. "You're so predictable. Whenever you hear the word no, in any context, you do whatever it takes to get to yes." He smirks. "Even if it means finding an uncanny double for the one woman in the world you wanted desperately but couldn't have."

Is he right about that? Have I been losing my mind over Georgina because she subconsciously reminds me of T-Rod—and I've got a score to settle? Or do I simply have a type—and Georgina is the most glorious version of it I've ever beheld in my entire life?

Unfortunately, "no" was the final answer in regards to my desire to fuck T-Rod. She's the Argentinian who got away, and always will be. Not emotionally, of course. I barely know the woman. But, God, how I've always wanted to experience her. And now, sadly, thanks to the rock on her finger and the babies who call her mommy, I never will.

My fascination with Theresa—you might even call it a low-key obsession—started the minute I met her. She was the highly organized, straight-laced twenty-one-year-old sent to Josh by a temp agency. And the minute I saw her, I wanted her. In fact, when I first saw T-Rod, I distinctly remember feeling like a nuclear lust-bomb had gone off inside me. The same thing I felt when I saw Georgina today.

Georgina.

Oh, God.

With T-Rod, it wasn't meant to be. Josh proclaimed her off-limits out of the gate—and not just for me, but for himself, too, and for all his friends—and by the time I decided to disregard his stupid proclamation, T-Rod's future husband was in the picture and my window of opportunity had decidedly slammed shut. But, this time, with sexy Georgina, she's not Josh's employee. Not his honorary little sister. And there's no would-be future-husband cockblocker slamming the door in my face. No, this time, with Georgina, it's smooth sailing for me to get to yes, yes, yes... In fact, there's not a doubt in my mind I'll be sinking myself inside her tonight—blissfully riding her, and myself, to four hours of heaven tonight.

"Aren't you about a decade too young to be having a midlife crisis?" Josh says, pulling me out of my reverie.

"Actually, my brain keeps saying that exact same thing. But, apparently, it seems other parts of my anatomy are running the show."

"Just be careful. The young ones fall hard." He snickers. "Probably because their brains aren't fully developed yet."

"Fuck you."

"Seriously, though. Tread softly, Rivers. I'm sure she's got huge stars in her eyes when she looks at you. You're gonna be able to manipulate her way too easily, so don't."

"She doesn't seem starry-eyed or manipulatable at all. I saw her earlier today, at that panel thing, sitting in the audience. I flirted my ass off from across the room for an hour and made it clear I wanted her to hang around afterwards and wait for me to get through my line, but she left anyway. I think that's what I like most about her—that she's willing to walk away. So rare these days."

Josh scoffs. "Sure, *that's* what you like most about her, you sick fuck. Clearly."

He indicates with his chin, where, at this moment, Georgina is bending down to grab something off a low shelf, gifting us with an insane view of her ass.

"Well, that and a few other things," I concede.

Josh laughs and sips his drink. "Is she a music student?"

"No. At least, I don't think so. She claims to be a journalism student, graduating next week. She said she went to that event today to meet CeeCee."

"She *claims*? She *said*?"

"I just think there's probably more to the story than that."

"Careful, Reed. Your paranoia is showing."

"I dunno, man. My gut keeps telling me she's got an agenda. Maybe she's a model on the side, and she's got her sights set on starring in RCR's next video. Or she's a dancer who'd ditch her big journalistic dreams in a heartbeat to back up Aloha on her next tour. I have no idea. All I know is, when I saw her at that event today, she zeroed in on me awfully fast, and came on like gangbusters. She's way too confident, and way too flirtatious with me, not to have an angle."

Josh shakes his head. "*She* zeroed in on *you*? Are you sure it wasn't the other way around, player?"

I shrug. "No, I'm not sure. That's my point. I'm usually sure when I'm the hunter, versus the hunted. With this girl, I don't know which way is up—who's got the upper hand. Who's got the bow and arrow. She's giving me whiplash in the best possible way."

Josh rolls his eyes. "Then enjoy it. No need to analyze it."

I sip my drink. "Oh, I'm enjoying it. Tremendously. But, still, my gut feels like she's got something up her sleeve."

Josh shrugs. "Maybe she thinks you could put in a good word for her with CeeCee."

I sip my drink. "Yeah, that could be it."

"If it's anything at all. Maybe, just maybe, she's a twenty-one-year-old journalism major who went to an event to meet CeeCee and unwittingly hooked a huge marlin on her line, when she hadn't even gone there to go marlin fishing. Maybe she's elated to catch the eye of a rich baller, who's not half-bad looking, who can take her backstage to meet Red Card Riot or Aloha Carmichael or 2Real or 22 Goats, any time he wants. Not to mention, take her to the best parties in town. And the best restaurants. Or to Paris on a whim. You're an exciting guy, Reed. To any woman. But especially to a kid like her." He claps my shoulder. "Stop being so fucking cynical. Not every woman in Los Angeles is looking to exploit you for professional gain. Some of them want to exploit you for your money, hot body, access to parties and private aircraft, and backstage passes."

I laugh. "You've gone soft on me, Faraday. Before Kat, you were even more paranoid than me about women's ulterior motives. You were a gold medal athlete in the sport of sniffing out gold diggers. We were brothers in paranoid arms, remember?"

"Yeah, before Kat, I was a paranoid asshat who didn't know the true meaning of happiness and wouldn't have known unconditional love if it bit me in the ass. So don't make my paranoia sound more glamorous than it was."

"Oh, for the love of fuck. Not this again. You swore at Henny's wedding you'd never again torture me with another speech about Kat 'saving you from—'"

"Thanks again for the generous tip, Mr. Rivers."

It's Georgina, standing before us with my credit card and receipt.

I smile and take my card. "You earned it." I motion to Josh. "Georgina, this is my best friend, Josh Faraday. Josh, this is Georgina Ricci. Bartendress extraordinaire. Aspiring journalist. Fellow UCLA alum, as of next week. Hustler. Chess enthusiast. Full-grown adult."

Josh laughs. "Hi, Georgina."

"Hi, Josh. Nice to meet you. And, for the record, I have no idea how to play chess."

Josh indicates the mess of drinks in front of us. "Looks like you know how to make drinks, though."

"I fake it pretty well. Reed figured out a clever way for us to hang out during a busy Thursday-night shift."

"That's Reed for you," Josh says. "The Man with the Plan."

"Oh? Wikipedia says he's The Man with the Midas Touch. Gasp. Is Wiki *wrong*?"

Josh chuckles. "No, he's that, too." He bats my shoulder. "Come shoot pool with us whenever you're done chatting up the bartender, brother. Take your time."

I open my mouth to tell Josh I'll follow him in two

seconds, just as soon as I say a proper goodbye to the lovely bartender, when a female voice shrieking my name behind me splits my eardrums. It's a voice I don't recognize. Not at all. But I know, instinctually, it's attached to someone I'm going to loathe, whoever the fuck she is.

Chapter 11
Reed

The woman shrieking my name is, indeed, a stranger to me. A young, blonde, high-strung one with a flash drive in her hand. After shrieking my name, she launches into an elevator pitch about her music, saying all the same things I've heard a million times before. She's a UCLA music student who saw me at today's event, she says. And, surprise, surprise, she's the next Adele.

"I don't accept unsolicited submissions," I say, putting up my palm. "No exceptions. And just a tip, Courtney. Don't compare yourself to Adele. Nobody is 'the next Adele.' You sound like a fucking amateur when you say that. Also—"

"Excuse me," Georgina says, and off she goes to the other end of the bar.

Fuck.

I'd forgotten Georgina was standing there, watching this entire exchange. Fuck! From Georgina's tone and body language, it's clear she thinks I'm being too harsh with this girl. But what am I supposed to do? Sit here smiling every time someone ambushes me during a relaxed night with friends? And more to the point, when I'm hitting on the hot-as-fuck bartender? If this girl hadn't bombarded me, I would have had a tantalizing "see you later, Cinderella" moment with Georgina. I'd have walked away from her on my own terms, leaving her wanting more. As it is, though, this girl is in my personal space, elevator-pitching me, while Georgina is standing ten feet away, looking upset.

"Enough," I say sharply to the blonde, cutting off her rambling. "When I told you I don't accept unsolicited demos a minute ago, that was your cue to fuck off."

The girl's mouth hangs open, just as Josh shifts his weight next to me, letting me know he thinks that was too harsh.

But fuck it. What this girl and Josh and Georgina don't understand—what *nobody* could understand, unless they've walked a mile in my shoes—is that I'm not on this earth to give out participation medals. I'm here to find and disseminate rare musical greatness, while also living my best life. And guess what? Pretending to give a shit every time some wannabe ambushes me with a demo isn't living my goddamned best fucking life!

I'm pissed as hell this blonde torpedoed my "see you later" with Georgina. And in the process quite possibly outed me to Georgina as the asshole that I am. But those aren't the main reasons I just told her to fuck off. In truth, the far less prickish reason for my behavior is that I'm helping this kid out. Teaching her something. If she truly wants to make it in music, she's going to encounter assholes far worse than me. On a daily basis, she's going to discover nobody will hold her fucking hand in this business. Not even if she's "the next Adele." Which she's *not.*

I glance at Georgina at the far end of the bar, making sure she's not overhearing anything, and to my relief, she's busy serving a customer. "Courtney," I say, "I'm doing you a favor here by not sugarcoating anything. Music is a brutal business, filled with savage, endless rejections that are going to crush your soul and disembowel your spirit and make you question your talent on a daily basis. And, to be perfectly honest, I can already see in your eyes you're not built to withstand any of that. Do you honestly think you are? Tell the truth. Swear on a stack of bibles you're up for that kind of abuse."

It's a test. If this kid caves, then my instinct about her is right: she'll never make it in the cruel world of music. But if she tells me to fuck off, if she says I'm wrong about her, and that she's going to hustle until her dying breath to prove me wrong, then, hell, maybe I've misjudged her. Maybe, if she pushes back like that, today will be her lucky day and I'll do something I never do: listen to her stupid fucking demo.

But, nope. Courtney doesn't push back. In fact, she does exactly what I'm expecting: she crumples, right before my eyes. "Sorry to... ," she murmurs, before scooping up her flash drive and sprinting away, tears pooling in her eyes.

"Jesus, Reed," Josh says. "That was a bit much."

"No, it wasn't." I pick up a mystery drink and take a long sip. "An Old Fashioned. Nice."

"Seriously, man. That was brutal."

"Yeah, well, tough shit. I can't go anywhere these days without someone trying to convince me they're the next Adele, Beyoncé, Laila, or Aloha. Or, if they're in a band, then they're the next Red Card Riot or 22 Goats. And guess what? *They never are.* Can I afford to waste five minutes, now and again, pretending to give a shit when someone approaches me with stars in their eyes? Maybe, though I wouldn't be happy about it. But, Josh, this shit happens ten times a day, every day. Am I supposed to waste a full *hour* out of every twenty-four on this shit? I bet even your mother-in-law, the nicest person I know, would tell me I'm well within my rights to shut this kind of shit down."

Josh sips a martini. "I strongly doubt my mother-in-law would be okay with you telling a young college student with stars in her eyes to fuck off."

My stomach clenches. "Okay, well. Maybe that one thing was a bit harsh. Do me a favor and don't tell your mother-in-law I said that, okay?"

Josh laughs. "Look, I get it. I can't imagine how annoying it would be to get bombarded like that all the time.

I'm just saying there are other ways to say what you did that aren't going to scar the kid for life."

"If me telling her to fuck off scars her for life, then she shouldn't even think of trying to make it in music."

Josh sighs. "Whatever. Don't mind me. I fully admit I've turned into a huge softie these days. You should see how Gracie has me wrapped around her little finger. If Little G cries a single tear, I'm wrecked. Kat's gotta play bad cop with her all the time, because I'm too big a pussy to do it." He chuckles. "That kid is so damned cute. Same with Jack."

I take a sip of my drink, and say nothing. Truthfully, I don't think I'm *that* different from Josh. Tears wreck me, too, but only when they're shed by someone I love, not a stranger in a bar. For fuck's sake, I've spent my entire life wiping my mother's tears, and where is she now? In Scarsdale, in the finest mental facility money can buy, painting with outrageously expensive paints I've imported for her from France. And all of it, to keep her tears away.

And when my baby sister got her heart smashed by her teenage love, and her tears wouldn't stop flowing, what did I do? Well, right after threatening to kill the bastard who broke her heart, I packed my sister off to the best college money could buy, three thousand miles away from the guy she couldn't seem to break away from on her own. All to keep her tears away.

And when my housekeeper, Amalia, cried for the first and only time in my presence—when that sweet woman broke down four years ago at my kitchen table and confessed her brother needed surgery and couldn't afford it and she was terrified of losing him—I not only wound up paying for the brother's *four* surgeries, I paid off his apartment lease for two years, too. All to keep sweet Amalia's tears away.

But some random chick in a bar cries because, waah, waah, the music industry is so hard? Because she's got a dream and I'm not rolling out the red carpet for her? Yeah, well, fuck her. I had a dream, too. And I mortgaged my soul, heart, blood, sweat, and tears to make my dream happen. I hustled and scrambled. And, yeah, I lied, too, on occasion, whenever truly necessary. But, most of all, I never gave up, no matter how many people told me I was crazy. No matter how many people said making money in music was impossible these days, thanks to streaming and illegal downloading and the new "singles instead of albums" culture. And now, here I am, laughing at all the naysayers, all the way to the bank.

Suddenly, I'm pinged with the thought of how supportive and awesome Josh and Henn have always been, which, of course, makes me curious about Henn's whereabouts through all this. I turn around and spot him at the pool table, happily playing a game of partners pool with three strangers. It's so fucking Henn, I can't help smiling about it.

"Come on," I say to Josh. "Grab as many of these drinks as you can carry, and let's shoot some pool. I'm in the mood to kick some ass."

"Well, you're not gonna kick mine. I've been sinking balls like a pro since we got here."

"Well, of course, I didn't mean *your* ass, dumbass. I meant *Henny's*. Come on."

As I start wrangling glasses off the bar, my gaze finds Georgina's on the other end of the bar. Instantly, my blood flash-boils at the way she's looking at me—like she wants to suck my dick. I smile, and Georgina looks away, her face blushing crimson. And, just this fast, I know a certain something about Little Miss Georgina Ricci... I'm not sure how much of my exchange with the blonde Georgina overheard, but I'm pretty sure it was enough for her to realize I'm maybe more of an asshole than she'd previously thought... Which is okay. Because, based on the heated look Georgina just flashed me before looking away, she very much *likes* assholes. Oh yeah, based on that scorching hot smolder, Little Miss Sexy-as-Fuck Georgina Ricci likes assholes... *a whole fucking lot.*

Chapter 12
Georgina

I put my phone down and sneak another peek at Reed across the crowded bar. For the past forty-five minutes, while I've been busy working, he's been playing pool with his two buddies. And looking scrumptious while he does. I shouldn't feel this attracted to the guy. Not when I've got a strong hunch he's actually a big ol' prick. A charming one, for sure. A sexy one. But a prick nonetheless. And yet, I can't help myself. My attraction to him isn't admirable. But it's primal and raw and, apparently, not going to subside until I scratch my freaking itch.

A customer flags me down, and I peel my eyes off Reed's hard ass to tend to him. When I'm done, I glance at Reed again, salivate over his ass for a bit—also, his forearms, biceps, and profile—and then grab my phone to find out if Alessandra has replied to my most recent text. She has.

Alessandra: It's not RR's fault that girl cried. All he said is he doesn't accept unsolicited demos. Which, btw, comes as no surprise to me. (I told you so.)

Me: That's all I HEARD him say to her. After I walked away, he said a lot more I couldn't hear. And, whatever it was, it made her run away crying. Is that what he's going to do to me when I give him your demo? Make me cry?

Alessandra: Not if he wants to have sex with you, which he obviously does.

Me: He should be nice to people, whether he wants to sleep with them or not.

Alessandra: He can't take every demo shoved at him, G. He'd suffocate underneath an avalanche of plastic.

Me: Well, I'm going to make him take yours, if it's the last thing I do. The only question is... WHEN should I bring it up? Tonight? And if so, before or after we have sex? Or should I gamble that I'll see him when he gets back from NYC and do it then? Gaaaah!!! DECISIONS, DECISIONS!!!

Alessandra: Follow your gut. As long as you promise not to prostitute yourself to help me, I'm happy.

Me: Dude. If you could see his ass right now, you'd know my desire to sleep with RR has absolutely nothing to do with you and your demo.

It's the truth. In fact, having Alessandra's demo in my purse has become the bane of my existence. An albatross around my neck. Although, of course, I'd never tell that to Alessandra. My phone buzzes again, and I look down.

Alessandra: Send me an ass photo, please.

Chuckling, I take yet *another* surreptitious photo of Reed, this one while he's bending over the pool table, and send it off to my stepsister. And then I glance at the clock. It's two minutes until midnight. Holy crap. Is Reed *really* planning to do something at midnight, like he said before? He did call me Cinderella, after all, but that was almost an hour ago... My phone buzzes again.

Alessandra: Dat ass! OMG!

Me: I know. I've been wiping drool off my chin all night. Hey, why aren't you sleeping? It's almost 3:00 there.

Alessandra: I couldn't sleep now if my life depended on it. I'm dying to see what's going to happen at midnight, Cinderella.

Me: Probably nothing, considering RR is no Prince Charming.

"Georgie," a male voice says, making me look up from my phone. It's Bernie, the owner of the bar... accompanied by none other than Reed and Reed's two friends.

"Oh, hi," I say lamely. I glance at the clock. Midnight on the button. "I didn't know you were coming into the bar tonight, Bernie."

Bernie claps Josh on his shoulder. "I wasn't planning on it, but then I got a call from this guy. Hey, Marcus! Come here!"

As we await Marcus, I glance at Reed, and the look of molten lust on his face sends arousal whooshing between my legs.

"What's up?" Marcus says.

Bernie introduces Reed and his friends, and explains that Josh used to work here many moons ago. "Reed wants to see Josh behind the bar again, for old time's sake. So, he's offered to pay for everyone's drinks until closing—at double our usual prices, just in case Josh is rusty." Bernie grins at Marcus and me. "He's going to tip each of you four hundred bucks, since you're both unexpectedly getting the boot for the rest of the night."

"The boot?" Marcus asks.

"You're off the clock," Bernie says. "Stick around and play pool or go home. Whatever you want. You're getting paid *not* to work."

"Wow, that's generous," I say, my eyes locked with Reed's. Holy hell, he's looking at me like I'm a sizzling steak on a plate, and he's a man with a fork and sharp knife. I keep my tone prim and proper. "Thank you, Mr. Rivers."

Reed smirks. "My pleasure, Georgina."

Bernie nudges Josh's arm. "I'll work alongside you, in case you've lost a step since your glory days. Come on."

"Lost a step?" Josh says playfully, following Bernie behind the bar. "I'm still in my prime, old man."

Laughing, the two men shoo Marcus and me out of the well, while Reed's other friend, the nerdy one, takes a stool. And, suddenly, I find myself standing on the customers' side of the bar with Marcus and Reed. Which isn't awkward at all.

Marcus looks suspicious as he assesses Reed. "I assume you did this because you're trying to impress Georgie."

"Marcus!" I say, shocked.

Marcus looks at me, his eyes blazing. "He's been ogling you all night, Georgie. Even when he's supposedly been playing pool, he hasn't stopped peeking at you."

My body zings with arousal, which is probably not the result Marcus was going for. Well, well, well. As I've been covertly ogling Reed from across the bar, he's been covertly ogling me?

Marcus turns to Reed. "I don't know who you are, but Georgina isn't going to fall at your feet, just because you're tossing out hundred-dollar bills like candy. Georgie's smart. *Special.* She's worth a hundred of the women you're probably used to picking up in bars by flashing your money clip."

"Marcus, stop," I say, putting my hand on his forearm. "I appreciate you looking out for me, but I don't need your protection this time. Truthfully, I've been ogling Reed all night, too. And not because of his money clip, but because we had great chemistry when we talked."

Marcus looks crestfallen. A knight toppled from his horse. The good guy, once again, *not* getting the girl.

My heart aching for Marcus, I turn to Reed. "Marcus is right about one thing, though. Your penchant for throwing around hundred-dollar bills is a bit much. Thank you for your generosity tonight. We both appreciate it. But if you keep throwing big money at me, I'm going to start wondering if you think I'm a stripper, rather than a bartender—which isn't something I want to be wondering."

Reed bites back a smile. "Sorry if I've offended you. Money was really tight for me in college. I waited tables and counted my lucky stars whenever I got a big tip. I just wanted to pay it forward."

Oh.

Well.

That was a pretty nice response.

And now I feel like an ungrateful bitch.

"Oh, yeah, thank you again," I say lamely. "Like I said, Marcus and I both appreciate your generosity a lot." I glare at Marcus, feeling annoyed he pushed me into making that embarrassing speech. "Right, Marcus? Reed has been incredibly generous, and we both appreciate it."

Marcus presses his lips together, clearly pissed.

I pat Marcus's shoulder. "I'm good, okay? I'm going to head off to enjoy this unexpected time off now. You should do the same."

Marcus looks heartbroken, but, after visibly recalibrating, he tells me to have a good time and stalks away with his big tips and unexpected two hours off.

"Are you two more than friends?" Reed asks.

"No."

"Much to his disappointment, I'm sure." He rubs his hands together. "But enough about him. Are you ready to head to my castle now, Cinderella? The clock has struck midnight, and your carriage—"

"Georgie!"

Oh, for the love of fuck, what now?

I turn around and palm my forehead. It's Bryce McKellar. The football star and Cling-on. The momma's boy who supposedly started believing in love at first sight when he saw me. He's here. And striding toward me with a bright smile on his face.

"Bryce," I gasp out, my heart rate spiking. "What are you doing here?"

Bryce hugs my stiff body. "You said you were working tonight, so I came by to say hi. I thought we could hang out when you get off."

I bristle. Bryce already asked me to hang out after work tonight, when I bumped into him on-campus, and I told him it wasn't going to work out. *But he came here, anyway?*

Bryce motions vaguely behind him. "I'm here with some teammates, so don't mind me until then. I can see you're busy... " His eyes drift to Reed and light up. "Hey, you're Reed Rivers!"

"And you're Bryce McKellar," Reed replies smoothly, extending his hand. "I've got season tickets. Congrats on last season. I can't wait for this upcoming one."

"Thanks. *Wow.* My sister is obsessed with you, man. What a trip."

"Your sister's a musician?"

"An amazing singer-songwriter. She plays piano. She's two years younger than me—going to USC, actually."

"Oh no. Yours is a house divided."

Bryce chuckles. "Yeah, she's a filthy traitor. But we still love her. Just barely, though." He chuckles. "Hey, how can I get my sister's music to you? You'd go crazy for it. She's the next Beyoncé."

"Unfortunately, I don't accept unsolicited demos, Bryce. No exceptions. But, as a favor to you, and only you, so don't tell anyone, I'll check out your sister's Instagram when I get a free minute."

"Really? Wow. Thanks!"

"Your sister's music is posted there?"

"Yeah. She always posts her stuff there."

Bryce tells Reed his sister's handle while Reed makes a note on his phone. And then, Reed shakes Bryce's hand and says, "Now, if you'll excuse me, I've got a hot date with a gorgeous woman."

"So do I, as a matter of fact," Bryce replies, winking at me. "It's been great meeting you."

"You, too. Kick ass next season."

"I will."

There's a beat. During which I feel like I'm going to pass out. Or barf. Or both. And then, both men say, "Georgina?" at the exact same time—a strange turn of events that would be comical, if it weren't so damned mortifying.

Of course, it's Reed, the man used to being king of the world on a whole other level than Bryce, who fills the awkward beat. Reed says, "Are you ready for our midnight date, my beautiful Cinderella?"

At Reed's comment, Bryce's face falls, full understanding crashing down on him—and I have to press my lips together to keep from giggling at his cartoonish expression. Not because I'm taking any pleasure in this awkward, embarrassing moment. But because it's now clear Bryce assumed I'd been taking Reed's drink order when he first walked up, not getting ready to head to Reed's house to bone him. And seeing him figure things out is genuinely amusing to me. But, also, simultaneously, rather unpleasant.

"I need a minute," I say to Reed. "Bryce? Can we chat for a second?"

Bryce looks like a deer in headlights. But he nods and follows me to a corner.

"I'm sorry," I blurt, before Bryce can speak. "I didn't know you were coming tonight. And I didn't know Reed would be here, either. I had no intention of humiliating you."

"You said you'd be getting off work at two thirty," he says dumbly. "It's only midnight."

"I wasn't lying," I say. "Without my knowledge, Reed arranged with my boss to get me off a couple hours early."

"*What?*"

I flinch at his sharp tone. If I felt like giggling at his reaction earlier, I don't now, as his shock seems to be morphing into anger before my eyes.

Lauren Rowe

"I met Reed earlier today," I say, my heart pounding. "At that event I was running to when we bumped into each other. But that doesn't matter. Even if I hadn't met him, I was going to call you tomorrow to tell you I don't think we're compatible."

"*Not compatible?*" Bryce says, like I've just said I think the world is flat. "But... we've got amazing chemistry. I told you—you're stone-cold wife material."

"But, see. That's the thing. I'm not. I mean, I might be one day. But not now. I'm not looking for a relationship, Bryce. And it's clear to me you are."

He looks disgusted as it dawns on him: *if she's not looking for a relationship, then she must be headed off with Mr. Music Mogul for a meaningless night of fun... which therefore means she's not even close to the wife-material kind of girl I thought she was.* "But isn't he, like... *forty?*" he blurts.

My jaw sets. "He's thirty-four."

"What the hell, Georgie? I know he's rich and connected and all that, but—"

"I don't care about Reed's money or connections. And screw you for implying that. We've got chemistry, plain and simple." God, I hope I'm telling the truth about that. Is it possible I'm being blinded by Reed's power and money and the fact that he has the ability to make Alessandra's dreams come true? I don't *think* that stuff is what's attracting me, and making me look past some kind of dickish comments, but I can't deny Reed's star power is part of his appeal. But only because he's so confident and sure of himself. I mean, if Reed weren't "Reed Rivers," but equally confident and commanding, I'm sure I'd still be willing to traipse off to his house tonight, for what's almost assuredly going to be the best sex of my life. Wouldn't I?

"Yeah, well, we have great chemistry, too," Bryce says. "And I'm not forty fucking years old."

86

"Okay, this is pointless. Like I said, I never intended to humiliate you. I'm sorry if I've wasted your time or embarrassed you. I've got to go now."

"With *him*?" Bryce grabs my arm to keep me from leaving, his dark eyes on fire. "He's not going to give a shit about you after tonight, Georgie."

Before the "fuck you" in my throat escapes my mouth, Reed appears at my side, anger wafting off his muscled frame. "*Release*," he says sharply, like he's a dog trainer ordering the obedience of his pit bull. "*Now*."

Instantly, Bryce obeys Reed, like a good doggie. But in one final show of defiance, he leans into my ear, right in front of Reed, and whispers, "I can do casual, if that's what you want. I just didn't think a girl like you would want that."

I don't acknowledge Bryce's insulting comment. Or his implication that "wife material" girls can't enjoy casual hookups, just like anyone else.

Reed's dark eyes are hard and his jaw clenched. He puts out his arm to me. "Ready, Cinderella?" He levels Bryce with a glare that makes my spine tingle. "It's time to go."

Relieved, I take Reed's arm. "I'm ready, *Prince Charming*."

I meant that last thing as a joke, of course. And Reed's smirk tells me he's taking it that way. Clearly, this man is nobody's Prince Charming. Least of all mine. Indeed, if there's such a thing as Prince Charming for anyone but my mother, I can't imagine he'd be a guy who brazenly cops to having no interest in doing anything but "seducing" women.

After I've linked my arm with Reed's, he puts out his free hand to Bryce, daring him not to shake it—daring Bryce to snub him because he's feeling territorial about a girl he barely knows—and thereby mess up his sister's chances at possible musical stardom.

For a second, Bryce stares at Reed's extended hand, but, quickly, he forces a smile and takes it. "No harm meant, man. It was just a misunderstanding."

"Totally understand. Have a great night."

"Thanks again for looking at my sister's Instagram."

"You bet," Reed says. "I'm looking forward to it." With that, Reed unlinks our arms so he can slide his strong arm around my shoulders, before confidently guiding me toward the front door.

As I walk with Reed, I feel swept away. Like I'm physically swooning. I inhale the scent of Reed's cologne, as well as his confidence. I register the strength and hardness of his fit body. The urgency and command of his grip on me. All combined, I'm feeling physically intoxicated by Reed in this moment, in the best possible way.

"Have you slept with him?" Reed says, when we're out of Bryce's earshot.

"That's none of your business." Okay, I can't help myself. "But, no, I haven't. Get this. Bryce and I haven't even *kissed*."

Reed chuckles. "Well, damn. He's awfully wound up about a girl he's never even kissed. Although, in the guy's defense, I could say the same thing about myself."

Butterflies release into my stomach. "Thank you. That's a nice thing to say."

"I'm a nice guy."

I snort. "That remains to be seen."

Reed chuckles. "I knew I liked you, Georgina. You don't pull any punches."

"Honestly, Reed, I still haven't decided if I like you. You're a bit of a mixed bag for me at the moment. But I'm most certainly attracted to you physically."

Reed shrugs. "Works for me. Like me or loathe me. It's all good. Just as long as you want to fuck me." He winks. "In fact, in my experience, it's often the ones who hate my guts the most who enjoy fucking me the most."

I say nothing. Because I've got a hunch he's right about that. I mean, look at me. I'm still peeved at the condescending way he spoke to me when he first walked up. More than a little wary about the way he treated that blonde girl. Not impressed by the way he looked at Marcus like he was dirt on the bottom of his shoe. And not certain if I was impressed or repelled by the way Reed took such obvious pleasure in cutting off Bryce's golden balls, and then dangling Bryce's sister's Instagram page in front of Bryce's face to keep him in line.

But even if the jury is still out on Reed's likeability— whether I ultimately decide I like him or loathe him, as Reed said—he's absolutely right: there's no doubt in my mind I want to fuck him like my life depends on it. More so, in fact, than I've wanted to fuck anyone in the four years since I started having sex.

Reed draws me into his muscled frame even closer, and whispers, "What'd you do to that boy, Georgie? Tell me the truth, as a cautionary tale."

"I did nothing, I swear. We met on campus. Talked and texted a few times. And that's it. For some reason, he seems to think it was love at first sight for us."

"No."

"Or so he said." I scoff. "Talk about a lady-boner-killer."

Reed smiles. "You don't believe in love at first sight, Cinderella?"

"No, Prince Charming, I don't. I frankly think the entire idea is ludicrous. But Bryce believes in it. Unless he was only saying that to me because he thought it was what I wanted to hear. Which would then make him horrifically bad at reading a girl's signals."

"Naw, he was being straight with you," Reed says. "Despite everything he's got going for him on the playing field, that kid's got zero game."

"And yet, he was willing to throw his supposedly instant love for me under the bus, to get you to listen to his sister's music. Love, zero. Ambition, one."

"Like I said before: everyone's got a price. You've just got to figure out what it is, and bribe them with it."

"I don't have a price."

He smirks.

"I don't."

He pats my head. "Okay, Georgie girl. You're the only person on Earth without a price." He chuckles. "It's times like this I'm reminded just how young you really are." He opens the door for me. "The truth is, sweetheart, if you think you can't be bought, that only means nobody's been smart enough to figure out your price yet."

Chapter 13
Reed

The cool night air envelops Georgina and me as the door of Bernie's Place closes behind us. I'm buzzing. Off-kilter. Feverishly lit up with my hunger for this woman's flesh—with my desire to explore and devour every inch of her, to breach her borders and push her boundaries—to claim her, conquer her, *ruin* her—until she's begging for mercy and crying tears of euphoria.

Only a few feet outside of the bar, a tsunami of lust washes over me. So much so, I stop walking, pin Georgina against the building's façade, and do the thing I've been aching to do since I first laid eyes on her: I press my hungry mouth to hers. And when she parts her lips and invites me inside with a soft and sexy moan, when my tongue enters her mouth and tangles with hers, when her body unmistakably bursts into white-hot flames against mine, I lose my fucking mind. Instantly, I'm a flaming pyre of greed and need. So overwhelmed with hunger for her, I can't remember my own name. Has a simple kiss ignited my body like this before? If so, I don't remember it.

My phone buzzes with an incoming text in my pocket, but I ignore it. Surely, it's Isabel again, insisting I call her. The same way she's been doing all night. But everything I needed to say to her, I said this afternoon. And even if I hadn't, nobody but Georgina exists anymore. Not in this moment. Right now, the entire world is Georgina and me, and nobody else.

I deepen my voracious kiss, my tongue demonstrating how my body is going to move inside hers when I get her into my bed, and she responds enthusiastically in kind, kissing me with as much passion and energy as I'm showing her. In short order, I'm so aroused, I can barely breathe. I push myself between her legs, yearning to burrow my throbbing cock inside her, and she moans her invitation for me to continue my assault. And so, I do. I press myself against her center, *hard,* still kissing her, yearning to massage that magical, delicious bundle of nerves that's going to drive her fucking wild when I get to it with my tongue, and Georgina slides her arms around my neck and grinds herself against my hard dick, making me even more desperate to sink myself inside her.

As our kiss continues, every atom inside me explodes into a fierce, unquenchable fire ball. Gasping for air, I grab Georgina's thigh and hoist it up, opening her to me like a blooming flower, and she shudders and grips my shoulder ferociously, like she's hanging on for dear life. We're a raging inferno now, Georgina and me. Both of us combustible in a way I haven't felt in a very long time. If ever.

Panting, I disengage from our kiss. But only because I'm acutely aware it's not nearly enough. *I want more.* And I can't get it on a sidewalk.

"We're fire," I murmur, brushing my lips against her soft cheek. "I can't wait to get you naked and kiss your pussy, just like that."

Her chest heaves. "Oh, God."

I kiss her again, simply because I can't resist, even though I know I'm only wasting our precious time at this point. And then, after we've forced ourselves apart again, we clasp hands and begin striding up the sidewalk like we're walking on air.

"Where are we going?" Georgina asks breathlessly.

"To a campus parking structure a few blocks away, to get my car, which will take us to my house in the Hollywood

Hills, where I'm going to strip you naked and fuck you like you've never been fucked before, for four straight hours, without a break, right up until the last nanosecond before I need to leave for the airport."

She says nothing. But her gorgeous hazel eyes tell me she's in favor of that plan.

We talk logistics. I ask if her car is parked somewhere around here. She says, no, she doesn't own a car. That she always walks to work, or takes the campus shuttle, and then Ubers home.

"If there's time later, I'll drive you home on my way to the airport," I offer. "If not, I'll call a car for you. I apologize, in advance, if I have to call a car. I'd prefer to drive you, of course."

"It's all good. Whatever we need to do to maximize our time together, that's what I want to do."

I flash her a wicked smile. "Have I mentioned I like you, Georgina Ricci?"

"You have." And that's it. She notably doesn't return my compliment. Which, frankly, turns me on even more. The last thing I need is for this firecracker of a woman to kiss my ass. Unless, of course, she's going to do it literally.

We walk in silence for a moment, electricity coursing between our hands, until Georgina says, "What did you say to that girl at the bar after I walked away? She looked upset."

"I told her I wouldn't take her demo."

"I heard that part. What did you say after that—after I walked away?"

"Nothing really. I told her music is a tough business. That she shouldn't compare herself to Adele." I shrug. "Some people don't handle rejection well." I pause. "Also, I told her to fuck off. But I did it nicely."

She looks shocked. "There's no 'nice' way to tell someone to fuck off. No wonder she cried."

"Josh said the same thing. But here's the thing, Georgie.

I get bombarded by wannabes all the time. Occasionally, I snap. So sue me." I snort. "Which also happens to me all the time, by the way."

She's quiet for a long moment as we continue walking toward campus, past storefronts and restaurants. And for a moment, I'm worried I've blown it. Scared her away. Miscalculated. Finally, she says, "You *never* take unsolicited demos—from *anyone*?"

"Correct."

"*Never?*"

"Never."

"*No* exceptions?"

I look at her, trying to read her. Does she have a demo for me, despite all her protestations earlier about her lack of musical ambitions? Is that it? "That's right. No exceptions."

"How'd you find Red Card Riot?"

"Someone I trusted told me about them."

"22 Goats?"

"Someone I trusted."

"Laila Fitzgerald?"

"One of my scouts found her and presented her to me. Same with 2Real. A scout stumbled across him on YouTube. And with Aloha, her former bodyguard had started working for me, and told me she was looking to switch labels. See? Not an unsolicited demo in the bunch."

"And yet, you agreed to listen to Bryce's sister's music."

"On her public Instagram page, you might recall."

"Isn't that the same thing, in the end?"

"No. An Instagram account is out there for anyone to see. It hasn't been curated specifically for me. Usually, the stuff there is pretty raw and not overly produced. Also, when I'm not physically taking something handed to me, it sets up lower expectations. It's less of a 'promise' by me to listen or follow up, and more of a casual, 'I'll take a look.'"

"Why were you willing to check out Bryce's sister's

music at all, though, but not that blonde girl's? Was it yet another perk of Bryce being a football star?"

We're walking hand-in-hand up the darkened sidewalk at a good clip now, both of us like horses sensing the barn is close. I'm bursting to touch Georgina. To run my hands and mouth all over her. I grip her hand more tightly in mine at the thought. "It was partly about Bryce being a football star," I admit. "But not in the way you think. Mostly, I wanted to neutralize Bryce when it came to you, as quickly and efficiently as possible."

"'Neutralize' him?"

I smile at Georgina—at her inquisitive, gorgeous face. "When Bryce first walked up, I didn't know what the situation was between you. For all I knew, you two were fucking, or maybe even in love."

She scoffs. "Uh, no. If I'd been in love with Bryce, or anyone else, I would never have so much as flirted with you."

I shrug. "Either way, I felt the need to neutralize him—to unequivocally get him out of my way. And what better way to do that than to show you, right out of the box, he can be bought—that he'd kick you to the curb in a heartbeat for the mere *chance* of getting his sister signed to my label?"

"You thought Bryce would choose his sister's music career over *me*, the great love of his life?"

"I had no idea. But I sure as hell hoped so. Which is why I said I'd check out his sister's Instagram. And, lo and behold, I found the guy's price on the first try. That's actually one of my favorite games. Figuring out someone's price and bribing them with it: watching with glee as they pick my offered bribe over something else they'd normally choose. Something they *should* choose, but don't because what I've offered is just too tempting. It never ceases to amuse me how easily people can be bought."

She shoots me a look of disdain. "One of your favorite games is playing the devil on someone's shoulder?"

"That's a great way of describing it. Yeah, most definitely."

"But you have other favorite games, too?"

I chuckle, but say nothing. Oh, little Georgina. You'll learn soon enough about my other favorite games.

For a long moment, we walk in near silence, the only sounds coming from the occasional car driving by and our brisk footfalls on the cement sidewalk.

Finally, Georgina says, "You said Bryce's status as a football star also figured in, although not like I think? What did you mean by that?"

I chuckle. "Man, you really picked the right major, didn't you?"

She makes an adorable face. "Sorry. When something fascinates me, I can't help asking a million questions."

She looks earnest and adorable right now. Beyond beautiful. Which makes me feel bad I suspected she was lying to me earlier about not wanting to be a pop star. Maybe Josh was right. Maybe Georgina is nothing but fascinated by me. Maybe she wants nothing but a hot night of sex with a baller. And who could blame her for that?

"Don't apologize," I say, just as we reach the parking structure. "I meant that as a compliment." We come to a stop in front of the elevator. I press the call button. "To answer your question about how Bryce's football-star status played into my thinking, I'd rather show you than tell you." The elevator doors open, and I lead her inside the box. "Do me a favor and call up Bryce's sister's Instagram, baby. I'm gonna teach you how to be a music scout for me."

Chapter 14
Georgina

After getting Bryce's sister's Instagram handle from Reed, I call up her page on my phone—trying desperately, as I do, not to let on that I'm a hair's breadth away from having a nervous breakdown. All night long, I've been filled with anxiety about how and when to tell Reed about Alessandra's music. And now, he wants to teach me how to be a "music scout"? Good lord, if I can't find a natural opening to mention Alessandra now, then I'm officially hopeless.

Shit. I feel like the stakes are higher now than ever. After that scorching hot, best-kiss-of-my-life kiss with Reed in front of Bernie's Place, I'm especially determined not to blow my chance to have sex with him tonight. But I can't help worrying Reed is going to feel betrayed when I finally pull out that flash drive. Will he think Alessandra's demo was my singular motivation this whole time? Will he view it as proof that I am, indeed, Bobby Fischer? Or has that amazing kiss worked the same kind of magical swooning spell on him that it worked on me, such that he'll be nothing but sweet and receptive when I finally pull out Alessandra's music? In short, I'm wondering if Alessandra's demo will provoke the same kind of benevolence Reed showed to Bryce... or the kind of wrath he showed to that cute little blonde at the bar.

"Well?" Reed says. "Did you find the sister's account?"

"Uh, yeah." I survey the endless selfies on Bryce's sister's page. "She's really pretty. She looks like Aloha Carmichael."

I show Reed my screen, and he nods his agreement.

"Okay, so, that's strike one against her."

"*Against* her?" My stomach drops. "I meant she looks like Aloha as a compliment."

The elevator doors open on the fourth floor of the structure, and we step out into the near-empty garage.

"I'm parked over here," Reed says, pulling me to the right.

My heart is thundering. "Reed, Aloha is gorgeous and one of the biggest stars on the planet, as you well know. How could looking like her be anything but a good thing?"

"Think, Music Scout. Why would I want to sign Aloha Two-Point-Oh, when the original is already one of my biggest earning stars? I owe it to Aloha to put all my Aloha-shaped eggs into *Aloha's* basket, not the poor man's version of her. There's only so much Aloha-style marketing and songs to go around. I would never want to dilute Aloha's market share."

I'm dumbstruck. I open and close my mouth, not sure how to respond. Now I *really* don't know what to tell him about Alessandra. Whenever I tell anyone about her, I always say she sounds like the lovechild of Adele and Laila Fitzgerald. But Reed is saying that would be a *bad* thing?

"But, still, Music Scout," Reed continues, "we'll press on. She's not 'out' after only one strike. There could be other factors weighing in her favor. Next up, tell me about her numbers. How many followers?"

I look down. "Almost ten thousand. That's good, right?"

"Is it? You tell me, Music Scout."

"Yeah, ten thousand seems like a whole lot to me."

Reed shakes his head. "Nope. It's not impressive. In fact, it's anemic and highly *un*-impressive."

Well, fuck. My stomach is churning now. Alessandra barely has a thousand followers. If this girl's following is anemic and unimpressive, what's Alessandra's? Pathetic? *Laughable*?

Reed says, "But that's not the end of the road for this

girl, either, Music Scout. If those ten thousand followers are actual people—not bots or ghosts set up to make her look good—if it turns out they're genuine, enthusiastic, and highly interactive fans—then that's something to consider."

"How do we know if they're real or not?"

"You'd have to audit her account. Look at the interactions on each photo and video. Click on the profiles of the interactive ones and see if they come off like real people with real lives, or fake accounts. Once you start looking closely, you can usually tell fairly easily."

I make a move to swipe at my screen, like I'm going to get started on what he's just instructed, but Reed stops me with a gentle touch.

"Not now, Music Scout. I'm just educating you, for later. That job could take a while, so we'll put it on the back burner for now. There's no point wasting our time on auditing her followers if she's got no talent. Or if she's got talent, but she's not a good fit for us. For now, we'll put a pin in that, say she looks *meh* on numbers, certainly not great, but there could be extenuating circumstances that will give her more of a platform in the future than the average bear."

Reed stops walking, and I follow suit, right in front of a breathtaking, gleaming black sports car. It's the kind you'd see on an actual racetrack, or in a spy movie. And, suddenly, I realize... *this is Reed's ride.* As in, the car he drove to get here today. On actual city streets. Holy shit.

"This is your *car*?" I blurt lamely.

Reed smiles. "One of them." He presses a button to unlock it, and a gentle chirp echoes throughout the empty cement structure.

"What is it?" I ask, slack-jawed.

"A Bugatti Chiron."

"A Bugatti... ?"

"*Chiron.* They vastly improved the Veyron with this model. It's got exponentially more pick-up."

"Well, thank God for that. I always say the Vey-whatever was a piece of shit."

He snorts.

"It's gorgeous," I say, in genuine awe. "A work of art."

"It is." He assesses his baby for a long beat. "If I didn't already have a hard-on because of you, Georgie, I'd have a hard-on looking at this car. I've got a thing for fast cars."

"And fast women," I say, like we're in a poorly written action movie. Because, come on, who could resist inserting that cheeseball line into this surreal moment, in front of *this* car?

Luckily, Reed gets my offbeat humor, apparently, because he laughs at my stupid joke as he leads me around to the passenger side. But just when I think he's going to open the door for me, he slides his palm onto my cheek, pins me against his gorgeous car, presses his hard-on into my clit, and kisses me deeply—this time, with even more heat and greed than the last time. And, once again, I'm instantly ravenous for him. My heart exploding, I slide my arms around his neck and grip his hair and kiss him the same way I'm going to fuck him at his house: without holding back.

"You drive me crazy," Reed whispers into my lips. "I can't resist you."

"Please don't."

His burning eyes scan my face for a long, heated, delicious beat. "Damn, you're gorgeous, Georgie."

I take a deep, steadying breath. "Damn, you're... mildly attractive, Reed."

He laughs—and so do I. Because, as we both know, Reed Rivers is drop dead gorgeous. His features aren't objectively perfect, by any stretch, in terms of symmetry. But the way they come together, the way his face is animated by his intelligence and wit and charm and *confidence*... the overall package of him is like catnip to this particular kitty. And I've got to think any other kitty who happens to cross his swaggering, strutting path.

After one more kiss, Reed opens the passenger door for

me, gets me situated in the luxurious leather seat, and shuts me in with a soft click. And the minute I'm alone in Reed's car, as Reed makes his way around the back to his door, I quickly google the car name he mentioned... and then gasp at the crazy words on my screen: *Bugatti Chiron. One of the fastest cars ever manufactured. Approximately 45 units sold worldwide per year. Price tag: $2.9 million.*

Holy crap! I'm sitting in a car worth three million bucks? I suddenly feel faint.

I swear I'm not going home with Reed because of his money. But, holy crap, it's not every day a girl sits inside a three-million-dollar machine. For God's sake, I've never been inside a three-million-dollar *house,* let alone a three-million-dollar *car.* Suddenly, I feel nervous to move a muscle inside this car. To breathe. What if I spontaneously combust—or barf or pee? The driver's side door opens and Reed slides into his seat. "Have you been dutifully scouring the girl's page to find a video for me, Music Scout?"

"Uh. No. But I will." I flip back to Instagram, my heart pounding in my chest.

"Here. Plug in," Reed says, holding up a cord. "We'll listen to her through my speakers."

My hands shaking, I plug my phone into Reed's offered cord.

"You okay?" Reed asks.

I wipe the flop-sweat off my forehead. "Yeah, I'm great."

But I'm a liar. I'm not "great." I'm feeling a bit sick, actually. Being in this car has made me realize just how successful Reed is. How big a deal it is that I've not only got his undivided attention, but we're *organically* talking about discovering new music, thanks to Bryce. What if I blow this chance for Alessandra? I can't do that. Not even for one night of the best sex in my life.

Reed starts his car, and its expensive engine purrs like a kitten. "Listen to that," he says lovingly. "Beautiful."

"Yeah, beautiful. At least, I think so. Honestly, I wouldn't know. I grew up driving my dad's 2004 Volvo, and I haven't needed a car of my own since I've been in school."

Reed chuckles. "I feel you. In college, I drove a '95 Honda Accord with a transmission that slipped and a passenger window that wouldn't roll down."

I chuckle, and he does, too. And, just like that, something passes between us. Something real. And sweet, believe it or not. Something that makes both of us smile like school kids with mutual crushes on a playground.

"Okay, cue something up already, Music Scout," Reed barks playfully, backing his glorious car out of its parking spot. "I've wasted enough time on this girl. I'll give her one more minute of my precious time, and then I'm going to focus on nothing but *you* until I have to drag my sorry ass to the airport."

"Okay, I'm looking... " I look up from my phone. "Actually, can I ask a quick question? What did you mean when you said 'extenuating circumstances'?"

We're headed down a ramp toward the garage exit now, but Reed glances away from the windshield to look at me quizzically. Clearly, he has no idea what I'm talking about.

"You said her Instagram followers aren't impressive, but there might be 'extenuating circumstances' to give her more of a future platform than the average bear?"

"Oh. Yeah." He turns out of the garage and we take off smoothly into the night. "This is what I mean about Bryce's football-star status coming into play. Assuming Bryce doesn't get injured this coming season, he'll almost certainly get drafted pretty high, and then quite possibly play in the NFL. Which means there's potential for him to have a huge, national platform in coming years, if he doesn't fuck it up. And you know who he'll almost certainly feature on his social media? His baby sister, the wannabe pop star. So, even if his sister's numbers aren't all that great now, she's got huge growth potential. Plus, she's young. Even putting her brother aside, I always keep in mind the young ones almost always need time to grow and develop."

I sigh with relief. Alessandra's nineteen. Would Reed consider Alessandra the kind of "young" artist he'd give a chance to grow and develop? "Interesting," I manage to say, even though my heart is crashing. "So, let's say a singer-songwriter has, I don't know, a thousand followers, and they're, say, nineteen... Then it's not totally impossible for you to want to sign them?"

"There are lots of factors to consider. That's precisely what I'm trying to teach you, Music Scout. In the end, it all hinges on talent." He smiles. "Unless, of course, the wannabe happens to look like you. I swear, I could Auto-Tune the shit out of you and make a mint. In fact, I think that'd be a fun experiment. You wanna try it?"

I laugh. "No, thanks."

"Worth a shot."

I bite my lip, trying to decide how far to push my luck. "So, um, a nineteen-year-old with a small social media following, but amazing talent, would still have a chance?"

Reed's smile fades. He turns away from the road and looks at me for a long beat with hard eyes, like he can read my damned mind. And I know I've messed up. Pushed too hard. Made him suspicious of me. But just as I'm about to throw my palms over my face and confess my sins, Reed returns his attention to the road and says, "That's exactly right, Music Scout. Nothing's impossible, if the artist's talent is mind-blowing enough. Now, to be clear, I'd strongly prefer a potential artist have a shit-ton more followers than a thousand. I mean, in this day and age, if they don't have at least 5k, then what the fuck is wrong with them? Are they stupid? Addled with crippling anxiety? See, the thing to understand is that the music industry is a *business.* You can't sit alone in your room, writing songs for yourself, and not sharing them with the world. I mean, you can, but that's what's called a *hobby*. The *business* side of music is about *selling* that music. Which means you have to *play* your songs for other people and get them to connect with the music and you—which then makes them want to *buy* the songs, or a ticket to your show. The *business* side of music is about *moving* people with your *art*— or, at least, your *charisma*. One way or another, it's about making people *feel* and *connect*. But not for art's sake. But because, in the end, you want them to *buy*. And that means every artist today, whether they're at the top of the game, or just getting started, is a salesperson, in addition to being an artist. If they can't hang with that, then they're not going to succeed. Not with me, or anyone else, and I don't want them—unless, of course, they look like you and/or hit me like a ton of bricks like Laila or 2Real or Red Card Riot or 22 Goats."

Fuck! This is *so* not good. Alessandra's voice is sensational. Her songs incredible. But she'd be the last person in the world to try to convince anyone of either. In fact, I think it's safe to say Alessandra is the worst salesperson who ever lived, when it comes to selling herself. Hence, the reason I'm such a vocal cheerleader for her. If I don't scream from the top of every rooftop about my stepsister, then who will?

"As an example," Reed says, apparently unaware I'm on the verge of having a panic attack mere inches away. "Let's say an artist has strong content, but for whatever reason, I'm on the fence about them. Maybe I love their sound, but I'm concerned they're too niche for the mainstream market. Or, maybe, I'm concerned they lack X factor as a performer. Well, in a case like that, a strong social media presence with diehard fans, even if their following is relatively small, like Bryce's sister's, might tip me over the edge to sign them, because that will convince me they've got what it takes to attract an audience. Plus, I can use their current fans as a test group. I can tailor marketing and branding to include whatever's been working for them, and expand on it." He shrugs. "If there's one thing I've learned in this business—in life, really—it's that the cult of personality—the 'cool kid industrial complex'—is very real and very powerful and should be exploited at every turn. The influencer culture is exactly what made the fiasco of the Fyre Festival possible. Did you see either of those documentaries, by the way? On the Fyre Festival? I was totally obsessed."

"Yeah, I watched them both. I was obsessed, too. I watched them back to back."

"Me, too," he says. "Which one did you like better?"

"The Netflix one, I think?"

He opens his mouth to respond, but I speak first.

"One more question, though. If that's okay."

Reed's jaw tightens. Ever so briefly. But he looks away from the road and smiles at me. "Sure thing. *Investigate* to your heart's content, Madame Journalist."

My stomach clenches. My gut is telling me to drop this topic and loop back to it later, maybe after we've talked about the Fyre Festival at length—but I'm so close now to gathering the courage needed to mention Alessandra, I simply can't leave it alone. "What if an artist is wildly talented, but super shy?" I ask. "What if she, or he, has virtually no social media presence, but their talent is out of this world? Would you still consider signing them?"

Reed shifts his hands on his steering wheel. "That's an exceptionally rare scenario. But, yes, on the rare occasion when I've been struck by lightning, I've signed the person, or band, on the spot, with no consideration whatsoever of their following." His jaw muscles pulsing, Reed shifts his car into high gear as we race down a long straightaway on Wilshire Boulevard. "Any other questions, Music Scout, or are you ready to play me something from Bryce's sister now?"

"Oh. Yeah. Sorry." I fumble with my phone. I wish Reed could see Alessandra perform in person, so he could experience the way her live vocals burrow into a person's soul. The way she evokes emotion with the subtlest of inflections. "Okay, I've found a video of Bryce's sister at a piano."

"Play it. I want to get this over with already."

My hand trembling, I cue the video, and two seconds later, the sounds of simple piano chords fill Reed's car, followed by... a beautiful voice. A breathtaking, soulful one that instantly sends shivers racing across my flesh. Oh, God. This girl is amazing!

"Okay, turn it off," Reed says, even before the girl has reached her first chorus. "I've heard enough."

My heart is galloping. "Enough to know you want to sign her?"

"Enough to know I don't. Turn it off, please. I'd prefer silence, so we can talk."

My lips smashed tightly together, I comply with his request, and the car becomes silent, except for the sounds made by Reed's fancy car.

"You barely listened to her," I finally say.

"I listened twice as long as I normally would, to give my new music scout plenty of time to make her assessment."

"Well, my assessment is she's *amazing* and you should have listened some more."

"She's got talent. No doubt about that. But she's not a fit for River Records. Best of luck to her. *Next*."

I can't believe it. Is he crazy? Deaf? She was soulful and moving. Lovely. Granted, the song she was singing might not be the stuff of global smashdom, but, surely, Reed heard enough to want to listen to another song.

"You thought she was lightning in a bottle?" Reed asks.

"I thought she was *possibly* lightning in a bottle. Enough to keep listening, to find out for sure."

He shifts his car. "And that's why you're a journalism major, and I'm me."

I repress the urge to flip him off and look out the passenger side window. Crap. If he didn't give this girl the time of day, then how long will he listen to my sweet Alessandra pouring her heart out?

"Georgina, she's a second-rate Laila Fitzgerald," Reed says. "And I've already got the original."

I bite my tongue, too pissed and flabbergasted to respond. I know it's irrational, but I'm feeling vicariously crushed for this girl—which, in turn, makes me feel crushed for Alessandra.

"Are you familiar with Laila Fitzgerald?" Reed prompts.

I roll my eyes. "Of course."

"And you didn't hear the similarity? The way she copied Laila's inflection? Georgina, she was literally *copying* Laila. She doesn't have a sound of her own. Doesn't know who she is. That makes her a hard pass for me. *Next*."

And the hits just keep on coming. Alessandra doesn't *try* to sound like Adele or Laila! She's been singing the same way since she was little! Is Reed saying Alessandra wouldn't be a legitimate prospect for him simply because she sounds like a combination of two fabulously successful artists?

"What's wrong?" Reed says. And when I look at him, he's doing that thing again. Staring at me like he can read my mind.

"Nothing," I say, but even as I say it, I know my tone is less than convincing.

Reed sighs. "Look, I'm sorry if you feel sorry for this girl. But move on. She won the lottery that I listened to her at all. I have a team of people I pay a lot of money to scout bands and artists for me, and then present their findings to me at weekly meetings. And you know why? Because I'm too busy and impatient to get eyeballs deep in this shit myself. I'm sorry if the reality of the music business seems harsh and heartless to you, but I know my business. And not only that, I have only one life to live, and finite hours in each day, and I can't waste valuable minutes on anything, let alone aspiring singer-songwriters who I know within seconds aren't going to be a fit. I know within the first ten seconds of a song if someone has a glimmer of a chance to make it onto my roster. The minute I know they *don't*, then I move on. Life is too fucking short to do otherwise. Do you understand?"

"Yes," I say softly, feeling like I'm being physically crushed by the weight of the music demo sitting in my purse. Why, oh why, did I have to have that damned thing in my purse tonight? This night would have been so much more fun, so carefree and sexy and glorious, if I had nothing on my mind but Reed's smoking hot body right now.

Reed pulls onto a side street, where we twist and turn in silence for a bit, until finally coming to a stop in front of a large metal gate. Reed pushes a button and the gate begins sliding slowly open. Silently, he drives through the gate and down a driveway, until parking at the top of a circular drive in front of an extremely large house nestled into the slope of a hill.

Reed turns off his fancy car's engine and turns to me, his brown eyes blazing. "For the love of fuck, just ask me already, Georgina. Let's get it out of the way, whatever it is, so we can move past it and have a great time together."

My heart stops. "Ask you what?"

"Whatever the fuck it is you've been scheming and plotting to ask me this entire car ride. Probably from the second you winked at me in the lecture hall, if I were a betting man." His eyes harden. "*Which I am.*"

Words won't form. I'm a deer in headlights. A thief caught with her hand on a combination lock. *Shit.*

"You want me to listen to a song, I assume?" he says, letting his hand drop from his steering wheel with exasperation. "'Someone' who doesn't have a big social media following?"

He's taken the air out of my lungs. Sent my heart rate galloping. I nod slowly, my cheeks burning. "I'm sorry."

"Is this 'someone' you, Georgina?"

"No."

He looks unconvinced.

"It's my stepsister, Alessandra. Well, my former stepsister. Her mom married my dad when I was eleven and she was nine, but they divorced a year later." I take a deep breath. "She's *so* talented, Reed. A true artist. I'd be thrilled and grateful if you'd, please..." I swallow hard. *Shit.* "Take a quick listen to her music and tell me what you think."

A small puff of air escapes Reed's nose. He shakes his head and looks out his driver's side window. "I knew it," he mutters. "It never fails."

I'm horrified. "Wait. No. You think Alessandra is the *reason* I came here with you tonight? She's not."

Reed swivels his head to look at me, his face nonverbally communicating he thinks I'm a fucking liar.

"Reed, I'm here because I'm genuinely attracted to you."

He bites back a scoff. "Do you just so happen to have Alessandra's music demo with you right now, Georgie, or do you want me to check out her Instagram page?"

Oh, fuck. "I... I have her music demo."

His chest heaves. "Wow. What a coincidence. Do you carry it around with you, everywhere you go?"

I feel tears threaten, but I stuff them down.

"Did you have it earlier today, when you went to the event to 'meet CeeCee,' and our eyes met, and *you* winked at *me*? Did you have your stepsister's music demo then, Georgina?"

I can't move. Or breathe. I've never felt so cornered in my life. So misunderstood... and, yet, so *guilty.*

Reed leans toward me, overwhelming me with his intensity. "Did you walk into that lecture hall today, hoping to give me that flash drive, Georgina? Tell me the fucking truth."

I open and close my mouth. And then slowly nod. "But it's not what you think. I genuinely went there to meet CeeCee, like I said, but since I knew you were going to be there, I *also*—"

He waves me off. "It's fine. I get it. You were multi-tasking. Killing two birds with one stone, right?"

My breathing is labored. I'm physically squirming in my seat. "Exactly. I didn't lie to you, Reed. I flirted with you only because I'm attracted to you. Not because of the demo."

He looks out the window again. "It doesn't matter, either way. Don't worry about it. I knew you were gaming me this whole time, so it's not like this changes anything. Frankly, it's par for the course for me, and a huge relief to finally have my hunch confirmed."

"Reed, listen to me. I haven't been 'gaming' you—"

He returns to me and his face is calm. Like he's wearing a Reed Rivers mask now. "It's okay, Georgina. I strongly prefer knowing someone wants something from me, rather than having to suffer through the exhaustion of them pretending they don't. God, I hate having to play along when they pretend they've never heard of me or any of my artists. To be honest, I don't have a problem with you letting me do filthy things to your body for four hours in exchange for me listening to your stepsister's demo. In fact, I think that's a fair trade-off. If you want to know the truth, one of my kinks is that I sometimes like to treat myself to a bargained-for exchange, just for the simplicity of it. The thing is, though, if I'm gonna pay for sex, whether with money or some other form of currency, I like *knowing* that's what I'm doing, rather than having a woman lie to my fucking face about it."

I'm livid. Beyond offended. In a flash, rage surges inside me, supplanting the arousal I've been feeling up to this horrifying moment. "You're calling me a whore," I say through gritted teeth, and to my shock, he doesn't correct me. He simply raises his eyebrows and tilts his head, as if to say, *If the shoe fits...*

And that makes me even angrier. "You asshole!" I seethe. "I wasn't going to sleep with you in *exchange* for you listening to Alessandra's music! They were two separate things!"

Reed flashes me yet another nasty look, conveying his disbelief.

"Fuck you," I spit out, the Italian in my blood taking over. "How dare you imply I'm willing to whore myself out to get something for Alessandra. How dare you!"

He chuckles. "How dare I? Save your indignation for your next performance, Georgina. The jig is up. You want something from me. I want something from you. There's no need to scream and act outraged about any of it. Let's talk like rational adults about the terms of this exchange and put this deal... to *bed*." He winks.

My jaw thuds to the floor of the car, even as my heart explodes with rage. "Asshole!" I unfasten my seatbelt with frantic fingers, swing open my door, and stomp away from Reed's fancy car, pulling up the Uber app on my phone as I go.

"Where the fuck do you think you're going?" Reed says, marching after me.

"Home. Call me crazy, but my lady-boner sags to my knees when an arrogant, self-entitled prick-asshole calls me a fucking whore."

"Sweetheart, trust me, if I fuck you hard enough while calling you that, you're gonna come harder than you ever have."

I whirl around, intending to slap him, but he grabs my arm and laughs. The bastard *laughs*.

"Fuck. You," I spit out, wrenching my arm from his grasp. "I wouldn't sleep with you now if you were the last man on earth!"

We're just inside the metal entrance gate of his driveway now, standing in the foggy darkness near a streetlamp. And, in this moment, I've never hated anyone as much as I hate Reed fucking Rivers.

"Stop being so dramatic," he says. "Nothing's changed. I admit I was thrown for a loop for a split-second, but I still want to fuck you. The only difference now is I'm aware I've

111

been your mark all along. Well, bravo, Georgina. Well played. But like I said, that's not a deal-breaker for me. I just like knowing the price list in advance, that's all." He looks me up and down. "The menu of options, shall we say, of what I'm getting in exchange for giving this stepsister's music a listen."

I ball my fists, forcing myself not to punch his smug face. "I'm not being *dramatic*," I shout. "I'm disgusted and enraged at you because you're a pig and a jerk who's treating me like a *whore*. Because I've suddenly realized: *I hate you*."

He laughs. "You *hate* me? And you're not being dramatic? Okay." He leans his broad shoulder against the post of the iron fence, and then puts a languid hand in his pocket. "Let me remind you: you're the one who's had an ulterior motive this whole time, as you've been winking at me, and kissing me, and pushing your tits at me at all the right angles, and—"

"Fuck off, Reed!" I shout. "Fuck off and *die*, you arrogant, rude, self-entitled piece of shit."

"Oh, my, my, my. And *I'm* the asshole here? Nice language, Georgina. Tsk, tsk."

I palm my cheek in mock horror. "Oh, no, did I hurt your sensitive ears with my filthy mouth, Mr. Rivers? Or does this cut even deeper than that?" I add my other palm to my face. "Oh, no. Did I hurt your actual *feelings*? This whole time, were you thinking I might *actually* be your Cinderella, and you might *actually* be my Prince Charming? Do you, like Bryce, believe in love at first sight?" I put my hands on my hips and narrow my eyes. "Or is it simply that this is the first time you can't have what you want, and it's killing you? That's what's got you so worked up, isn't it—knowing you're *never, ever* gonna fuck this epicness?" I motion to my body. "Too bad, sweetheart, because I promise I would have been the best you've ever had."

His nostrils flare. His chest heaves. And thanks to the massive boner straining inside his pants, there's no question my punch has landed. "Okay, enough," he says. "Stop acting like a petulant child and come inside. It's cold out here and you're pissing me off."

"Sucks to be you, I guess. I've already called an Uber."

"Cancel it. We're going inside now. I'm gonna listen to one of your stepsister's songs—*one*—but only if you promise not to have a fucking tantrum if I tell you she's not a fit. And then, in exchange for me listening to that *one* song, we're going straight to my bedroom, where I'm gonna rip off those clothes, tie you to my bed posts, and fuck you like you've never been fucked before. So hard, you'll be seeing stars. So well, you'll be crying for mercy and coming harder than you knew was possible."

He's going to tie me to his bed posts? My traitorous clit pulses sharply at the imagery. But, still, in my white-hot rage, I stay the course. "You're not gonna do any of that," I spit out. "And you wanna know why? *Because I don't fuck assholes.*"

Reed's eyes are on fire, his indignation from a moment ago now replaced by white-hot lust. "Come inside and play me the goddamned fucking song, Georgie, so I can fuck your brains out, for both our benefits. We don't have all night and I'm losing my fucking mind over you. Not to mention my fucking patience, too."

I scoff. "I'm not going inside with you. And I'm not going to play my stepsister's music for you, either, because you don't deserve to hear it."

He sighs and looks at his watch. "Can we fast-forward this part, please? Unfortunately, I'm flying commercial and can't delay my flight."

I look down at my phone. "My Uber is one minute away. The longest minute of my life."

"Cancel it," he commands. "For the love of fuck, you've come this far. Use your head, Georgina. The chess game is over. I said *yes* to listening to a song." He sighs. "Fine. If you cancel the Uber and come inside right now, I'll listen to *two* songs."

"Oh, you're *begging* me now? Negotiating against

yourself? How delicious. Well, beg all you want, Mr. Big Shit. The answer is still no. Because no matter how great Alessandra is—and trust me, she *is* great—you're going to say she sucks, just to push my buttons. That's clear to me now. You're a Defcon one level button-pusher, Reed Rivers. I realize that now. And I'm not willing to play your stupid game of chess."

He drags a palm over his stubbled face, looking tormented. "Sweetheart, stop acting like a bratty little child. You're out of control. I'll listen and give my honest opinion, good or bad. I promise, I'm fully capable of separating business and pleasure. *Because I'm an adult.*"

Rage rises inside me again at his obvious implication: *that I'm not.*

"If your stepsister is a fit, then I'll say so. Of course, I will. Because that would benefit me." He smirks. "Although, in the interest of transparency, I should probably admit pushing your buttons is rapidly becoming my new favorite game."

I let out a primal shriek of rage that makes Reed laugh, which only pisses me off more. "Stop being so goddamned condescending!" I shout. "This isn't a joke. This is my stepsister's *life*. Her dream. And you're making a mockery of it. Plus, you've repeatedly impugned my character!"

Reed's eyebrows shoot up at my dramatic last comment, and, I must admit, I think maybe my word choice and intonation were both a little over-the-top. But, whatever. I'm so fucking angry, I press on, letting myself feel whatever I feel and say whatever angry, babbling, bizarre thing pops into my head. "You're not the only 'adult' who can separate business and pleasure, Reed. Yes, I went to that event with Alessandra's demo in my pocket. That was the business side of things for me. And, yes, I planned to give it to you, if the opportunity fell into my lap. And, yes, maybe I flirted with you a little more aggressively than I normally would have, at first, simply because I was so shocked and excited when I realized I'd caught your eye. But guess what is also the truth?

The *pleasure* part of this equation for me. Namely that, by the time I served you that tenth drink, I wanted you, Reed. I wanted to come home with you, and let you do literally anything you wanted to me, for no other reason than I wanted to experience the pleasure of it."

"Liar," Reed says. But before I can smack him, he adds, "You knew you wanted to fuck me by the *third* drink."

I know he's trying to calm me down with humor. But it's too late for that. The man basically called me a whore. There's no coming back from that. "Maybe even the first," I say. "But now? Congratulations. I wouldn't fuck you if you paid me."

"Interesting choice of words."

I grit my teeth. "It was a figure of speech. I meant I wouldn't fuck you if you were the last man on earth. Is that clear enough for you?"

He sighs. "Okay, it's time for you to stop acting like the hotheaded, impetuous twenty-one-year-old you are, and come inside. It's cold out here, and I'm hard as a rock for you. Let me bribe you, sexy Georgina. I promise you'll like giving me your end of the bargain."

My traitorous clit pulses again. This time, thanks to the look of molten lust on Reed's face. There's no way I'd say yes to him, obviously—let alone yes, yes, yes. But I can't deny my body wants to, even in the midst of my mind's rage and disgust.

But before I've said a word, I'm saved by the bell. Or, rather, by the blinding headlights of my Uber shining onto Reed's chiseled face.

"Perfect timing," I say smugly, turning away from Reed. "*Ciao, stronzo.*"

I wave to the driver on the other side of the gate to let him know I'm coming, but Reed grabs my shoulder.

"Tell him to leave," Reed commands, his voice brimming with intensity. "Come inside with me and play me the demo. Let me show you what your body can do, Georgie."

I whirl back around. "I already know what my body can

do. You wanna see?" Glowering at him, I flip him the bird with both hands. "Pretty cool, huh?"

Reed leans against the gatepost and chuckles. "Wow. Tell me how you really feel about me, baby."

"There aren't enough middle fingers in the world to tell you how I really feel about you, *baby*."

He grimaces playfully. "So heartless."

"It was never my 'heart' that felt attracted to you, so it's not a big loss."

"Tsk. So rude. You'll catch more flies with honey. Didn't your momma ever teach you that?"

No, she didn't, asshole, because my mother is fucking dead. But if she were here, there's no doubt in my mind my fiery, fabulous badass of a mother would be applauding me for flipping you off, ya big dick. In fact, she'd be flipping you off, right along with me. I don't say any of that to Reed, of course, but it's sure as hell what I'm thinking.

Wordlessly, I turn around and inspect the metal gate, my anger at an all-time high. First, this arrogant piece of shit tells me I'm "play-acting confidence in my mother's heels," and then he tells me my momma should have taught me to play nice in the face of flaming assholery? Well, fuck that. And fuck *him*. "How do I get through?" I yell, pounding on the iron gate with my palm. "Help me out of here or I'm gonna climb over this gate and fall on my ass, and then sue *your* ass for negligence and false imprisonment!"

Calmly, Reed slides a key into a lock on a pedestrian side gate, and I stomp through the opening without so much as a thank you. But when I reach the other side, I realize I can't actually storm off without trying one last-gasp attempt at helping Alessandra. Even though, obviously, anything I say to Reed at this point will fall on deaf ears.

I turn around. "My stepsister's name is Alessandra Tennison. Her Instagram handle is *TheRealAllyT*. She barely has any followers and no brother destined for the NFL. She's just a shy, sweet, incredibly talented nineteen-year-old who's finishing her sophomore year at The Berklee College of Music in Boston. Her father died a week after her eighth birthday, after going out for an early-morning jog and getting mowed down by a texting driver. And her happiness, her dreams, mean everything to me. A shit-ton more than any one-night stand with a manipulative, arrogant asshole." With that, I whirl around, march to my Uber, and throw myself into the backseat.

"Georgina?" the driver says, per safety protocol.

"Yes. Please, go."

As the car takes off, I steal one last look at Reed. He's standing on the other side of his slatted gate, one of his forearms laid flush against it, and his forehead resting on his arm. His eyes are two hot coals, smoldering in the dim light of the nearby streetlamp. His dick is plainly bulging behind his pants. As hard as a rock, like he said earlier. And for a fleeting moment, I'm a bit pissed at my values, not to mention my Italian temper, for making me miss out on what was almost certainly going to be the hottest hate-sex of my life. *He was planning to tie me to his bed posts*? Holy hell.

As I stare at Reed from the backseat of the departing Uber, seriously questioning my life choices, my temper, and my penchant for sometimes missing the forest for the trees, Reed shoots me a clipped wave in farewell, his cocky body language shouting, *It's your loss, baby!* And that pisses me off, all over again. Without a thought in my head, I raise both middle fingers into the air out the back window before turning around and taking several deep, shaky breaths... before, finally, letting the anger and embarrassment I've been holding back seep out of me in the form of big, soggy tears.

Chapter 15
Reed

"R eed!" CeeCee says brightly, picking up my call. "How's my favorite music mogul?"

"Fantastic, thanks. I just landed in New York, and I'm on my way to meet up with the Goats at their hotel."

"Oh, how I love the adorable Goats! Tell them I said hello."

"I will. They're kicking off *Good Morning America's* summer concert series on Monday."

"How wonderful."

"What about you, CeeCee? What's my favorite media mogul-*ess* up to this week?"

"Well, sadly, I'm not in New York escorting 22 Goats to *Good Morning America*. You've got me beat there. But I've got a few exciting things lined up before I'm scheduled to jet off to meet my darling Francois in Bali."

"Oh, God, I love Bali. Where are you staying?"

She tells me about her trip's itinerary for a bit and then says, "Thank you again for yesterday. Angela was thrilled with the lineup of the panel—particularly, that she was able to snag a superstar like you as the event headliner."

"I wasn't the headliner. *You* were. I was just another panelist."

"Ha! Don't attempt false modesty with me. I didn't have a line out the door afterwards. Did all those students want to ask you questions about the music industry, or did they just want to flirt with you?"

"Actually, most of them wanted to give me their music demos."

"Of course, they did. And... ? Did you discover anyone particularly intriguing?"

My stomach clenches. Did CeeCee notice me losing my shit over Georgina? Is she fucking with me by asking me that? "No, not really," I say, my heart pounding. "I don't accept unsolicited demos, as you know."

"Yes, and I think that's wise. If word got out you did, you'd need bodyguards twenty-four-seven, not just at music festivals. All the more reason I'm grateful you were willing to subject yourself to the onslaught yesterday."

"It was my pleasure. Anything for you."

"Aw, thank you. That's wonderful to hear because, actually, there's something else I'd like you to do for me: give me an in-depth interview for *Dig a Little Deeper*."

I chuckle. "Not this again. Anything but *that*."

"Why are you being so stubborn about this?"

"Why are *you*? Surely, you've got A-listers lined up around the block, wanting to get featured in your new magazine. Why do you keep coming after me?"

"Because everyone else has already been profiled a thousand times. You, on the other hand, are a glamorous man of mystery. You're enigmatic, Reed. Inscrutable. We can all see you're living an enviable life, or so it seems, but what's behind the curtain? What does it take to keep all those plates spinning? And how much has your past influenced your current success? The world knows, generally speaking, you've had to overcome a lot to get where you are, and yet, you've never once been interviewed about any of it."

And I never will, I think.

"Come on, Reed. You never let anyone peel back the layers of your onion. Let me be the first."

"I'm quite content being an unpeeled onion. But, thanks."

119

"I'm envisioning a cover story, honey. An up-close headshot on the cover with those gorgeous eyes of yours, front and center, staring into the reader's soul... It'd be an interview bursting with my admiration and love for you. I'd show you as the inspiration you are."

"I'm not an inspiration."

"Yes, you are. And yet, nobody knows it because you always seem so polished. Let down your guard a little bit, and I promise it'll be the best interview of your life."

"CeeCee, nobody needs to know the nuts and bolts of me. How hard I've worked to get here. What I've overcome. Let them think I walk on water and bathe in Evian and shit diamonds and fuck supermodels every second of my golden life. *That's* my brand—which, by the way, I've meticulously cultivated in order to sell a shit-ton of music over the years."

CeeCee sighs with disappointment. "I think an in-depth interview would be even better for your 'brand.' I truly do. It'd be a win-win."

"I'm sorry," I say. "It pains me to say no to you about anything, love. In some ways, you've been more of a mother to me than my own. But—"

"Now, see! That's exactly the kind of thing I want to talk to you about in an interview! You've never said anything like that to me before. And now I'm dying to know what you mean."

I look out the car window at the bustling streets of Manhattan. "I'd be happy to tell you over drinks some time. *Off* the record."

"I'll hold you to that. So, what can I do for you, my dear?"

"Nothing."

"You called *me*, remember?"

"Oh. Yeah. I just called to tell you how much I enjoyed doing the panel, despite all the griping and bitching I did this past week about having to do it."

"Aw, I'm so glad."

"Icing on the cake, I wound up chatting with your friend, Angela, about being an expert witness on this stupid copyright infringement lawsuit I've got to defend, and she just now emailed Leonard and said she's reviewed the case in detail and she's happy to do it."

"Fantastic! You'll love Angela. Your jury is going to adore her."

"The case won't get to a jury. Some moron-band nobody has ever heard of is claiming Red Card Riot stole a chord progression that can be found in everything from Mozart to Bruno Mars."

CeeCee scoffs. "God, I hate people."

"I would have told you all about it yesterday, but you took off without so much as a quick goodbye."

"Sorry. You were being mobbed by kiddies, and I only had a short window to grab a coffee with an old friend."

Bingo. Finally, we get to the good stuff. "Oh yeah? Who?"

"Gilda Schiff. An old friend from college. She's a journalism professor at UCLA."

My heart is suddenly thrumming. "Hmm. The woman I saw you leaving with looked a bit younger than an 'old college friend.'"

"Oh, your eagle eye noticed that gorgeous creature who left with Gilda and me, did it, all the way from across that huge lecture hall?" She chuckles. "The college kiddie with us was one of Gilda's journalism students. Apparently, she had the bright idea to attend a music school event to meet me and try to land herself a writing job."

"With *Rock 'n' Roll*?"

"No. Georgina has her sights set on *Dig a Little Deeper,* though she said she'd take any opportunity."

My heart rate increases, yet again, just hearing Georgina's name. In a torrent, I'm suddenly remembering

Georgina's "greatest hits" from last night. Our amazing kisses. The way her tits peeked out of her tank. The way her hazel eyes flashed with homicidal rage when she told me off in front of my house, making me hard as a rock. And, finally, the way she hurled herself into that Uber, and then flipped me off with both hands as her car peeled away. And all of it, despite the fact that anyone else would have stayed and kissed my ass—not to mention, come inside and sucked my dick—to advance her stepsister's cause.

I clear my throat, my breathing shallow. "So, are you going to hire her?" I ask, trying to sound as nonchalant as possible. "I gotta think her worming her way into meeting you at a music school event is a point in her favor. It shows she's capable of thinking outside the box, don't you think?"

"Oh, absolutely. And being able to think outside the box wasn't the only point in this young woman's favor."

You can say that again.

"She's a treasure, Reed. An absolute gem. Funny and engaging. Charismatic and confident. An excellent writer, too. I just finished reading her writing samples, and I was duly impressed."

My eyebrows rise. I didn't see that one coming, I'm ashamed to admit. Gorgeous, witty, magnetic, sexy, curvaceous Georgina is also an excellent writer? Well, I'll be damned.

CeeCee continues. "She's still a bit green, of course. Definitely needs some real-world experience. But with some guidance, I think she's got potential to become a top-notch journalist."

My heart is crashing in my ears. Holy fuck, I want this for Georgina. "It sounds like the event was a win for us both, then. I found myself an expert witness for a frivolous lawsuit, and you found yourself a newbie journalist to hire."

"Actually, no, I don't think it's going to work out for me to hire her, I'm sad to say."

My heart stops. *No.* "Why not? From the way you've been talking about this girl, it seems like hiring her is a no-brainer."

"It would be, if only I had the right position for her. But, unfortunately, I don't."

I take a deep breath to make sure my voice doesn't sound over-eager. "Surely, you could move things around to make a spot for her. Good talent is hard to find."

"The problem is we don't hire kids straight out of college for *Dig a Little Deeper.* Only seasoned professionals. And at *Rock 'n' Roll,* which she said wasn't her first choice, anyway, writers with no experience are required to funnel through an unpaid, three-month internship as a proving ground before we even think of offering them a paid position on the writing staff."

Another deep breath. "Okay, so, offer her an unpaid internship at *Rock 'n' Roll.* Let her hone her chops and earn her way to a paid gig."

"Why are you fighting so hard for this girl? In fact, why are you even wasting your time talking to me about her at all? Normally, you'd have brushed this topic aside faster than a sneeze."

"No, I wouldn't."

"You absolutely would. Is it because she's so beautiful? Or didn't you happen to notice that with your eagle eye from across the lecture hall?"

Shit. "I didn't notice that, actually. I only saw her from the back." *Fuck.* "Maybe yesterday's panel inspired me to want to give back."

"Uh huh."

I audibly shrug, hoping it sounds authentic. "Maybe yesterday's event made me remember what it was like when I was first starting out, and every bit of mentorship meant so much to me. Especially yours."

"Mmm hmm. What aren't you telling me, Reed?"

"Nothing. I'm just trying to help a young woman with a dream, out of the goodness of my heart—thereby helping my dear friend. You said she's got something special, and I want you to have the best people on your staff because I love you so much."

She laughs. "Wait. There's *goodness* in your heart?"

"That's what you took from everything I just said to you?"

She laughs again.

"Hell yeah, there's goodness in my heart," I mutter defensively. "It's just hard to notice because it's hidden underneath so many mysterious, enigmatic 'layers' of my onion."

She hoots with laughter.

"Seriously, Ceece, you should hear the way you've been talking about this girl. You're obviously smitten with her."

"Oh, I am. She was exceptional, Reed. The brightest, most charming and charismatic newbie I've met in a long time. Maybe, ever. I sat across the table from her in that coffee place and thought, 'Anyone this girl interviews wouldn't stand a chance. She'd get them to spill *all* their secrets in the first five minutes.'"

I smile to myself. Truer words were never spoken. "Well, there you go," I say breezily. "Don't let someone like that get away."

CeeCee sighs. "The thing is, I'd feel like an asshole offering Georgina an unpaid internship. After Georgina left the coffee place, my friend, Gilda, told me Georgina's father recently battled cancer, and Georgina needs a paid position after graduation to help him afford some expensive medication he still needs to take."

My stomach drops into my toes at this unexpected revelation.

"Under the circumstances," CeeCee continues, "I'd feel terrible offering Georgina an unpaid internship. Actually, I was thinking of picking up the phone and trying to help her get a paid position somewhere else."

"What? You can't do that. Break your rules and hire this girl for pay, CeeCee."

"I can't. My hands are tied. If I make an exception for Georgina and let her bypass the internship program, my staff would flood me with résumés, insisting their best friends and nephews should get the same treatment."

"It's your company. Surely, you can make an exception, just this once."

I hear a slapping noise. Like CeeCee's just slammed her palms onto her desk. "Okay, Reed. That's it. What the fuck aren't you telling me?"

My heart stops. "Nothing. You just seem particularly moved by this girl, and I don't want you regretting your decision later. To be honest, I'm moved by her, too—by this thing with her father. I know what it's like to want to do whatever it takes to help a parent in need."

CeeCee is quiet for a moment in the face of my unexpected comment. I never talk about my mother. And now, in this one conversation, I've referred to her *twice*. Surely, CeeCee thinks the sky is falling.

"I really *was* moved by Georgina," CeeCee says wistfully. "Even before I found out about how she helps her father. She was truly lovely, Reed. A diamond in the rough. Plus—and I probably shouldn't admit this, but—the fact that she's so gorgeous and sexy would make her hugely effective if I were to assign her to interview musicians for *Rock 'n' Roll*. I know it sounds sexist, and maybe a little underhanded of me, but the fact remains that interview subjects, especially male musicians, tend to open up like steamed clams with really stunning interviewers, as I'm sure you've noticed yourself over the years."

I chuckle. "Why do you think I've always opened up the most with *you*?"

She snorts. "Always, such a charmer. Seriously, though, without even realizing what they're doing, horny musicians always turn themselves inside out, trying to impress the really gorgeous ones, which never fails to translate into interview gold."

I pause for a moment. Long enough to make it seem like I'm weighing what I'm about to say. "I tell you what, CeeCee. I'm going to give you a gift, because I love you and also want to help this girl. I'm going to make a six-figure donation to one of your favorite cancer charities—the one that supports family members of those affected by cancer. They can use part of my donation to set up a grant for this Georgina of yours—the equivalent of three months' salary, plus whatever might be needed to pay for this expensive medicine her father needs. That way, you can officially hire Georgina for the usual *unpaid* internship, as far as your payroll department and other employees are concerned, but she'll actually get paid on the sly. *Boom.* Georgina and her father win. You win. *Rock 'n' Roll* wins. Everybody wins."

"Everybody wins but *you.* Why would you do this?"

"Because I'm a good guy. Because I love you. But, mostly, because you said she'd be particularly good at interviewing musicians and that gives me an excellent idea."

"Ha! I knew there had to be a catch."

"What would you say if, in exchange for my generous donation to one of your favorite charities, *Rock 'n' Roll* does a special 'River Records issue,' featuring nothing but my artists?"

"I'm so relieved to find out you have an ulterior motive for your generosity. For a second there, I felt extremely disoriented."

"My motive isn't *ulterior.* It's *parallel.* Yes, I want to get something out of this, but I *also* want to do good. For you and this 'diamond in the rough.' Seriously, what's the downside of my proposal? It's a no-brainer."

CeeCee is quiet. Thinking. Processing. Trying to figure out what she's missing here. Why I'm bending over backwards.

"I'll roll out the red carpet for this girl," I say. "She'll have full access to everyone on my roster, all at once. I've never done anything like this before, and I'd only ever do it for you."

"It wouldn't just be her," CeeCee says, and, instantly, I know I've got her. "I'd have to assign several people to the issue. Plus, I'm sure I'd write a few pieces, too."

I smile broadly. "Whatever you want, as long as the newbie works on nothing but the River Records issue during her summer internship."

"Why?" CeeCee asks, her tone instantly suspicious.

"Because I'm paying her fucking salary, that's why."

"Oh."

CeeCee is quiet for a long moment. And I don't blame her. It's highly unlike me to bend over backwards to help a stranger. But not outside the realm of possibility, I'd think, considering all the benefits that will flow to both CeeCee and me from this arrangement. Obviously, I've omitted to tell CeeCee the foremost benefit that will flow to me. My top reason for doing this. Namely, that this arrangement will undoubtedly lead to me fucking Georgina at some point during the summer—which, in this moment, is something I want for myself more than I want my next breath. Certainly, more than I want the two hundred grand I'm planning to donate to CeeCee's cancer charity. But, so what if I haven't told CeeCee that part? Omitting that *one* particular nugget of information doesn't make what I *have* mentioned any less true.

"Okay," CeeCee says. "I'll agree to the special issue—"

"Wonderful."

"*On one condition.*"

I hold my breath.

"It absolutely *must* include a full-length interview of *you*."

I exhale with frustration. "CeeCee."

"We can't do a River Records issue without an interview of Reed Rivers. It can be a simple two-pager, if you like, but an interview of you is non-negotiable.*"*

Again, I look out the window of my limo, just in time to see the bushy trees of Central Park coming into view. "All right," I concede. "I'll sit down for a basic *one*-pager, including a five-by-seven photo of me to take up space."

"A *two*-pager, including a three-by-five photo. That's my final offer."

Fuck. I say nothing for a moment, mulling my options.

"A two-pager can't, by its very nature, be as in-depth as the five-pager I've been dying to do for *Dig a Little Deeper.* Plus, don't forget, this would be for *Rock 'n' Roll,* so it will be fluff. Mostly."

"So, it'll be like the 'Man with the Midas Touch' interview?"

I can practically hear her devious smile. "No, it'll be meatier than that. For God's sake, Reed, for that one, the only really personal thing you said was you're not interested in marriage or children. I'll need a lot more than that for a River Records special issue. But, still, yes, the piece will, by necessity, be *basically* on-brand for *Rock 'n' Roll.*"

I roll my eyes at my predicament, even though CeeCee isn't here to see it. "Okay. Fine. A two-pager. But it's not going to 'peel back the layers' of my onion too far. I'll give a little something more than last time, but my deepest layers will stay firmly unpeeled."

"Deal. We'll peel back only *one* layer of your onion."

My driver honks his horn and screams at a yellow taxi that's stopped immediately in front of us to let its passengers out.

"Ah, New York," CeeCee says. "I can hear it from here."

I chuckle. "There's no place quite like it. So, will this Georgina of yours interview me for this onion-peeling interview?"

"Do you *want* Georgina to be the one to interview you?"

I pause long enough to make it seem like I'm genuinely considering the question. "Yeah, that's probably a good idea. She might bring a fresh perspective and voice a more seasoned writer wouldn't. Plus, you already interviewed me for that 'Midas Touch' piece. Might be fun to switch things up."

"I agree. I was actually going to suggest she do it. I've got a hunch she's going to be particularly talented at peeling back your layers, my dear."

Another wave of paranoia washes over me. Seriously now, did CeeCee notice me losing my shit over Georgina—and she's been fucking with me this whole conversation? "Just make sure she knows she's only allowed to peel back *one* layer of the onion," I say, hoping my voice sounds playful and calm. "No additional layer*s* shall be peeled during the course of this interview."

"I'll be sure to tell her. No worries, sweetie. Hey, would you be willing to give Georgina a work station at River Records for the summer—just for ease of access?"

Ease of access. Oh, God. I've got such a dirty mind. Upon hearing those words in reference to Georgina, my brain can't help but imagine myself opening Georgina's olive thighs and sinking myself deep inside her—getting to feel the Nirvana I've been waiting ten fucking years to feel, ever since I first laid eyes on Georgina's double a decade ago and felt an urgent, animalistic desire to fuck the living hell out of her.

"Reed?"

"Yes. A work station for Georgina would be fine with me. Talk to Owen about it. Just as long as we're clear that she's *your* employee. Not mine. I don't want my artists thinking this girl is a shill for our marketing department. It's

important they know she's a *bona fide* reporter for *Rock 'n'
Roll,* interviewing them for an important special issue. *You're*
her boss. Not me. I want them to take her seriously."

"Of course, Reed. So do I. You know I'd never allow my
magazine to be used as a propaganda arm of your label. This
issue is going to have journalistic integrity, even if it happens
to work to your label's and artists' extreme advantage, as
much as it works to mine." She clucks her tongue. "Oh
goodness, my mind is already racing with a thousand ideas.
When will you be back from New York? Let's have dinner."

"Not before you head off to Bali, unfortunately. We'll
have to do it when you get back. In the meantime, feel free to
call Owen to arrange logistics and scheduling. Let's get this
special issue cooking with gas."

"Fabulous. Georgina mentioned she's graduating on the
twenty-second. So I'll get her on-boarded the very next day,
right before I head off to Bali."

My limo stops in front of the Ritz Carlton, right across
from the Park, and a doorman in white gloves promptly opens
my car door. "I've made it to the Goats' hotel. I gotta hang
up."

"Bags, sir?" the doorman says, and I motion to the trunk
before striding toward the double doors of the hotel lobby.

"Have fun in Bali," I say. "Say *bonjour* to Francois for
me."

"I will. I'll call the cancer charity now, right after we
hang up, and email you the info for the donation. Oh, and,
Reed. One more thing."

I stop walking, just inside the doors of the hotel, my heart
pounding. Is this it? Is she going to tell me she's sniffed me
out?

"Let's make sure all the horny musicians on your roster
treat this young woman with respect and professionalism,
okay?"

I sigh with relief.

"I know you didn't get a good look at her as she was walking out of the lecture hall, but, trust me, she's stunning. And as we both know, musicians aren't always the most restrained members of the male species when it comes to beautiful women."

I smile to myself. *The same could be said of music executives.* "Don't worry," I say. "Owen and I will make it clear to everyone: the newbie reporter is off-limits."

"Thank you. Georgina has worked her way through school as a bartender, so I'm sure she's quite adept at fending off horny heathens. But, still, it never hurts to remind everyone she's there to do a job, and not to get hit on right and left."

My blood simmers at the thought of any of my guys making a move on Georgina. But a couple of them, in particular. "We're on the same page," I say through clenched teeth. "I promise, CeeCee, if any of my guys hit on your summer intern, they're going to have to answer to *me*. And, I guarantee, it won't be pretty."

Chapter 16
Georgina

"He was such an asshole!" I say to Alessandra. And, of course, I'm talking about Reed.

It's my graduation party. A few hours ago, while clad in a traditional cap and gown, I accepted my diploma, posed for a smiling photo, and became the first person in my family to graduate from college. And now, my small extended family and a few longtime family friends have gathered in my father's two-bedroom condo in the Valley to celebrate.

At the moment, Alessandra and I are standing in Dad's small kitchen by ourselves, sent in here by Aunt Marjorie to slice up the cake. But since this is Ally and me we're talking about, we've long since forgotten our assigned task, and we're doing nothing but gabbing, gossiping, and laughing together. All the things we always do when we get together, whether in person or on our phones—but especially in person. And especially when it's been months since we've been together in the flesh.

Alessandra leans her slender hip against the counter, her blue eyes shining. The late-afternoon sunlight streaking through the kitchen window is bringing out the auburn highlights in her dark, curly mop and highlighting her glorious freckles. Her smile is as sincere and warm as ever. Her lavender aura every bit as peaceful and serene as usual—every bit as much as my blazing-red aura is fiery and passionate.

"Maybe you hurt Reed's feelings and he was just, you know, lashing out as a defense mechanism," Alessandra says,

132

causing me to snort-laugh. "I'm serious," she persists. "From what you've described of your chemistry with him, and the crazy fireworks that went off for you when you kissed... I don't know, honey, maybe you're underestimating the fireworks that went off for *him*."

Again, I snort.

But Alessandra won't let it go. "Even if Reed's rich and powerful and older, and used to banging supermodels—"

"Actresses, mainly, I think. Probably models, too. But actresses and daughters of famous people seem to be in most of the photos with him."

"Okay, whatever. My point is Reed is still a man. And men fall for you, Georgie. That's a fact. It's your superpower."

I scoff. "Men want to have *sex* with me."

"Only because you push them away emotionally, so they'll take whatever they can get."

The image of Shawn's phone screen that fateful morning pings my brain. The memory of how I stumbled across those sickening strings of texts and photos—the exchanges between Shawn and several women that made it painfully clear he'd been running around on me for quite some time, with multiple women, when I'd been nothing but faithful and supportive. And, worst of all, he'd done it all while my life was falling apart and I needed his love and support and faithfulness the most. I feel a deep ache remembering my hot tears I shed that horrible morning... and then a glint of pride, even though I probably shouldn't, thinking about that bad thing I did when my tears turned to fury.

"I haven't *always* pushed men away emotionally," I say. I run my fingertip through a blob of icing on the corner of the cake and slide my finger into my mouth.

Alessandra sighs sympathetically. "I know, honey. I'm just saying maybe it hurt Reed's feelings, more than you realize, when he found out you had an agenda the whole time, so he acted like a dick to mask his hurt feelings."

I put my palm up. "Okay, you gotta stop now. You're crediting Reed with way too much humanity. The man thinks he's a god among men, the immortal ruler of everything he surveys, and he was simply pissed I wasn't falling at his feet like all the other mortal girls. I didn't hurt his feelings, if he has them. Did I bruise his ego? Probably. But that's it. Feelings weren't involved for either of us. He made it clear from the start he wanted to bring me to his house for nothing but sex, and I made it clear I was super down for that plan. The End."

Alessandra pops a bite of cake into her mouth. "Don't sell yourself short, Georgie. You have a way of making people *feel* something. It's your gift. The gift of genuine, and often instant, connection."

I shake my head. "Not this time. If you met Reed, you'd understand. He's unapologetically on the prowl. He flat-out said he didn't want to 'date' me, only 'seduce' me." *And tie me to his bed posts.*

"He actually used the word 'seduce'?" Alessandra asks.

"He sure did."

She chuckles. "Wow. Was he wearing a suit with a skinny tie and holding a gimlet when he said it?"

We both giggle at the old-school imagery. But, if I'm being honest, my laughter is tinged with wistfulness. Regret. Yearning. Because, damn, Reed rocked that old-school, sexy word—*seduce*—like nobody's business.

"The crazy part is," I say, "Reed didn't sound like he was doing a *Madmen* parody when he said it. Somehow, it came across as nothing but hot." I bite my lip. "Actually, after being subjected to so many drunk fuckboys and their fumbling attempts at hitting on me, it was thrilling to have such a suave older man come on to me like some kind of old-school movie star." I sigh at the sudden flood of memories wracking my brain. The cocky look on Reed's face when he said he didn't plan to date me. The way he called me Cinderella. And, of course, our amazing kisses... Oh. I suddenly realize Alessandra is staring at me, her eyebrow arched. "What?"

My stepsister flashes me a snarky look. "If you could see your face right now... Georgie, you don't hate Reed. You still totally want to screw him!"

"No, I hate him with the fiery passion of an erupting volcano... *and* I still totally want to screw him."

We both burst out laughing.

"But don't mistake hate-lust for genuine feelings," I add. "Not on my end, and certainly not on his. He flat-out said he's 'non-committal' about relationships. Which, by the way, is a lovely way of saying he's a commitment-phobe. Which is great with me, of course. I told him, 'Hey, you're non-committal? Cool, dude, because so am I.'"

"That you are." She takes another bite of cake and snickers. "Sounds like you two are exactly each other's types, huh? Or, at least, Reed is yours: emotionally unavailable and smoking hot."

Sighing, I pick up a fork and steal a bite of cake off Alessandra's plate. Because, really, what can I say to that accusation? Reed is, indeed, precisely my type. The most perfect example of it I've ever encountered. A glittering paragon of suave, cocky, unattainable male perfection, with a side of assholery, like nothing I've encountered before. "I'm sorry, Ally. I can't believe I screwed things up so badly for both of us. I wish I'd handled things differently that night. For both our sakes."

"It's that Italian temper of yours," she says, rolling her eyes. "Getting you into trouble, once again."

"I know. I'm sorry."

"I'm kidding. You have nothing to apologize for, especially not to *me*. If Reed was rude and disrespectful to you, then I'm thrilled you told him off. Never think you have to take shit from any man, even a rich and powerful one, especially not to help *me*. My time to shine will come soon enough, baby girl. I know it. And when it does, I won't take crap from anyone. And I certainly won't prostitute out my beloved sister-from-another-mister to get ahead."

Oh, my heart. If I didn't already love this beautiful girl, I would have fallen head over heels in love with her now.

I look out the window of my father's small kitchen at the cloudless blue sky, trying to gather my thoughts. Ever since I got home from Reed's the other night, I've felt a powerful ache growing inside me. An overwhelming sense of regret gathering steam. And now, I can't help wishing I could rewind the clock and do things differently that night. "The thing is... " I say. "It's not like, before Reed implied I was a whore, I'd thought he was my Prince Charming. It's not like the horrible things he said to me outside his house shattered my illusions about him."

I look down at my hands, feeling my cheeks redden with shame. I'm not proud of myself for wishing I could rewind the clock and follow Reed into his house that night—where I'd then let him tie me up and fuck me like an animal for four hours straight, in exchange for him listening to Alessandra's demo. But, if I'm being honest, that's exactly what I've been wishing these past few days, now that I've had some time to reflect.

"What are you saying?" Alessandra asks, her eyebrow arched.

"I'm saying... Reed already had a horrible opinion of me that I wasn't going to shake, no matter what I said or did. So, in that case, why did I even bother trying to convince him my intentions were pure? I should have kept my eye on the prize and done exactly what he expected of me—fucked him as payment for him listening to the demo. At least, that way, we both would have gotten what we wanted out of him."

Alessandra smiles. "Actually, Georgie, it sounds to me like you did the *one* thing you could have done to change Reed's mind about you. Plus, bonus points, you did it in style—with your two middle fingers raised to the sky. So classic."

I giggle. "You should have seen the look on Reed's face as I was driving away. He was so fucking pissed at me."

"Hey, ladies." It's my father, coming into the kitchen. And his voice makes us girls both straighten up. Dad strides across the small kitchen and puts his arm around my shoulders. "Aunt Marjorie sent me in here to ask about the cake. She suspects you two girls have gotten to chatting and completely forgotten why you came in here."

Alessandra and I giggle and nod.

"Guilty as charged," Alessandra says.

Rolling his eyes, Dad picks up a knife and begins cutting the cake for us. "Ally, would you mind distributing slices to everyone? There's something I want to talk to Georgie about."

"You betcha, Pops," Alessandra says.

The three of us load cake slices onto a tray for Alessandra, who then breezes into the living room to expertly deliver them like the part-time waitress she is.

When Alessandra is gone, Dad turns to me and smiles proudly, his eyes instantly moistening. He places his hands on my shoulders, a sure sign an emotional speech is coming. It's not a rare occurrence with my father—watching him become overcome with emotion. He's always worn his tender heart on his sleeve, my Dad. It's the thing I love most about him.

"You're my pride and joy, Georgie," he says, tears threatening. "You know that, right?"

"I do, Daddy. Thank you for always telling me that. And for doing without so much, for so long, so I could get a college education."

"It's what Mommy and I both wanted for you. We wanted you to be able to make a living doing something you feel passionately about."

My eyes are glistening now, along with Dad's. God, I wish my mother were here to witness this proud and happy day.

Dad reaches into his pocket and pulls out a small box.

And, instantly, I know what's inside. My mother's wedding ring. Instantly, I hurl myself into my father's arms and burst into tears. And so, of course, my emotional, tenderhearted father cries along with me.

"You always said you'd give it to me on my wedding day," I mumble into Dad's shoulder.

"I realized your mother would want you to have it today," he whispers into my hair. "She came to me in a dream last night and told me to give it to you. She said, 'Georgie doesn't need a man to make us proud. She's already the woman we've raised her to be.'"

I sniffle. "That sounds just like Mommy."

Dad pulls back from our hug and wipes his eyes. "You know I'm hoping you'll have a family of your own one day, but only because I want you to experience the kind of love story I had with your mother. I want you to experience the kind of unconditional love I feel for you, Georgie."

"I know, Daddy. I love you, too."

"But that doesn't mean you need to get married or have babies to make me and your mother proud, or to be the woman we dreamed you'd grow up to be. Without going to college myself, I didn't fully understand how proud I'd feel today. How amazing it would feel to watch you—" He presses his lips together, too choked up to continue. Which makes me choke up, as well. And for a moment, we're both silently swallowing air and wiping our eyes.

Finally, Dad gathers himself enough to open the box, and I gasp at the sight of the diamond-encrusted ring inside, the one I remember my mother always wearing with such pride on her lovely hand. Beaming with his love for me, my father says, "*Amorina*, today, you're exactly the woman your mother and I always dreamed you'd be. Wear this ring, and let it always remind you of that."

I slide the ring onto the ring finger of my right hand, but it's too big. I try my middle finger next, and smile when it's a perfect fit. "Isn't it pretty?" I say, holding up my newly decorated hand. "Now, I'll look like a queen whenever I flip someone off."

"*Georgie.*"

I giggle. "Aw, come on, Dad. You know it's perfect Mommy's ring fits my middle finger, instead of my ring finger. We both know I'll get far more use out of it this way."

Dad sighs. "You're still sure you 'never' want to get married?"

I purse my lips, considering. "No, I think I'm over that. I only felt that way right after your divorce from Paula. But only because you and Paula made marriage look like an exceedingly stupid thing for anyone to do."

Dad rolls his eyes. "That's an understatement."

"I think nowadays I'm open to *maybe* getting married one day. Just not until I've gotten my career going. And certainly not before age thirty. I only want one kid, though, so I don't need to be in any rush."

Dad looks satisfied. Maybe even relieved. And I totally get it. It's not that my father believes marriage and babies is the only endgame for a woman. Not at all. He's a traditional guy in some ways, but not about that. No, I think in addition to him wanting me to experience a love like he had with my mother, and the love he has for me, he simply wants to feel confident I'll be safe and protected, and loved unconditionally, my whole life, even after he's gone, whether his departure from this earthly life comes way sooner than either of us would want, or, God willing, decades from now.

Dad takes my hand and gazes at it, perhaps thinking about the happy day, so many years ago, he married a nineteen-year-old spitfire who, tragically, wound up leaving this earth far too soon. He says, "She's smiling down on you right now, you know."

"I know," I say. "I can feel her. She's smiling down on you, too, Daddy. *Always.*"

Lauren Rowe

I put my palm on my father's face, letting my mother's ring brush his stubbled cheek, and then kiss his other cheek tenderly.

I'm not lying about my mother *always* smiling down on him, by the way. Even when Dad stupidly married Paula, in the midst of his grief, I know my kind-hearted mother was in heaven, cheering him on. Wanting him to find love again. Wanting him to feel joy after so much sorrow. True, it wasn't true love for Dad and Paula, to put it mildly, but I'm positive my mother didn't hold it against my brokenhearted father for blindly stumbling through his pain in that way.

"Don't worry about me, Daddy," I whisper. "I'll always be okay. I'm a fighter. A *hustler*."

He chuckles. "A *hustler*?"

I wink. "All good things come to those who hustle." My phone buzzes in my pocket. I pull it out, check the screen, and whoop. "This is the call I've been waiting for, Daddy! Oh my God!"

"I'll give you some privacy," Dad says excitedly. He beelines for the door of the kitchen. "Good luck!"

When he's gone, I hastily answer the call, my hands shaking and my heart thrumming in my chest. "Hello, this is Georgina."

"Hi, Georgina," a woman says. "This is Margot, CeeCee Rafael's personal assistant."

Oh my God! *This is it.* The call I've been waiting for since I walked out of that coffee date with CeeCee. I collapse into a kitchen chair, praying this woman is calling with happy news.

"Hello, Margot. How are you?"

"Couldn't be better. CeeCee was wondering if you might be able to come to the office tomorrow morning at ten? Sorry for the late notice, but she's traveling internationally the following day, and she wants to personally give you some great news. It's about a job opportunity she has for you. I think you'll be pleased."

140

I squeal, making Margot chuckle. But before Margot responds to my exuberance, a male voice in the background on her end says something to her. "I'm sorry, Georgina, can you hold for a minute? So sorry."

"Sure."

And she's gone, leaving me on hold listening to Katy Perry tell me I'm a firework.

Okay, Georgie, I say to myself. *Don't get too excited. You might have to turn down whatever CeeCee offers you.*

Sadly, it's the truth. I've done my research, and therefore know *Rock 'n' Roll* never hires recent college grads for paid positions. Indeed, there's a mandatory *unpaid* three-month internship for college grads, which the company uses as a proving ground. If it weren't for Dad's medical expenses, I'd take anything offered to me, whether paid or not. Anything to get my foot in the door. Hell, I'd be this assistant's unpaid assistant, if that's what was offered to me. But the reality remains, I can't afford to take an *unpaid* job, for more than a few weeks, given Dad's situation.

Of course, Dad always says it's not my job to take care of him financially. "I'll be able to pick up carpentry work again any day now," he always says. But that seems like a gigantic stretch to me, given the lasting side effects Dad has been experiencing from his treatments.

Dad also likes to say he could sell the condo, if worse came to worst. But on that score, Dad's equally full of shit. I've seen Dad's bank statements. I know he's upside down on this place—meaning any profit he might make from selling it would go straight to the bank.

"I'm back," CeeCee's assistant says. "Sorry about that. So, does ten o'clock tomorrow work for you?"

"Yes. It's perfect. Thank you."

"Please, don't be late," the woman says. "CeeCee's schedule is jam-packed tomorrow, since she's headed to Bali the following day. She's moving things around to squeeze you in, simply because she's so excited to talk to you in person about the job offer."

My heart leaps, even though my brain knows it probably shouldn't. "I'll make sure to get there fifteen minutes early."

The woman gives me the address for tomorrow's meeting, plus some parking instructions, and then signs off by saying, "Don't be nervous, okay? I think you're going to be extremely happy with what CeeCee offers you."

Chapter 17
Georgina

Oh. My. Freaking. God.
I can't believe my ears.

I'm sitting across from CeeCee in her luxurious office. CeeCee is seated in a white leather chair at an expansive glass desk, looking like a baller in a black pant suit and badass earrings, while I'm sitting across from her in my only pencil skirt, trying not to shriek uncontrollably at what she just said. Holy fucking crap, CeeCee Rafael wants to hire me for a *paid* internship at *Rock 'n' Roll*!

"I know you had your heart set on *Dig a Little Deeper,*" CeeCee says, leaning back into her beautiful throne. "But if this internship goes well during the summer, who knows where it could lead."

I babble stupidly for much too long about my euphoria and gratitude. About dreams coming true. I ask if there's someone at the cancer charity I can thank for the grant CeeCee has unexpectedly arranged for me, and, holy fuck, for my father's medication, too, and she tells me, nope, she'll forward my effusive thanks to the powers that be.

Handing me a tissue for my tears, CeeCee says, "I hope you're not upset at Gilda—Professor Schiff—for mentioning your father's illness to me. She only told me so that I could think outside the box in terms of arranging payment for you."

Again, I babble into my tissue, using far too many words to say, in essence, I'm so, so grateful, to CeeCee and Professor Schiff and the amazing cancer charity.

CeeCee clasps her manicured hands and places them on her glass desk. "So, do you want to hear about your assignment for the next three months, my dear?"

I wipe my eyes one last time and put the tissue into my lap. "Oh my gosh. *Yes*."

CeeCee flashes me an excited smile. "For the next three months, Georgina, you're going to be working *exclusively* on a singular, exciting project." She pauses for effect. "A special issue of *Rock 'n' Roll* devoted solely to the artists and inner workings of one record label... River Records!"

My jaw drops along with my stomach. *No*. This can't be happening. The best news of my life has just turned into the worst. CeeCee is hiring me to work exclusively on an issue devoted to Reed River's label... for the next *three* months? It's a catastrophe!

"Don't worry, you won't be the only one writing for this issue," CeeCee says, apparently misreading the look of panic on my face. "I'm also assigning a couple of seasoned writers, too, who'll contribute content and also mentor you. Plus, I'll write a few pieces for the issue, too. But, make no mistake about it, Georgie, your job is to interview the shit out of as many River Records artists as you can personally manage throughout the summer and turn those interviews into fresh, fun, original content. I want you to think outside the box and really run with it."

Holy fucking hell. My mind is racing with thoughts, all of them centering on Reed fucking Rivers. Does he know CeeCee has assigned me, the woman who double-flipped him off the last time he saw her, to this special issue? If he doesn't already know, will he get me kicked off the project the minute he finds out?

For several minutes, CeeCee details her vision for the issue. And, slowly, despite my panic about Reed, I begin to feel swept away by the excitement of it all. We brainstorm ideas for a bit, our mutual enthusiasm mounting. And, finally,

CeeCee says, "And, of course, what would a special issue about River Records be without an in-depth, featured interview of the man at the helm of it all, Reed Rivers?"

And there it is. The two little words I've been dreading since CeeCee first told me about this assignment: *Reed Rivers.* If Reed doesn't know about me being assigned to the project, he's going to find out soon enough. And when he does, will he pick up the phone and tell CeeCee to send someone else— someone who didn't tell him to fuck off and die, and then peel out in an Uber while he stood in front of his house with a raging boner poking the front of his pants?

"Is something wrong, Georgina?" CeeCee asks.

I shake my head. "No. I'm just feeling a little woozy due to excitement. This is a doozy of an opportunity, CeeCee. A doozy with a capital 'oozy.'"

CeeCee giggles. "Yes, it is."

"Um. Out of curiosity," I say, "how much of this idea has been cleared with Mr. Rivers?"

"All of it. Nothing happens at River Records without Reed clearing it. You'll find that out soon enough. He's extremely hands-on."

Hands-on. In a flash, my body remembers what it felt like to have Reed's greedy hands on me as he kissed me. I'm suddenly remembering the scent of his cologne. The delicious roughness of his stubble. The death grip of his palms on my ass that made me delirious with arousal... *He wanted to tie me to his bed posts.* My cheeks hot, I clear my throat. "So, he's already agreed to do the interview... with me?"

"He has."

"But I mean... with *me,* specifically?"

CeeCee tilts her head like Scooby Doo sniffing out a snack.

"I mean, does he know I'm a newbie?" I add quickly. "Does he know I'm straight out of journalism school, with no experience?"

CeeCee nods. "Yes, Reed and I talked about that very thing, and he smartly recognized, as do I, that you'll bring a fresh, exciting energy and voice to the project." She smiles kindly. "Don't be nervous, Georgina. I'm sure, after seeing Reed on that panel, you're a bit intimidated. And I don't blame you. He's incredibly successful and confident. And his communication style is blunt and unapologetic, to say the least. But he's a very good friend of mine, and I can honestly say he's a sweetheart underneath all that swagger. Plus, he trusts my judgment. And I've told him I've got a lot of faith in you."

A shudder of nerves sweeps through me. "I hope I'm able to prove you right."

"You will. It was when you talked about bartending during our coffee date that I knew you'd be a fantastic interviewer. Like I told you then, bartending is just another form of what a journalist does. As a bartender, you've honed the art of talking to people. Listening to them. Making connections in a short amount of time and getting them to open up. Now, you'll be taking those skills and simply putting the experience down on paper—which your writing samples, and Gilda's high praise of you, lead me to believe you'll be able to do with ease."

"Thank you so much. I didn't really think of bartending being related to journalism in that way. But I think you're right."

"Of course, I am." She leans forward conspiratorially. "I'm most excited to see how you're going to handle Reed's interview. I have a strong feeling he'll be uncharacteristically chatty with you."

I press my lips together, suddenly feeling sick. Shit. Is this my cue to come clean? To confess to CeeCee that Reed likely won't be uncharacteristically chatty with me, because, surprise, the last time I saw the man, I kissed the hell out of him, rubbed my aching clit against his huge dick like a cat in heat... and then left him standing at his front gate with not only blue balls, but, almost certainly, a firm desire to never lay eyes on me again?

"I feel like I should tell you something," CeeCee says, taking the words right out of my mouth. She leans back into her chair again. "For the past two years, ever since I first conceived of launching *Dig a Little Deeper,* I've been begging Reed to give me a full-length, in-depth interview for that magazine. But he's always said no." She steeples her manicured fingers. "You might not know this, but Reed's father was a notorious white collar criminal who killed himself in prison when Reed was nineteen or twenty. His father's case was extremely high profile. All over the news. And yet, Reed never, ever talks about it. Certainly not publicly, anyway. And not with me, despite the fact that I've known him ten years. And yet, I think that's the one thing the world would be *most* fascinated to hear him talk about."

I swallow hard. "Yeah, I think I read something about that on Reed's Wikipedia page."

Shit. I clamp my mouth shut, instantly regretting I let it slip I've already read up on Reed. But, thankfully, CeeCee doesn't seem to notice my blunder.

Without missing a beat, CeeCee says, "Of course, the friend in me would never push Reed to talk about his father, if he doesn't wish to do so. But the journalist in me wants you to be aware of the existence of this dynamic, just in case it happens to come up. If, by some chance, Reed slowly opens up with you throughout the summer, and you get the chance to expand the scope of your initial interview—to 'dig a little deeper,' shall we say, beyond what we'd normally expect to write about in *Rock 'n' Roll*—then I want you to run with it, without hesitation."

I process CeeCee's words for a moment. "Are you saying if I'm successful in getting a really in-depth interview of Reed, you'll publish it in *Dig a Little Deeper,* instead of *Rock 'n' Roll?*"

CeeCee shrugs. "I'm saying I'm open to the idea. Of

course, I've got no interest in tricking Reed. That should go without saying. He's my friend and I love him. What I'm saying, however, is that, if it turns out Reed is responding well to you, and you see an opportunity to go more in-depth with him than originally thought—with his consent, of course—then I want you to seize that chance."

I bite my lip, my mind whirring and clacking. "If I do get something amazing out of Reed, something that knocks your socks off, and you wind up publishing it in *Dig a Little Deeper...* would you hire me for that magazine?"

CeeCee shrugs nonchalantly, but I can tell by the twinkle in her eye, I've asked the exact right question. "I can't answer that without reading the piece first." She weaves her fingers together. "But, yes, of course, I'm open to the *possibility* of hiring you at *Dig a Little Deeper* after your summer internship, *if* you prove to me you've got the chops for it."

I'm lightheaded. Dizzy. Overwhelmed with ambition and excitement. "I'm going to knock this out of the park, CeeCee. You'll see."

She chuckles. "Darling, I truly believe you will."

We talk about the logistics of my job for a bit. The fact that some guy named Owen, and not Reed, will be my contact at the label—which, admittedly, calms my nerves about the whole thing.

Finally, CeeCee says, "Okay, let's talk turkey about the animals in the zoo for a bit, shall we?"

"The animals... ?"

"The musicians you're going to be interacting with on a daily basis, and partying with, and making friends with, all summer long. Because that's what always happens with musicians. They invite the writers to party with them, and peek into their lives, even if it's just for one crazy day. And, of course, you'll always say yes to any invitation, because the best interviews happen off-the-cuff, in the moment, when you're a part of *their* lives."

I nod.

"The downside of all that, of course, is that, sometimes, they forget you're there to do a job, rather than be their groupie."

"Ah."

"I'm sure this won't come as a shock to you, Georgie, but musicians, especially ones of the male variety, aren't known for being particularly restrained around women, especially exceptionally attractive women, like you."

I blush. "Thank you."

She leans forward in her chair. "Don't take any shit from them, Georgina. You're not a sex object. You're a professional journalist for an esteemed magazine. Party with them. Have a blast. Be their friend. But never forget they need you as much as you need them. That's how this machine works. It's symbiotic. The musicians make the music, yes, but they'd be nothing without their fans. And they need *publicity* to get and keep their fans. They need *mystique* and validation, which my magazine provides to them better than anyone else. You're every bit as powerful as they are, Georgie, I promise you that. You got that?"

"Yes, ma'am." I flex my arm muscle, and she chuckles.

"I've made it clear to Owen you're to be treated with professionalism and respect, by *everyone*. I don't care how big a star any particular guy might be, if someone hits on you and makes you feel uncomfortable, then you're to go straight to Owen or to me, and we'll set the brute straight, without a moment's hesitation. You understand?"

"I do. Perfectly. Thank you so much for looking out for me. But don't worry. I was a bartender, remember? And a waitress before that. I've handled 'animals at the zoo' many times, and still managed to walk away with great tips."

"You see? I told you bartending was a perfect training ground." She picks up a pen and fidgets with it. "Any questions, my love? I've got to run off to a meeting in five."

149

I bite my lip, weighing the pros and cons of asking the question on the tip of my tongue, and finally decide it's going to be a long summer, if I don't ask it. "Yeah, just one question." I clear my throat. "What if I'm partying with someone and having a blast and befriending them, like you've told me is smart to do... and what if someone flirts with me, or hits on me... and I actually *like* it? *A lot.* What happens then?" My cheeks bloom with embarrassment. "I mean, I don't want to do anything unprofessional. Or cross any forbidden lines. It's just that... if I find someone insanely attractive, and I'm single, and so are they, am I allowed to make it clear I *like* being hit on by this particular person, or would that be considered unprofessional and a big no-no?"

Thankfully, CeeCee doesn't look the least bit shocked or appalled by my question. Only amused. Indeed, so much so, she's smiling from ear to ear. "Have I mentioned I really like you, Georgina?" She laughs heartily. "Sweetie, go for it. Insanely hot men grow on trees in the music industry, and you can always do whatever the hell you want with them, just as long as it's what *you* want to do, for *you*, and not because you think it's required for the job." She smiles slyly. "To be honest, I can't even count the number of times I've slept with a musician I met on the job. And some of them were huge household names, too." She winks. "This was all long before I met my beloved Francois, of course. But, whew! I've definitely had my fun out in the field. And I don't regret a single minute of it." CeeCee makes a big show of looking right, and then left, as if she's about to tell me a secret in a crowded room. She leans forward, a naughty expression on her face. "In fact, I've conducted some of my most 'probing' interviews while lying buck naked next to my interview subject... in bed."

My jaw hangs open, practically clanking onto CeeCee's glass desk, and she giggles uproariously at my expression.

"Have fun, Georgie," she says, smiling brightly. "As

long as you never lose sight of the fact that you're there to get me lots of compelling and fresh content for *Rock 'n' Roll*—and, perhaps, something spectacular for *Dig a Little Deeper,* too, if the stars are aligned. As long as you do that, then whatever else you might do along the way, simply because you're young and gorgeous and you only live once, is your own goddamned business."

Chapter 18
Reed

A s my driver takes us down the long, tree-lined driveway of my mother's facility, I look out the car window and let my mind drift. Not surprisingly, it lands on Georgina. *Again.* The same way it's been doing this entire past week. Once again, I find myself thinking about Georgina's flushed cheeks as she told me off in front of my house. And then her flashing hazel eyes, and raised middle fingers, as she drove away in that Uber.

I can't believe that crazy woman ditched my ass, even though she *knew* it was in her stepsister's best interest for her to stay and kiss it. Not to mention, for her to come inside and suck my dick. And yet, hotheaded, sassy, glorious Georgina Ricci got into the backseat of that car and left me in her dust, her two middle fingers riding sky-high, and her integrity firmly intact. *And I haven't stopped thinking about her since.*

"Mr. Rivers?"

I blink and realize we've arrived at the front of the mental facility—a posh place in Scarsdale, an affluent town about forty-five minutes outside the City, that boasts a "bed and breakfast"-type vibe for its patients. I check my watch while unlatching my seatbelt. "This is going to be a quick visit this time, Tony. So don't drive off to buy a pack of cigs or anything. I want you here when I come out, ready to haul ass to La Guardia."

"I'll be here."

Inside the lobby, I show my identification to the attendant, per protocol, even though everyone knows me. After signing the log, I leaf through the past few weeks of signatures, making sure my mother's best friend since childhood, Roseanne, has visited as frequently as our contract requires. With relief, I discern Roseanne has, indeed, held up her end of our bargain. And also that my saint of a little sister visited yesterday with my little nephew in tow, exactly as she told me she was planning to do as the three of us strolled through the Central Park Zoo earlier this week.

"You don't have to visit my mother," I said to my sister in front of the elephant enclosure. "She's never even acknowledged your existence. Fuck her."

"*Reed*," my sister chastised. "Don't say that about your mother."

"I'm just saying you owe her nothing."

"It's not about me *owing* something to her. It's about me doing something nice for a lonely lady in a mental hospital. I often do what I can to brighten the day of a perfect stranger, so why not your mother? You've mentioned several times she doesn't get a lot of visitors, only you and that 'friend' of hers you have to pay. And you've also mentioned she never stopped loving our prick-ass father, despite their nasty divorce and everything else."

"She was always his doormat. I don't know if you can rightly call that 'love.'"

"Well, either way, I think it might be nice for a lonely lady to get to see a cute little baby who has her ex-husband's DNA inside him. The same DNA as her own beloved son. Maybe seeing my baby will remind her of happier times in her own life."

I felt a mix of emotions right then, during that conversation with my sister in front of the elephants. First off, I felt shame at my secret knowledge that the words "beloved son" probably didn't apply to me, at least if you were to ask my mother. But, mostly, I felt awed by my sister's selflessness. Not that I should have been surprised, really, since compassion is her defining characteristic. But, still, as I stood there with my sister and my sweet little nephew, watching an elephant dunk its thick trunk into a trough of water, I had this distinct thought: *How the hell does this girl have Terrence Rivers' DNA inside her, the same as me, and yet, unlike me, she doesn't have a single asshole bone in her body?*

I close the facility's logbook, having finished my inspection of it, and return it to the attendant at the front desk. And then, I make my way down the familiar hallway toward Mom's room—the biggest one at the facility, with the best view of the garden. But when I poke my head inside Mom's room, she isn't there.

I turn to leave, figuring Mom must be at yoga, or perhaps painting in a hidden corner of the garden, when a canvas by the window catches my eye. I walk toward the easel, bracing myself for my inevitable exasperation when I survey it, and audibly groan when I make out the details of the scene depicted. *Fuck.* It's yet another happy family portrait. *And I want to smash it against the fucking wall.*

To an outside observer, this painting, like all the others, would likely seem like nothing but a pleasant idyll. A lovely tribute to family. And if it were a one-off, or a two-off, or even a hundred-off, I'd probably agree. In reality, though, as I know too well, this painting is actually anything but a pleasant idyll. No, it's a physical manifestation of my mother's unwell, hyper-fixated mind. Evidence of what doctors call my mother's "perseveration."

In short, my mother's got an obsessive compulsion that prompts her to pick up a paintbrush, every week of her life, and paint yet another iteration of this exact scene, with only a few small variations and variables, over and over and *over* again.

Indeed, no matter how many times her doctors, therapists, "best friend," or I encourage my mother to, please, *please*, paint something else—*anything else*, for the love of fuck—Eleanor Rivers always paints the same thing. An idyllic depiction of her family at rest or play, enjoying some pleasant sunshine without a care in the world.

This time, Mom's portrait depicts a late-afternoon family picnic in a park surrounded by gorgeous cherry blossoms. As usual, Mom's painted herself as a young mother. This time, Mom's avatar is seated on a red blanket with her two small sons: my older brother, Oliver, who's holding an ice cream cone and looks to be about seven or eight, and me, holding a lollipop, looking to be around five or six.

Mom always paints Oliver the same way—looking like he's around eight years old—even though, in reality, he drowned in our backyard swimming pool at age four, when I was two. Mom also gives Oliver some sort of treat in every painting. An ice cream cone, as with this one. A piece of candy. A shiny new toy. A puppy. A kite. A kitten. A butterfly net. Apparently, one of Mom's greatest pleasures is showering her ill-fated older son, in paintings, with all the little gifts she never got to give him in real life.

Scattered around Mom and her two happy sons are Mom's three younger sisters and mother, all of them clad in merry, pastel dresses, and all of them gaily spinning cartwheels and jumping rope... even though, in real life, tragically, all four of them died in a horrific house fire when Mom was barely sixteen.

Mom had been babysitting a neighbor's three children at the time of the fire, mere blocks away. When word of the blaze got to Mom, she frantically sprinted home, hell-bent on hurtling herself inside the burning structure and saving everyone she loved so much from catastrophe. But, alas, by the time she got to the house, it was already abundantly clear it was too late. Four of the only five people my mother loved in this world were already gone.

As for the fifth person in this world my mother loved, her father, he was a traveling salesman on a trip at the time, marooned that fateful night with a flat tire about two hours away. Or, at least, that's what Charles Charpentier swore to investigators, when no witnesses could confirm his whereabouts, one way or another.

To this day, I think my mother mostly believes her father's version of events, which is why she always includes him in her happy family paintings. Including her father in her paintings is my mother's way of declaring to the world: Charles Charpentier's sole surviving child rejects the wicked rumors about him—the whispers that swirled around Scarsdale immediately after the fire, and then continued swirling endlessly, long after the man killed himself on the one-year anniversary of the tragedy.

According to my grandfather's doubters, Charles Charpentier was a compulsive gambler who'd arranged to burn down what he'd *thought* would be his empty house that fateful night, in order to collect insurance money and pay off his mountain of debts. To my mother, on the other hand, her father was a tragic figure who lost *almost* everything that horrible night, all at once... and, tragically for her, the only thing that remained, the man's eldest daughter, simply wasn't enough to keep him from putting that gun to his head and pulling the trigger.

Interestingly, Mom always places her father off to the side in every painting—as if he's watching his family's revelry from a distance, but not participating in it. I think Mom keeps her father at arm's length in this way, each and every time, because, in the deepest recesses of her unwell mind, she's not sure what to think about him. Consciously, she's decided to believe in his innocence. But, subconsciously, I'm guessing she's got her doubts. Perhaps she includes her father's figure in her paintings, in the first place, as a declaration of love and support for him... but she then feels compelled to set him apart, away from her beloved mother and sisters, as a show of loyalty to them... just in case, on the off-chance, the incessant whispers and gossip about her father were actually true.

"She's in the yoga room," a voice says. And when I turn

around, it's one of the nurses. Tina. A middle-aged woman in blue scrubs who's worked here forever.

"Thanks," I say. "I'll look for her there."

Tina comes to a stop next to me, her eyes trained on Mom's canvas. "No grandma this time? Poor Grandma hardly ever makes the cut."

"Mom's grandmother should be grateful to make it into any of Mom's paintings. By all accounts, Grandma was a raving bitch."

Tina chuckles.

"My guess?" I say. "Grandma won't make it into a painting until Christmas."

"Christmas?" Tina says. "Dang it, I hope not. We've got a pool about when Grandma's going to make her next appearance, and I put my ten bucks on Thanksgiving. If Grandma shows up to eat turkey, I'll win a hundred bucks."

"Sorry, I wouldn't count on it, Tina. Apparently, Grandma hated my mother's cooking and told her so, repeatedly. So, I'm thinking the last thing Mom would want to do is give Grandma a seat at the Thanksgiving table, only to let her bitch about Mom's turkey being too dry."

"Shoot."

"But, hey, I guess it's *possible* Mom could paint Grandma at the Thanksgiving table, to let her rave about how *perfect* everything is. Mom's been known to paint revisionist history a time or two. Or *forty-two billion.*"

Tina points. "Who's the baby? I don't think I've seen him or her in one of your Mom's paintings before."

"I believe that's my nephew."

Tina grimaces, apparently assuming the baby must be deceased, if he's making an appearance in an Eleanor Rivers original.

"He's alive and well," I clarify quickly. "My sister brought him to visit yesterday for the first time."

"Oh, I was off yesterday." She peers at the tiny blonde

figure as he plays with a red ball in the hinterlands of the grassy park. "Wow, one meeting with him and your mother's already put him into one of her paintings? He must have made quite an impression. It took me working here eight years before your mother finally made me an ice cream vendor in one of her paintings."

I shrug. "She's always loved babies. It's when they get to age seven or eight that she has no fucking clue what to do with them."

Tina flashes me a look of sympathy, before returning to the canvas. "Why do you think your nephew is way off in a corner like that, so far away from everyone else? I would have thought she'd at least let one of her sisters throw that ball to him."

"Your guess is as good as mine," I say. But I'm a liar. I know exactly why my mother has banished my nephew to a far corner: it's a sign of his paper-thin connection to "her" family. But why would I admit that to Tina? Especially when, like Tina said, the fact that Mom's included him at all, after only one visit, is a sign of progress, however small.

"She adores you, you know," Tina says. "She talks about you all the time."

I smile politely and shove my hand into the pocket of my jeans. But I know the truth. If my mother talks about me at all, it's only to brag about my money. The truth is, my mother isn't capable of loving me in the way other mothers love their children. But that's okay. She doesn't need to be capable of it. I've long since stopped hoping for, or expecting, motherly love from her. All that matters to me now is that she is, in fact, my mother, and that *I* love *her*. All that matters is she's on the short list of people I'd do anything for, protect until my dying breath, and love unconditionally, forevermore, whether she's capable of returning my devotion, or, shit, even simply *liking* me... or not.

Chapter 19
Reed

In the yoga room, I discover Mom at the front of the class with her boyfriend, Lee—a paranoid schizophrenic who's so heavily medicated, I've never heard him say more than four words during any given visit. At the moment, the class, including Mom and Lee, are attempting to do the Warrior Two pose, although what they're managing, to be generous, isn't exactly the stuff of yoga instructional videos.

"Reed is here," the instructor says to Mom, making her turn around. And when Mom sees me standing in the doorway, she claps, rises from her pose, and makes her way over to me.

When Mom arrives, I squeeze her frail body into a tight hug and tell her I love her. She doesn't return the words, but that's not a surprise. She once told me those words aren't in her vocabulary, because whenever she says them, someone dies. So, really, I suppose I should consider my mother's refusal to tell her only living son she loves him a gift. She's merely trying to save her son from dying, after all. And there's nothing wrong with that.

"I can't stay long today, Mom," I say. "I have to catch a flight back to LA for a concert. For work."

For Georgina.

Again, the force of nature that is Georgina Ricci flashes across my mind. I imagine her showing up backstage tonight at the RCR concert, excited to begin her first day on the job with a press pass around her neck... and then being greeted at the backstage door by... *me*. Oh, God, I can't wait for that delicious moment when our eyes meet again. When she realizes she's got to play nice with me, whether she likes it or not. In truth, I've been obsessing about it all week long.

"*LA*," Mom says with disdain. "I never should have let Terrence convince me to leave my family here in Scarsdale to move to LA. That was the beginning of the end for me."

I take a deep breath and bite my tongue. Mom says something like this every time I visit, and it's a whole lot of crazy. First, let's be real here: the fire was the beginning of the end for her. Doesn't she realize her family perished long before she even met Terrence Rivers? Which means my father didn't "convince" her to leave her family, or anyone else, to move to Los Angeles. Actually, as far as I understand it, my thirty-five-year-old father convinced his deeply troubled, but stunningly beautiful, pregnant nineteen-year-old bride to leave Scarsdale, in the hopes she'd be able to leave her traumas far behind, and embrace the new life growing inside her. To begin a new chapter, in a new place, with a new husband.

Or, shit, maybe Mom is simply acknowledging she would have preferred to stay in Scarsdale forever, with the ghosts of her dead family, than move to California and become the mother and wife, and then, unhinged ex-wife, she ultimately became.

Either way, the comment annoys me whenever Mom makes it, because it's my mother's dead family that presently ties her to this facility in Scarsdale. And that's a huge fucking inconvenience for me. I've begged Mom, more times than I can count, to let me move her to an even better facility in Malibu—a place right on the cliffs overlooking the glittering Pacific Ocean. But, no. She won't do it. No matter what I say or do, or how many brochures of the Malibu facility I show her, Mom says she won't leave her "family," ever again. Plus, she steadfastly refuses to leave Lee, her "boyfriend," so, it's a double non-starter. Of course, I've offered to move Lee to Malibu, along with her, on my fucking dime, by the way—which wouldn't be cheap—but she always says Lee won't leave his brother, who apparently lives in the City. A fact she's apparently been able to extract from a man so medicated, he constantly drools down his chin and says not more than six words a day.

"You have to stay for lunch," Mom says brightly to me. "They're serving chicken pot pies. Your favorite."

They're not my favorite. In fact, I rarely eat carbs. "Maybe next time," I say. "I've got to keep this visit short, like I said."

Mom frowns. "Your last visit was short, too."

"No. Last time, I spent the entire day with you. We watched *Jeopardy* and played Scrabble. Remember?"

She shakes her head. "No. Last time, you had to leave because of some awards show."

Oh my fucking God. The Grammys thing was *months* ago. During my most recent visit, Mom had a terrible meltdown, so I stayed the entire day with her, holding her hand. Listening to her talk. Trying, and failing, to make her smile. And then, finally, when she calmed down, we watched *Jeopardy* and played fucking Scrabble. And, by the way, I did all of this, even though I had so much on my plate at work, I hadn't slept more than three hours a night in a week.

And while I'm cataloging recent visits in my mind, the visit before the most recent one was a long one, too. During which, as I recall, I joined Mom's yoga class, let her win in checkers, *and* listened to her read mind-numbing poetry by Sylvia Plath. But, of course, Mom doesn't remember my last two extra-long visits. All she remembers is the time, months ago, I had to make it quick because Grammy nominations had just been announced, and my artists had collectively received more nominations than ever before—and I had to blow out of here to manage the happy chaos of my life.

"Come," Mom says, putting out her hand. "I want to show you my painting."

I take her hand and let her lead me to her room, and then "ooh" and "aah" as she shows me the picnic I've already seen.

Simply to make conversation, I ask, "Once you finish filling in the grass and trees, will it be complete? Or is there something else you're planning to add, after that?"

Shit. Tears instantly well in Mom's eyes. "I can't finish the grass and trees because I'm out of the right color green!" she blurts. "And the only place they sell it is Sennelier!"

And that's it. She melts down. Which is so fucking crazy, I can't stand it. Sennelier isn't Mars, for fuck's sake. It's a renowned art store in Paris, with an easy-to-navigate online store—the place I order all Mom's uber-expensive art supplies. And yet, she's just said the name of the place like it's located in another dimension.

I grab a tissue off Mom's nightstand and hand it to her. "I'll order whatever you need online, Mom. There's no need to cry."

"How? You can't help me because you're going back to *California*."

I can't help chuckling at the way she just said "California," as if she'd said the word "Satan" in its place. "Mom. Take a chill pill, would you? I'll pay whatever it takes to get it here overnight. Come here. Watch this." I pull her sobbing frame to the bed and sit her down, the same way I've done countless times. Calmly, I get onto my phone and head to the French art store's website—a site I've already bookmarked for easy access—and then place an outrageously expensive order for rush delivery of every single shade of green in their store. "See? *Aucun problème, madame.* Whatever your heart desires, I'll always get it for you. No need for tears." I put my arm around her frail shoulders and hug her to me and she cries a river of tears—a torrent that obviously has nothing to do with her needing a few more

162

tubes of green paint. As Mom's tears continue flowing, I covertly check my watch. *Fuck.* "I've got to go, Mom," I say, my stomach twisting. "I really can't miss my flight."

"Because you have to go to *California.*"

"Because I need to work."

"But you haven't had lunch yet."

"Next time. I'll eat on the plane."

She sits up and levels me with her dark, piercing eyes. "You're staying for lunch, Reed Charlemagne," she declares. "I won't take no for an answer."

I take a deep breath and bite my tongue. God, how I hate that fucking expression. She's said it my whole fucking life, as long as I can remember, and whenever I hear it, no matter the situation, the only thing I want to do is scream "No, no, no, motherfucker!" like a toddler with a very dirty mouth. But, because I'm an adult, and I really shouldn't call my mother a motherfucker, I take another deep breath, squash my instinct to rebel, and say, "I'll stay for a quick lunch. But no dessert. I've got to watch my girlish figure."

Sniffling, Mom wipes her eyes. "You don't have a girlish figure. You're a strong, muscular man. Just like your father."

"It was a joke, Mom. It's called *sarcasm.*" I rise from the bed. "Stay put. I need to make a quick call to arrange a later flight, and then we'll head to the dining room."

"But you're coming back?"

"Yes, I'll be right back. I promise."

Pulling out my phone, I dip into the hallway.

"Howdy, boss," Owen says, answering my call.

"Change of plans, O. I need a new flight to LA, about an hour and a half later than the original one. Book me private, if necessary. I don't care how much it costs, just as long as I make it to the RCR concert before it starts."

"What's up?"

"My visit with my mother is taking a little longer than planned. We're going to enjoy chicken pot pies together."

"How lovely. My favorite."

"Believe me, I wish you could be here to take my place. So, listen. Since I won't make it to the arena as early as planned, you're going to have to be the one to greet the new *Rock 'n' Roll* reporter when she arrives."

"No problem. I met with her yesterday and showed her around the office. Her name is Georgina. She's great."

Georgina. In a flash, I'm flooded with images of her again. Those earth-quaking kisses. Her mouthwatering tits peeking up from her tank top. Her ass in those tight jeans when she bent over. And, of course, those blazing hazel eyes as she raised her middle fingers into the sky.

I clear my throat. "Personally escort her around backstage, okay? And do *not*, under any circumstances, leave her alone with Caleb. You got me? That's your top job. If you fuck that up, I swear to God, you're fired."

I can hear Owen smiling on his end of the line. As he well knows, there's virtually nothing he could do, or not do, to get canned by me. Which is why I feel comfortable threatening him with it all the time, but only to emphasize when a particular task is especially important.

"I got it, boss," he says. "Georgie gets no alone-time with Caleb."

"I can't emphasize this enough, O. Georgina is *exactly* Caleb's type and he just broke up with some airheaded supermodel, so he's gonna be especially on the prowl. A thousand bucks says he's gonna pounce on Georgina the second he gets a clear shot. So, for the love of God, make damned sure he doesn't get a clear shot."

"So, you've seen Georgina, then?"

Shit. I remain mute, feeling like I've been caught red-handed.

"So... hmm," Owen says. "I'm sensing Georgina might not only be *Caleb's* exact type. Could it be she's also someone *else's* exact type, too...?"

I grimace sharply to myself at my implicit admission, but, nonetheless, forge ahead in a businesslike tone. "I'll be heading straight to the concert from the airport," I say evenly, "so be sure to tell the LA car service about the change in my itinerary."

"Will do, boss. No problem. Enjoy the chicken pot pie with your momma. I'll text you the new flight info. And don't worry, I'll make sure Georgina meets the entire band, all at once."

"Good. Don't fuck it up, O. Your job depends on it."

"Yes, sir."

After hanging up with Owen, I text the change of plans to my driver, Tony, out front, and then return to my mother's room. When I get there, I find my mother staring blankly out her window at the garden.

"Mom?"

She doesn't flinch.

I place my palm gently on her shoulder. "Ready to eat, Mom?"

She turns her head. "Who'd you call?"

"Owen."

"The gay man who works for you?"

"The gay, smart, loyal, reliable, funny, organized, creative man who works for me."

"I like that you have a gay male secretary."

"Owen's not my secretary. He defies traditional description."

"So do I."

I laugh. I meant that Owen's *job* defies traditional description, thanks to everything he does for me and the label. But Mom's retort was too funny—and accurate—to correct. "That's true, Mom. You most definitely defy traditional maternal description."

"Have I met Owen?"

"No. But guess what? His last name is French. *Boucher*."

She gasps. "Butcher! He's from France?"

"Not Owen himself. But somewhere along the line, someone in Owen's family tree was French. He told me about it once, but I forget the details."

"Yet another reason for me to meet this man. My instinct tells me Owen Boucher and I would be kindred spirits. He's got a French butcher somewhere in his family tree and I've got a French carpenter in mine. We're soulmates."

"Owen's name is 'yet *another* reason' you're soulmates?" I say. "What's the first reason?"

"He's gay," she says matter-of-factly. "And I'm an artist. Artists and gay people always get along. We share a common understanding of what it means to be an *outsider* in this dark and lonely world."

I smooth a lock of her gray hair. "Maybe I should bring Owen the Butcher here to have chicken pot pies with Eleanor the Carpenter some time, eh? You two can sit in the garden and talk about art and sexuality and Sylvia Plath and being *outsiders* until your heart's content."

"And our French lineage."

"That, too."

"I'd like that." She frowns sharply. "Seeing as how my son hardly ever visits me because he's too busy going to rock concerts and awards shows in *California*."

I close my eyes and pray for strength from a God I don't believe in. "I visit as much as I can. If you'd let me move you to—"

"I'm not moving to Malibu, Reed. My home is here."

My gaze drifts to Mom's painting again. To my nephew on the outskirts of the grassy park—the first new "family" member she's ever painted. And it's enough to keep me from going completely mad. Barely, yes, but it is. "If I bring Owen to visit, will you promise to include him in your painting that week?"

Mom shrugs, as noncommittal as ever. And I know in my heart, even if I were to fly Owen to Scarsdale to have chicken pot pies with her, even if they were to have the best conversation in the world about art, sexuality, 'outsider-ism,' Sylvia Plath, and France—a torture I'd never subject Owen to, by the way, unless I were paying him a hefty bonus—she wouldn't paint him in that week's opus. Because he's not family, and she'd need *years* to shift gears enough to let an outsider, even an exceedingly pleasant gay one, intrude in her reality.

I also know something else as I stand here with Mom. A thought I quickly stuff down and push away the moment my brain conjures it: no matter how many "Owens" I might arrange for my mother to talk to, or what fancy French paints I might buy for her on rush delivery, none of it will ever be enough to make her love me. At least, not like most mothers love their children. Not the way she loved a certain four-year-old who never grew up to become imperfect in her eyes, who never grew up to remind her of his father, Terrence—a dashing, charismatic, broad-shouldered man who, many moons ago, promised to take care of and love a gorgeous, tempestuous teenager named Eleanor... but, instead, only wound up shattering her already broken heart.

Chapter 20
Reed

I slide into the backseat of the car picking me up from LAX and confirm with the driver he's taking me to RCR's concert at the Rose Bowl. Logistics sorted, I pull out my phone to answer the million and one unread emails and texts requiring my attention. But I can't concentrate on them for shit. Because... *Georgina.* Yet again, that woman has hijacked my thoughts. Only this time, now that my body senses it's once again in the same city as hers, that I'm mere minutes away from actually being in Georgina's glorious presence again, I literally can't think of anything but her.

If only I hadn't been a pussy and agreed to stay for lunch with my mother, I would have arrived at the stadium in plenty of time to personally greet Georgina when she arrived, her shiny new press pass around her neck. Damn. I really wanted to see the look of excitement and anticipation on her face in that moment, and then watch with amusement as her features instantly morphed into anxiety when she saw me and realized that, maybe, those double-birds she flipped me a week ago weren't such a good idea, after all. Oh, God, that moment was going to be such a turn-on for me. But thanks to those chicken pot pies, and my eternal soft spot for my mother, I missed it.

Plus, I've missed out on some other good stuff, too. For instance, being the one to show Georgina around backstage and introduce her to everyone. I very much wished to do that, not only to be helpful to Georgina, but to communicate to

168

every fucker within a mile radius, especially a certain drummer for RCR, that Georgina is *mine*. Not to be touched. Not to be flirted with. Off-fucking-limits. *Mine, mine, mine.*

Plus, of course, I very much wanted to be able to pull Georgina aside, after initially letting her twist in the wind for a bit, to clear the air about the other night. After some reflection this past week, I've come to realize I *might* have overreacted a bit when I found out about her stepsister's musical aspirations. But I also think Georgina fucked up, too. Royally. And I'm interested to see if, after a week of her own reflecting, Georgina is ready to own up to her part in the way things blew up between us. Is she going to hold tight to her prior indignation with white knuckles, or admit she flew off the handle like a fucking lunatic and apologize to me, as she should? Frankly, I'm dying to know.

I'm going to fuck her, either way, of course, whether she doubles down on her "fuck you's" or has the good sense to start kissing my ass, now that she realizes it's in her best interests. But I'd be lying if I didn't admit I'm hoping to witness another round of fiery sass from feisty Georgina, just for the pure entertainment of it. Oh, and also because watching her fly off the handle makes me so fucking hard, it physically hurts.

"There's a VIP entrance at the back," I say to my driver as we approach the Rose Bowl's parking lot. And, five minutes later, he's pulling up to the restricted-access loading zone in the back. Sure enough, I spot Owen standing curbside, awaiting me as instructed. At the moment, he's staring at his phone while smoking a cigarette. Being punctual and reliable and humble and patient. You know, being Owen. "Right here," I say to the driver, while simultaneously shooting off a text to Owen: *Look up. I'm here.*

When Owen looks up, it's just in time to see me barreling out of the parked car and marching with urgency toward a large metal door.

"Tip the driver and get my luggage delivered to my house, would you?"

"Aye, aye, Captain."

"Where's Georgina?"

"Greenroom B. I left her in the care of a PA, talking to the entire band."

"All four of them?"

He nods. "Plus, Leonard and his daughter and a gaggle of her friends."

I breathe a sigh of relief. Caleb couldn't possibly make too much progress with Georgina in a crowd like that. "Perfect."

Leaving Owen behind to figure out my luggage and the driver's tip, I breeze past a security guard posted at the VIP door—who, lucky for him, lets me pass without stopping me for my ID—and then, once I'm inside the stadium, begin marching like a madman through familiar hallways toward a back elevator.

Georgina.

Goddammit. Now that I'm this close to her, I'm feeling consumed by a physical craving to kiss her again. Once I finally fuck her, I'm positive this mini-obsession that's been building inside me all week will quickly fade. But until then, it's here, baby. In full force. Like a raging boner that won't go away until it at least gets a hand job.

Nearing the greenroom, I hear female laughter, and my heart seizes.

Georgina.

I stop outside the doorway to catch my breath. Rake my fingers through my hair. Drag my palm over my stubble. And, finally, enter the room like I own the place. But, shit, I don't see Georgina anywhere. Fuck!

"Reed!" my attorney, Leonard, calls to me. And I'm instantly trapped. Fuck, fuck, fuck!

Still glancing around for Georgina, I greet Leonard, and

then his euphoric teenage daughter, and her equally excited friends. I say quick hellos to the guys of Red Card Riot, and clench my jaw when I realize only three of the four are here: Dean, Emmitt, and Clay. *Caleb is nowhere to be found.*

On any other day, I'd be thrilled to find Caleb Baumgarten—the drummer the world knows as "C-Bomb"—absent from a room I'm standing in, thanks to a longstanding beef between us. But this one time, Caleb being MIA, when Georgina is also nowhere to be found, is evoking near-panic inside me.

"Where's Caleb?" I bark at Dean, the lead singer and guitarist.

"Whoa, chill, man," Dean says, laughing. "We've got plenty of time before showtime."

"Where is he?"

"He left a while ago with some newbie reporter for *Rock 'n' Roll*." Dean flashes me a knowing look. "It's her first day on the job, so Caleb gallantly offered to take her for a little pre-show 'tour' of the backstage area."

Motherfucker. I knew Caleb would be all over Georgina like white on rice, sooner rather than later. But *this* fast? It's a fucking record, even for him.

I say my quick goodbyes to everyone, bark at a shocked production assistant to take extra-good care of Leonard and his daughter's party, and then I'm gone, out the door and racing down the cement hallway.

I poke my head through a series of doors, all while brushing off repeated requests for my attention. "Not now," I bark at whoever. "Ask Owen about that."

Finally, I hear it. The sound of Georgina's laughter. It's muffled. Coming from a distant dressing room. But it's most definitely her.

I pick up my pace. Burst through a door. And there they are. Georgina and Caleb. Sitting mere inches from each other, face to face. Georgina's on a couch, looking star-struck and flushed.

Caleb looks like a bearded shark at feeding time, his jacked, tattooed body draped over an armchair, his green eyes on fire.

When I enter, the pair jolts in surprise. Georgina, God bless her, lurches back at my intrusion, her body conceding it's mine, even if her brain doesn't know it yet.

Caleb, on the other hand, smiles like a sniper and leans *toward* Georgina when he sees me, his ripped body staking its claim.

My gaze moves from Caleb's bearded smile to Georgina's panicked eyes. And when our gazes mingle, when Georgina's hazel eyes meet mine, I feel the same explosion of chemistry, fire, and attraction I felt between us in that lecture hall—and then again, even more so, at the bar. And, yet again, when we walked outside Bernie's Place, and I pinned her against the building and pushed my raging boner against her and kissed the living hell out of her, overwhelmed by the nuclear bomb exploding inside me—the powerful yearning I felt to claim, conquer, own, *desecrate.*

Georgina's chest heaves at the sight of me. And, instantly, I know the same forest fire raging inside me at the sight of her is burning out of control inside her, as well.

"Time to go," I bark at Caleb.

But Caleb only scoffs. "There's plenty of time before we hit. The opening band hasn't even—"

"You're missing an important VIP meet and greet."

Caleb waves his tattooed knuckles. "This is way more important than that. Georgie isn't a groupie, man. She's a writer for *Rock 'n' Roll,* assigned to do an interview of the band, and of me in particular. She's joining the tour this whole week, starting tonight, so we can hang out and she can do a really cool in-depth interview of me."

No.

Fuck no.

There's so much "fuck no" about everything Caleb just said, I can barely keep myself from hurtling my body across the room like a missile, wrapping my hands around his tattooed neck, and squeezing the life out of him. Did Owen approve everything Caleb just said? If so, he's fucking fired. For real, this time.

"Hi, Mr. Rivers," Georgina says, rising from the couch, her hand extended. "I'm Georgina Ricci from *Rock 'n' Roll.*" She proudly holds up the press pass around her neck. "CeeCee told you about me, I hope? I'll be working exclusively on the River Records special issue. I'm really, really excited about it, Mr. Rivers."

Her eyes are pleading with me. Begging me not to throw her out, along with Caleb. And it suddenly occurs to me she has no idea how I fit into this new job opportunity of hers. Did I have a hand in her getting this assignment—or was it given to her against my will? Obviously, Georgina's wondering where we stand after the other night. Am I going to help her during this summer internship... or fucking torture her?

"I'm excited you're here, Georgina," I say warmly, attempting to put her at ease. I shake her hand and my flesh tingles at her touch. "CeeCee has said some great things about you. I'm excited about the special issue, and glad you're working on it."

Her shoulders soften, her expression conveying, *Well, that went a whole lot better than I feared it would.*

I peel my eyes off Georgina to glare at C-Bomb. "Time to go, Caleb. Those VIPs were promised a photo op with the *full* band. Everyone's waiting on you."

He languidly pulls out a box of cigarettes. "They'll survive. I'm gonna chill here with Georgie until showtime. We need to chat a bit about ideas for my interview." He winks at Georgina. "It's gonna be sick."

I take a deep breath. "You're contractually obligated to show up for 'designated VIP meet and greets,' Caleb. And I'm hereby designating this one as a contractual obligation."

Caleb lights his cigarette and takes a long drag off it, his green eyes shooting daggers at me. But when it's clear I'm not going to budge, and that this could get a tad bit embarrassing for him in front of Georgina—because, come on, we both know I own his fucking ass at the end of the day—Caleb slowly rises from his chair and stretches his hulking frame. "Duty calls." He smiles wistfully at Georgina. "See you later."

"Have a great show," Georgina says. "Don't worry. We'll have plenty of time to talk this week."

"I'm throwing a party in my hotel suite after the show. Why don't you come and see how the band blows off steam after a show? Spoiler alert: there's alcohol involved."

She chuckles. "I'd love to. Thank you. Spoiler alert: I like alcohol. I bartended in college."

"Hey, yet another thing we have in common! You know how to make drinks, and I know how to drink 'em."

"*Hey.*"

He beams a huge smile at Georgina that makes me want to lurch over to him, take his stupid Mohawk in my fist, and slam his smug face, repeatedly, into the floor until it's a bloody pulp. But, somehow, I force myself to stand still, not moving a muscle. Not even breathing.

Caleb says, "I'll tell my PA to get your phone number during the show, so I can text you the info for the party. Are you staying at the Ritz, with all of us?"

Georgina blushes. "Oh, gosh, no. I'm booked at budget hotels this week. But never more than five miles from where you guys are staying, so it'll be easy for us to connect."

"Fuck that, dude. I'll book you a room at the Ritz tonight, on me, so you can party with us and only have to stumble a short way to your bed afterwards."

A puff of disdain escapes me involuntarily, and Caleb smiles, letting me know he's heard it, and is thoroughly enjoying having this exchange with Georgina in front of me.

"Wow... that's certainly not necessary... " Georgina says about the offered hotel room.

"I insist," Caleb says, ever the gallant fucking gentleman.

"Wow. Thank you. Okay."

"Caleb," I say sharply, a hair's breadth away from committing an extremely bloody form of murder. "*It's time for you to go.*"

Caleb smirks, winks at Georgina, takes another long drag off his cigarette and finally saunters out the door, but not before turning at the doorframe and shooting me a quick, nonverbal "fuck you, bitch." Which, of course, I return in kind. Fucking punk-ass little bitch prick.

When Caleb is gone, I march to the door and close it behind him, breathing deeply to banish my homicidal thoughts. Finally, I turn to face Georgina—the woman who's relentlessly invaded my thoughts and dreams and masturbation fantasies this entire week. Damn, she looks even hotter than last week. As ripe as a peach.

Georgina fidgets under my intense, silent gaze, looking like she doesn't know if I want her to stay or go. If I want to kiss her or spank her or tell her to get the fuck out or to hop onto my cock. And so, I decide it's time to make things crystal clear to her. Right fucking now.

"Sit down, Georgie," I say sternly, my jaw clenched. "We need to have ourselves a little chat."

Chapter 21
Reed

A s I cross the room toward Georgina, muted music from a distant part of the stadium begins wafting through the walls of the small room—the sound of the opening band, kicking off their short set.

I unbutton my suit jacket and take the armchair across from Georgina. The one formerly occupied by Caleb. I place my ankle on my knee. And exhale. "Congratulations," I say calmly.

"On what?" Her gorgeous features are etched with anxiety. Obviously, she's wondering where things stand between us, given her fiery, early-morning exit from the front of my house a week ago.

"On the new job," I say. "And your graduation. I presume you graduated last week, as planned?"

She nods. "I'm officially a UCLA alum. Go, Bruins. I'm actually the first college grad in my family. My dad couldn't stop crying." She presses her lips together, like she's forcibly keeping herself from rambling further.

I can't help but smile at her adorableness. "That's awesome," I say. "I'm sure your parents are insanely proud of you."

Something flickers across her pretty face that makes me question my words. Have I just unwittingly highlighted the age gap between us—come off like a friend of her father's? Or could it be her parents *aren't* proud of her, for some reason? I can't imagine that's the case, but I suppose it's possible they wanted her to study something other than journalism?

When I don't speak for a long moment, but instead opt to stare her down and revel in her obvious anxiety, Georgina puts her hands into her lap, like she doesn't know what to do with them. She bites her lower lip. Fidgets. And then, "How was New York?"

"Busy, productive, fun, exhausting, and highly lucrative."

"Oh. That sounds good."

"It was. Very good."

I fall silent again, enjoying the way my silence turns her breathing shallow. The way it brings a flush to her cheeks and cleavage. Yeah, I'm being a bastard. Making her sweat, simply to amuse myself. Well, and also to punish her a tiny bit for the way she double-flipped me off. For fuck's sake, Georgina was the one with a music demo in her pocket. Not me. She was the one with a hidden agenda. And yet, she had the audacity to flip *me* off and screech away in an Uber, leaving me standing there, after I'd stooped to *begging* her to come inside? When was the last time I begged anyone for anything? And yet, Georgina made me do it, just that fucking fast. Well, never again. That's for fucking sure.

"So you wanted to have a little chat... ?" she prompts, her voice tight.

I pick at a piece of lint on my suit jacket. "Yes." I pause again, for dramatic effect. "This plan for you to join RCR on tour this coming week?"

She nods.

"It's the first I'm hearing about it, and I don't approve. You'll have to find something else to do this week. Tagging along on RCR's tour is off."

"*What?*" she blurts. For a moment, she gapes like a fish on a line, before shouting, "You can't do that, Reed!"

"I just did."

"CeeCee cleared the whole thing with Owen! Owen helped arrange it!"

"And Owen works for *me*. Well, he used to. If he arranged that shit show of an idea, then he's fired."

She turns pale.

"I'm joking. Owen is bulletproof. Ask anyone."

"Reed, you can't call everything off. CeeCee is excited about the idea, and so am I. And so is the band. Just now, when I was talking to all four of them about it in the greenroom, they said—"

"I don't give a flying fuck what the band said. The plan wasn't cleared through me. And I don't like it. I think it's an unoriginal, tired idea that's already been done a thousand times. Ever seen *Almost Famous*?"

She's flabbergasted. "Well, granted, we might not be inventing the wheel here, but who cares? Readers will eat it up. What fan wouldn't want to tag along with RCR on tour, through me? It's every music lover's fantasy. A once-in-a-lifetime chance to peek behind the—"

"Stop trying to sell me. It's dead. Move on."

She consciously shuts her gaping mouth. "But... Reed, I've got hotel rooms booked for the entire week!"

Oh, Georgina. I resist the urge to chuckle at her indignation. Her naiveté. As if the tragedy of a few unused hotel rooms would stop the world spinning on its axis. If I'd forgotten Georgina is only twenty-one, I was just now reminded of it. "Hotel room reservations are almost always refundable," I say calmly to my little kitten, trying not to smile at her lack of real-world experience. "And if not, then I'll reimburse *Rock 'n' Roll* for any expense, seeing as how the rooms were booked after coordination with Owen. Who, to be clear, will be out of a job after this, I promise you that."

Again, she looks pained.

"Kidding again. Get used to it. It's a running joke."

Georgina rubs her face, distraught. And, for a moment, I

feel kind of sorry for the poor little thing. She looks like a possum caught in an iron trap. Like a little lamb being carted off to slaughter. But, to my surprise, after a few deep breaths, she visibly gathers her strength and straps on her warrior's armor. Suddenly, the simpering twenty-one-year-old vanishes, supplanted by the same fierce superhero I witnessed in front of my house the other night.

Georgina's eyes are sharp now. Her nostrils flaring. After one more deep breath, she puffs out her spectacular chest and lets me have it. "I won't let you do this," she says, her eyes ablaze. "CeeCee made it *very* clear to me *she's* my boss, not *you*. She also said you explicitly agreed we're not churning out propaganda for River Records here—we're independent *journalists*. You've expressly agreed CeeCee's got full editorial control, and CeeCee, my *boss*, has decided I'm touring with RCR this entire week."

A faint smile lifts the corners of Georgina's indignant mouth, like she thinks she's dealt me a death blow with her little speech. And, once again, I find myself fighting not to smile. Holy shit, she's fucking adorable. Irresistible. Feisty. Glorious. Oh, how I wish she could sing, even a little bit. Because the girl's got star power in spades, in a way truckloads of wannabe actresses and models and pop stars would kill for. "Everything you've said is exactly right," I reply. "Especially the part about you being *CeeCee's* employee, not mine. In fact, I wouldn't have agreed to this arrangement if it created any kind of employer-employee relationship between you and me." I lean forward, my eyes on fire. "And do you know *why* I didn't want you as my employee, little Georgina?"

Her chest rises sharply. Her nostrils flare again. She shakes her head.

I smile. "*Because I never fuck my own employees.*"

Georgina's lips part with surprise at my obvious implication, left unsaid: *but I have no problem fucking one of CeeCee's.*

Lauren Rowe

"Well, news flash," she says, narrowing her eyes. "You're not going to fuck me, either, no matter whose employee I am." She leans forward, cutting the distance between us in half. "And do you know *why* you're not going to fuck me, Mr. Rivers?" She's close enough for me to see the caramel flecks in her hazel eyes. To smell her shampoo and moisturizer and toothpaste. *"Because. I. Don't. Fuck. Assholes."*

I can't help smirking at her bald-faced lie. "Well, so much for you fucking C-Bomb, then. That's a relief."

She clenches her jaw, clearly annoyed, but says nothing.

I cock my head. "So, that's your clever way of telling me, yet again, that *I'm* an asshole?"

"Seems like a logical deduction to make from what I just said."

"Well, that's an interesting interpretation. Between the two of us, I think any reasonable person would say *you* acted like a far bigger asshole the other night than *me*."

Her eyebrows furrow sharply. "Are you high? You were a colossal dick to me, Reed."

"Oh, really? Huh. I didn't tell anyone to fuck off and die. And I'm certainly not the one who had a demo in my pocket the entire time we were flirting. Just a boner, which certainly doesn't qualify as a hidden agenda."

"Ha! You want to talk about hidden agendas?" she booms, her glorious temper rising and reddening her cheeks. "Every word out of your mouth that night was a lie, designed to get you into my panties. You think it's not a hidden agenda to pretend to give a rat's ass about what a woman says, to pretend to care about having a conversation with her, for the sole purpose of 'seducing' her? I know you're a hundred-and-five and all, but we kids these days call men like you 'fuckboys,' Reed. *And it's not a compliment.*"

"Getting you into my bed wasn't my *hidden* agenda, Georgina. It was my expressly stated goal. I explicitly told you, straight-up, I wasn't interested in dating you. Only

180

seducing you. Maybe you 'kids' today aren't familiar with the art of seduction, so let me translate for you. The entire purpose of it is getting to the *fucking* part. So, please, enlighten me. Tell me, what was I hiding from you that night? Name one fucking thing."

She opens and closes her mouth, at a loss for words.

"I thought so," I say, leaning back in victory.

"Okay, Mr. Rivers. Listen up, you arrogant prick. I'm going to explain what happened the other night, *once*, without leaving anything out. And then I'm going to move on and never speak of this again, because I'm already sick to death of the stupid topic." She takes a deep breath, apparently trying to keep her temper under control, and every cell in my body strains with desire for her. "I wasn't using you that night, Reed. I was genuinely, sincerely, outrageously attracted to you, from the first second I saw you. I assure you, I wanted to get 'seduced' by you, every bit as much as you wanted to seduce me. And, for the record, yes, I was fully aware 'seduction' was a euphemism for 'fucking.' Aware of and quite thrilled about it."

I'm breathing deeply. Trying not to let on how intoxicating she is to me—that she's already won me over, and then some.

"To be honest," Georgina continues, crossing her arms. "I bet I wanted to have sex with you, even more than you wanted to have it with me. Because, heck, you can have sex with anyone in the world—just by snapping your fingers, Mr. Big Shit Music Mogul. For you, banging some nobody student-bartender isn't a big deal. Just another Thursday night. But, for me, getting 'seduced' by Reed Rivers, going to his fancy house in his fancy car, was a *very* big deal. And before you call me a gold digger, I'm not. Why would I care about your money, when I was in it for nothing but one night of sex? But who wouldn't feel swept away by you and your glamorous life? You made me feel like I was in a movie. I haven't slept with that many guys in my life. And certainly never anyone as experienced and exciting and dashing as you. I'm not saying I gave a shit about you, personally, okay? Even as we were driving to your house, I wasn't sure I liked you. But one thing I was positive about: I sure as hell wanted you to do filthy things to me—with absolutely no strings attached, I might add—simply for the fun of it."

Every word out of her mouth has been music to my ears. And to my cock. And not a huge surprise, to be honest. Of course, Georgina sincerely wanted to fuck me that night—for all the reasons she just set forth. She's a journalism student, after all, not an aspiring starlet—a whole different breed of woman than the ones I'm used to encountering. Plus, even the best actress in the world couldn't have faked Georgina's reaction when we kissed. The way she bucked and jolted into me, and then kissed me back with a passion that took my breath away—like she was drowning and I was oxygen. Or, fuck, maybe it was the other way around, and she was the oxygen. Either way, Georgina's passion that night reflected back to me everything I was feeling in that moment—like every atom in my body had been doused in lighter fluid, and then set ablaze by the torch that was Georgina Ricci.

Which is probably why... maybe... now that I'm thinking about it... I reacted the way I did when I first found out about the demo. For a split-second there, I irrationally thought maybe Georgina *had* been the world's best actress, and that she'd played me expertly the whole time, even during our nuclear-bomb of a kiss. And I didn't like how that made me feel. But now... now that I've had time to process and reflect, now that I'm seeing the earnestness in her eyes, I know for certain she's telling me the truth. Of course, she is. Which means I really was an asshole that night. But realizing I was an asshole doesn't mean she wasn't one, too. And it certainly doesn't mean I'm inclined to let her off the hook. Not yet, anyway.

"So, you expect me to believe it was pure coincidence you had your stepsister's music demo in your pocket that night?" I ask.

Georgina rolls her eyes. "Will you stop being a stubborn dickhead for a second and just listen to me? Holy hell, you're even more stubborn than me."

I bite back a smile.

"I'd never heard of you before the event. On my walk there, Alessandra told me about you during a phone call. So, because I *love* my stepsister, and always want her dreams to come true, I loaded a flash drive with her best songs the minute I got to the lecture hall, just in case the chance to hand it to you fell into my lap. Wouldn't you have done the same thing for someone you love? God, I hope so... or else you're an even bigger dickhead than I think you are."

This time, a huge smile spreads across my face. When was the last time anyone spoke to me like this? T-Rod, I'm pretty sure. In Maui, several years ago during Josh's wedding week. Anyone since? I truly don't think so.

"The truth is, having that demo in my purse the whole time we were talking at the bar turned out to be an albatross around my neck. Of course, I wanted to come through for Alessandra, but I didn't want that demo to screw up my own chances of getting 'seduced.' Which, yes, I fully realize, is exactly what wound up happening. The bottom line is I wanted to have sex with you, Reed, because you made my ovaries vibrate. Was I *also* hoping you might be willing to take a few minutes of your precious time to listen to my stepsister's songs? Yes. So sue me. But, I swear to God, my desire to help Alessandra wasn't a 'hidden agenda.' It was an agenda that ran *concurrently* with my own."

I smile. How could I not? I'm the guy who's paid money to a cancer charity to get this girl here, after all, because I want to fuck her so badly. But *also* because of some other motivations that run *concurrently* with my desire to fuck her. Things like my genuine desire to help Georgina and her father, and to get CeeCee a promising new employee, and my artists some great publicity. But, yeah... mostly, because I want to fuck Georgina. "Thank you for explaining all that to me," I say. "For what it's worth, while I was making your ovaries vibrate, you were making my balls vibrate."

She can't help smiling at that. "Thank God for small mercies."

"Look, I admit I gave you a bit of a harder time the other night than you rightly deserved. And for that, I sincerely apologize."

She looks shell-shocked. And then deeply pleased. "Thank you. I accept your apology."

There's a beat, during which the opening band hits the last, crashing drumbeat of their short set.

"What about you?" I say.

"What about me... what?"

"What do you apologize for?"

She pulls a face that says, *Not a goddamned thing.*

"You don't think you have anything to apologize for?"

She twists her mouth. And then says, begrudgingly, "I'm sorry I double-flipped you off. It was rude of me. One middle finger would have sufficed. This one. With my new pretty ring on it."

She flips me off, singularly, and I can't help chuckling, despite myself.

She shakes her head and exhales. "Okay, yes, I *maybe* went off the rails a teeny-tiny bit. But, honestly, I'm proud of myself for telling you off and leaving when I did. I chose my integrity over my libido. If choosing my integrity over sex with a smoking hot asshole isn't 'adulting,' then I don't know what is."

"Mmm hmm. Because you never, ever fuck assholes."

"Correct."

"Not even the smoking hot ones."

"Correct again."

Chuckling, I shake my head. "You're such a liar, Georgina Ricci. And a terrible one, at that. I'd bet anything, literally anything, you *only* fuck smoking hot assholes. In fact, I'd bet a million bucks you'd rather fuck an exciting, smoking hot, bad-boy asshole, than some nice, boring, God-fearing *football star* with a Captain America smile any day of the week."

She rolls her eyes, plainly annoyed I've invoked Bryce McKellar to make my point. But then she makes a face that tacitly admits I've pegged her exactly right. Yep. This girl is a fireball who's hopelessly attracted to assholes like me, the ones who throw lighter fluid on her flames, whether she likes it about herself or not.

A genuine affection for her rises up inside me, an attraction to her feisty, flawed, adorableness. And I suddenly can't help smiling at her from ear to ear. To my surprise, she returns the gesture, flashing me the most genuine smile she's graced me with since we chatted at the bar... and, just that fast, something passes between us. Respect. Understanding. Georgina knows I see through her hotheaded, drama-loving bullshit, and I know she sees through my button-pushing, keep-you-at-distance bullshit. We're the same, Georgina and me. Two bullshitters, buried beneath hardened outer layers. Two people who recognize themselves in the other. At least, in this moment, it sure feels like we do.

In a distant part of the stadium, the crowd roars, signaling Red Card Riot has just walked onstage. And a few seconds after that, we hear the band launch into the first song of the night—an instantly recognizable, global smash off their second album called "Ready or Not."

"Well, that's my cue," Georgina says, popping off the couch. "Good chat, Mr. Rivers. When I get back from touring with RCR at the end of the week, I'll call to schedule your interview."

"Sit down, Georgina."

She freezes.

"I said sit the fuck *down*. You're not going on tour, and we're not even close to finished with our little chat."

Chapter 22
Reed

Georgina sits back down on the couch, looking like a petulant teenager who's just been grounded from going to a concert with her girlfriends. "Come on, Reed. This tour is my best chance to get an amazing interview out of C-Bomb."

I can't believe my ears. "You still think you're interviewing C-Bomb?" I say, barely containing my disdainful chuckle. "Sweetheart, no. That's off, too. *Obviously.*"

"*What*? No!"

"You can interview the full band, if you like, *after* they return from tour in a month. I'll set that up for you. But the mini-tour *and* the one-on-one with C-Bomb are both off."

Georgina balls her hands into fists of frustration and bangs her thighs, morphing from a grounded teenager into a toddler being denied an ice cream cone. "But CeeCee specifically assigned me to interview C-Bomb, as my top priority. She said everyone always interviews the frontmen of bands, like Dean, and never the drummers. She said C-Bomb, with his bad-boy persona and muscles and beard and crazy hair, will make an eye-catching cover boy and sell a shit-ton of magazines. She said you'd *love* the idea!"

I'm floored. None of what she just said makes any sense. CeeCee knows I loathe C-Bomb with the force of a thousand suns. And yet, she told Georgina I'd "love" the idea of him being a featured interview in the issue—and our fucking *cover* boy? Ha! I can't fathom a more ludicrous statement. So, why the fuck did CeeCee say any of it? Why did she send Georgina straight to C-Bomb, on day one, as her "top priority," when she had to know I'd nix the idea from jump street? I blink rapidly, trying to reboot the faltering computer in my brain. "CeeCee said I'd 'love' the idea of you interviewing C-Bomb?" I ask slowly, simply because it's so preposterous, I'm not sure I heard her correctly.

Georgina nods furiously. "And, don't forget, you agreed to give CeeCee full editorial control, so really, it's up to CeeCee whether I interview C-Bomb, not you. And CeeCee says *yes*."

I scoff at the ridiculous notion. "CeeCee has full editorial control regarding the artists I make available to her. But, see, since I own every band and artist on my label, *I* decide who's made available. And I'm not making RCR available to you until they get back from tour—and, even then, not as individuals, only as a full band."

Oh, she's livid now. "But, why?" she booms, her eyes bulging. "Why, why, *why* are you doing this to me?"

"I'm not doing anything to *you*. I'm protecting my brand. The tour idea isn't original or fresh enough. And C-Bomb isn't a good interview subject or representative of his band or my label, as an individual. My job is to sell RCR's upcoming album. And to do that, I want Dean's blue eyes front and center, because *Dean* is the one who sells records and tickets and posters for walls."

"So does C-Bomb! He was *literally* on my wall when I was a teenager, Reed! And he hasn't been interviewed a fraction as much as Dean."

My heart is galloping. Georgina's confession that she had Caleb on her teenage wall is driving me fucking crazy—and most definitely having the exact opposite effect she's intending. But somehow, I manage to keep my voice calm and professional as I say, "I don't want an interview of C-Bomb for sound business reasons. Conversation over."

Georgina grunts in frustration. "Lies, lies, lies! Stop bullshitting me, Reed. You don't want me going on tour with RCR, or talking to C-Bomb, because you think he'll make a move on me!"

"No." I lean forward, my eyes blazing every bit as much as hers. "I don't want you going on tour with RCR, and talking to C-Bomb, because I *know* he'll make a move on you."

Fuck.

Why'd I say that?

At my confession, Georgina leaps up and points at me in the armchair. "I knew it. Ha!" She crosses her arms. "Well, so what if he does? You and I aren't dating. In fact, you've made it clear you've got no intention of *ever* dating me. Which means you get no say on who, besides you, gets to try to *seduce* me. I'm an adult, Reed. And so is Caleb. You might own Caleb's *band*. But you don't own Caleb, the *man*. And you sure as hell don't own *me*."

My body feels like it's short-circuiting. I'm feeling so jealous, so possessive, so turned on by the fire in her eyes, I can't think straight. Did Georgina have sexual fantasies about Caleb as a teenager? Did she practice kissing her pillow, while pretending it was Caleb? "Caleb can't have you," I say evenly, my heart raging in my ears. "Nobody on my roster can have you. In fact, nobody on planet Earth can have you, until this thing between us has run its course."

She stares for a long beat, flabbergasted. And then throws her head back and bursts out laughing. "The ramblings of a madman. Nobody on *Earth* can have me until you've grown tired of me and thrown me away? Gosh, what a lovely offer, Mr. Rivers. But, no, thanks. You don't get to have me. You don't get to plant your flag in me vis-à-vis the entire fucking *world*. And you most certainly don't get to screw with my job, just because you want to fuck me and I've turned you down. That's illegal, you know. I've got rights. Or haven't you been following the news lately? That kind of shit isn't allowed anymore, Reed.'"

Oh, Jesus fucking Christ. "Georgina, I have no intention of screwing with your job. On the contrary, I only want to help you do it. I want this special issue to be a grand slam, every bit as much as you do. But don't, even for a minute, forget your *job* is to write about *my* artists. You're in *my* house now, Georgina, which means you're going to play by *my* rules, whether I want to fuck you or not. Which, to be clear, I do. Very much. I don't deny that. But that fact doesn't change the fact that you'll toe the line when it comes to my artists. And not just you. Anyone who wants to interview my artists, whether they're from *Rock 'n' Roll* or any other publication, whether I want to fuck them or not, always, *always* plays by my rules in my house. No exceptions, not even for you."

She puts her hands on her hips. "God, you're so full of shit. There's no 'sound' business reason for you to put the kibosh on the C-Bomb interview. You're feeling jealous and territorial. Plain and simple. You might as well have pissed on my leg when you walked in here and found me with him, you looked so freaking jealous."

She's absolutely right. But there's no way in hell I'd ever admit that. "Find something else to write about this week," I say. "I'm done talking about this."

Georgina lets out an exasperated sigh and sits back down on the couch. "Reed, listen to me. I need this tour. CeeCee said she'll consider everything I write this summer as an audition for me to write for *Dig a Little Deeper.*" Emotion threatens at the mere thought of it, but she swallows it. "I know I could get an *incredible* interview of Caleb, if only I had the chance to hang out with him for a full week."

"I have faith you'll find some other amazing person or topic to write about, if you put your mind to it."

She takes several deep, calming breaths. And then drags

her palm down her face. "I didn't want to have to play the sympathy card here, but you leave me no choice. I was *really* counting on those free hotel rooms this week. Please don't mess that up for me because of petty jealousy. Please."

"What are you talking about?"

She tilts her head back and sinks into the sofa, her body melting in adorable surrender. "I had to vacate student housing on graduation day. My student loans are all used up, and I'm told I won't get my first paycheck for this job for about three weeks... " She sighs. "I've got, like, seven dollars to my name right now, so I was counting on a week with no expenses to get back on my feet. Before I got this job, I was going to move back home with my dad in the Valley, so I could help him with his expenses. But now that I'm going to be spending so much time in Hollywood, commuting like that won't work. I was hoping to take this week, with no expenses, to figure out a cheap living situation for the summer. Maybe a friend's couch. A room to rent."

My heart twists. It's so rare for Georgina to drop her tough-girl routine. But whenever she does, I find her all the more alluring. "I'll book you a hotel room for the summer—on me," I say simply. "Something within walking distance of my office."

She sits up. "Seriously?"

"Sure. I wish all life's problems were this easy to solve."

She's absolutely elated. She hops up like she wants to hug me, but abruptly sits back down, her cheeks flushing. "Thank you so much, Reed." She fans her blushing face. *"Thank you."*

My heart skips a beat at the look of pure joy on her face. "You're very welcome, Georgina."

In a heartbeat, the expression of joy on her face is replaced by one of skepticism. "Not to look a gift horse in the mouth, but why, exactly, are you doing this?"

"Because it makes sound business sense," I say, lying

through my teeth. "You'll be able to maximize your time this way. Plus, you'll be relaxed and close by. All good things for the special issue, in the end."

Her skeptical smile turns absolutely breathtaking. "Liar," she says softly. But she's said the word playfully. Affectionately, even. And it sends a flock of butterflies whooshing into my stomach—which is a shock to me. I haven't felt the cliché of "butterflies" too many times in my life. And when I do, they usually feel foreign and strange to me. But, holy fuck, this time, I'm feeling them and thoroughly enjoying them.

"You ready to stop screaming at me and watch the rest of the concert with me?" I say. "We can watch from the wings." I rise, assuming her answer is yes, yes, yes... but quickly realize I've miscalculated. Georgina's not standing with me. Indeed, she's staying put and shaking her head.

"Fuck," I mutter, sitting back down. "Now what?"

Everybody's got a price.

I say it all the time and know it to be true. But something tells me Georgina Ricci's price ain't a free hotel room a few blocks away from River Records.

Chapter 23
Reed

Seeing as how you won't let me go on tour or interview C-Bomb," Georgina says, her eyebrow arched, "you owe me something as good or better."

"I'll let you interview RCR and also Dean, individually."

"Not good enough. Dean's been interviewed a trillion times. He's so good at being interviewed by now, I'm sure I'll be able to chat with him for twenty minutes at the party tonight and walk away with an entire interview all sewn up."

I can't believe my ears. "You still think you're going to that party tonight? Georgina, obviously, that's off, too. Same as everything else."

She throws up her arms. "No!"

"Yes."

"But Caleb invited me!"

"And I'm uninviting you. I thought you understood the party being cancelled was part and parcel of everything else I've cancelled."

"Okay, that's it. The last straw. I quit." But she doesn't move. She just sits there, stewing. Thinking. *Strategizing.* Finally, she visibly lights up with an idea. "What if I took off my press pass and went to that party tonight as a civilian? Not as a reporter. Just as Caleb's personal guest. I could do that, and you couldn't say boo about it."

My heart rate spikes. *Fuck.* The clever girl's found herself a loophole. *Fuck me.*

Georgina smiles wickedly, and I know I've done a shitty job of maintaining a poker face. Indeed, whatever she just saw flicker across my face, it's egging her on.

"You know what?" she says, sitting up. "That's exactly what I'm going to do. Throw away my press pass and go to the party tonight as a civilian. And not only that, I'm going to throw away my press pass for the entire week, and start my job a week later than originally planned, and go on the tour, too. Why should I be an official reporter on the tour"—she levels me with her blazing eyes—"when I can be Caleb's... *groupie?*"

Oh, for the love of fuck. She's evil. A shark smelling blood. A demon.

Georgina licks her lips. "Band members are allowed to bring guests on their tours, right? I bet that's even stated in their contracts. So, fine, I'll just be Caleb's personal guest for the entire week and all my problems will be magically solved." She snaps her fingers. "Don't forget, C-Bomb offered to get me a hotel room at the Ritz tonight, on his dime, just to make things easier on me after the party. Wasn't that sweet of him? So, I'm thinking, maybe, if I ask him really sweetly to get me rooms in every city along the tour, he'll do it for me. Do you think he would? I bet he would." She drapes her arm across the back of the couch. "And if not, then, gosh, maybe he'll be willing to let me crash in his bed... every... single... night."

Oh, my fucking God, she's diabolical. Pure, unadulterated evil. A force of nature. A human asteroid hurtling toward my planet. How did I not see this coming? I'm normally brilliant at predicting my opponent's tactical maneuvers. But this time, I must admit, Georgina Ricci has outplayed me. I clench my jaw, forcing myself to keep a poker face. But, damn, this diabolical woman just laid down a royal flush to my two pairs and I'm losing my fucking mind.

"What was that groupie's name in *Almost Famous?*" she asks breezily.

I force myself to sound nonchalant. "Penny Lane."

"That's right. I bet I'd get a ton of great content for *Dig a Little Deeper*, if I pulled a Penny Lane this whole week with Caleb." She swipes her palm through the air in front of me, like she's imagining her name in lights. "'My Tantalizing Week as a Badass Drummer's Penny Lane.' By Georgina Ricci." She smiles wickedly at me and lowers her hand. "Gosh, with a scintillating title like that, I bet the article would fly off shelves. It'd probably be the best-selling issue of *Dig a Little Deeper* yet, doncha think?"

Oh, she's good. But, still, as I sit here staring at her, I'm starting to smell her panic. To make out the chinks in her armor that betray the panic bubbling frantically underneath all that gorgeous bravado. Her shallow breath. Flaring nostrils. The crimson in her cheeks. Ah, yes. Despite this little show she's putting on for me, gorgeous Georgina is actually terrified I won't call her bluff, but will, in fact, let her walk out that door to become C-Bomb's groupie this week. Now that I'm smelling her delicious fear, I'm positive she doesn't want to do it. Doesn't want to be his, whether she had his poster on her wall as a teen or not. *If* she did, at all. God only knows what this demon would be willing to say to fuck with me. But, no, either way, this girl is dying to be *mine* and nobody else's. I'm sure of that now, thanks to the way her heart is visibly crashing behind her incredible tits.

Should I let her twist in the wind a little bit longer? Let her panic boil over? Yes, I should. Unfortunately, though, I'm too worried I'm wrong about her not wanting to fuck Caleb to risk it. Taking a long, deep breath, I drape my elbow over the back of the armchair, matching her posture. "I'd strongly urge you against pursuing a 'Penny Lane' strategy with C-Bomb. You might get one scintillating article out of it, but you'd likely torpedo your career. It's a marathon, not a sprint, baby."

"Would an article like that torpedo C-Bomb's career?"

"Of course not. An article like that would add to his mythos as a sex god."

"That's sexist."

"Maybe so, but that's life. He's the drummer in a rock band, and you're a brand-new baby journalist who needs to be taken seriously."

She presses her lips together, conceding I've just scored a point in our game of table tennis. A point she's awfully glad I've scored, if I had to guess.

"Plus," I say, "is doing an end-run around me, the CEO of River Records, really in your best interests, long-term? Even if the other night had never happened between us, even if I had no designs on you for myself—which, to be clear, I do—do you honestly think it would be wise for a summer intern at *Rock 'n' Roll* to defy a direct order from the founder and CEO of the very label she's been assigned to write about? Tread carefully, Miss Ricci. Think about the full consequences of your actions. No more flying off the handle."

Her chest heaves. And her nostrils flare. And I know she's pretty much crapping her pants at her predicament—and the corner she's painted herself into. "All right," she says. "I'll put my Penny Lane piece on the back burner... *for now.* But only if you offer me something that's as good or better. Because there's no way in hell I'm going to call my boss, who isn't *you,* by the way, and say the assignment *she* gave me is off because, oh, gosh, the CEO of the label I'm assigned to write about wants to fuck me, and therefore doesn't want me to be alone with Caleb Baumgarten.'"

And... she's back. Guns blazing. Damn. I must admit, I'm proud of her for pulling that rabbit out of her hat at the eleventh hour. Deeply impressed, as a matter of fact. "That one-on-one interview of Dean?" I say. "It'll be a full-day thing at his compound in Malibu. In fact, if I ask him to, I'm sure he'll give you a tour of the place. Maybe even cook for you. Stir-fry, probably. That's his specialty. Plus, Dean loves to surf, so we could do a photo shoot of him on the beach with his board, and he could talk about how much inspiration he derives from the ocean. Surely, a clever girl like you could parlay all that into something deep and meaningful that CeeCee would run in *Dig a Little Deeper.*"

Georgina sniffs like my offer is shit. But it's got to be tempting to her. Dean is a global rock star. A revered musician, songwriter, and heartthrob. And yet, he's not a famewhore, which means he doesn't do a whole lot of in-depth interviews—preferring, instead, to do a thousand and one superficial ones—only whatever publicity is minimally necessary to sell the band's latest release.

"You're not concerned I'm going to have sex with Dean if I spend the day with him at his compound in Malibu and eat his stir-fry and watch him surf?" she asks, her brow arched wickedly. "He's not too shabby to look at, if you haven't noticed."

"I'm not worried."

It's the truth. Dean's not a threat to me. For one thing, he's a good guy. Not an asshole, like Caleb. And if there's one thing I know about my Georgie girl, she likes herself a good asshole. Also, Dean's not on the prowl. He's been in love with the same girl his entire life—the girl he wrote his band's debut single about years ago—Shaynee—and she's recently re-entered his life. And, finally, even if Dean's heart weren't otherwise engaged, he's the kind of guy who'd respect an off-limits designation by the head of his fucking label, unlike Caleb. In short, the guy's not a threat to me, any way you slice it.

Georgie doesn't flinch. "Well, that's a lovely offer, Mr. Rivers. Thank you. I'll take you up on all that. But it's still not enough to keep me from calling CeeCee and ratting you out. If you want me to call my *boss* and tell her I'm not going to fulfill the assignment she gave me, because Reed Rivers wants to fuck me so badly, then you're going to have to give me more." She gazes at her manicured fingernails, as if she's suddenly bored as hell. "Frankly, Reed, if Dean is all you've got to 'bribe' me with, I'd just as soon throw my press pass into the trash and become C-Bomb's personal Penny Lane. I'm sure CeeCee wouldn't mind me starting my job one week later than originally discussed, to get a meaty article like that."

Exasperated, I lean back into my armchair. "All right, Meryl Streep. Cut the crap and just tell me your price. You've obviously got one in mind. Put your cards on the table and tell me what it is."

"Whatever do you mean?"

I lean forward sharply. "You know exactly what I mean."

"Ooooh. As in, 'Everybody's got a price'?"

"What's yours?"

A smug smile spreads across her gorgeous face. She leans forward, giving me a lovely view of her tits in her low-cut blouse. "My price? Well, Mr. Rivers, it's *you*, of course."

"Well, damn. That's an easy one, baby. Lock the door and bend over the back of that couch, and I'll give you every fucking inch of me."

Again, she doesn't flinch. "No, I want to *write* about you, Mr. Rivers. I want you to give me an in-depth interview, suitable for *Dig a Little Deeper*."

I burst out laughing. "No."

"*Yes*."

"Didn't CeeCee tell you? She's already asked me to do that a hundred times, and... " I trail off.

CeeCee.

Of course.

Why didn't I figure this out sooner?

Georgina is CeeCee's unwitting pawn. CeeCee sent Georgina to Caleb, as her top priority, because she knew it would turn out exactly this way. CeeCee knew I'd get jealous and possessive and nix the idea... and that Georgina, clever girl that she is, would be smart enough to exploit my reaction and use it as leverage. Fucking CeeCee. I have to admit, the woman is brilliant, even though I'm pissed at her right now.

"An interview with me is already part of the deal for the special issue."

"Yes, I know, but I want you to give me something more in-depth—a wide-ranging interview that breaks new ground with you. Something covering both business and personal topics. Something on-brand for *Dig a Little Deeper.*"

I scoff. "No."

Georgina rises and strides toward the door. "All right, then. Goodbye. I'm going on tour with Caleb, as his Penny Lane."

She's bluffing and I know it. There's no way in hell she could have felt what I did when we kissed and still want to fuck Caleb, or anyone else who isn't me, any more than I want to fuck anyone who isn't Georgina.

When I say nothing behind her, Georgina calls out over her shoulder, still striding toward the door, "I'll see you in a week, Mr. Rivers—that is, if Caleb hasn't fucked me to death by then."

Oh, Jesus Christ. I'm ninety-nine percent sure she's bluffing, but on the off-chance she's not... "Georgina!" I shout, much more loudly than I mean to say it. "*Stop.*"

She freezes at the door, her back to me.

I'm quaking. Flooded with adrenaline. Arousal. Jealousy. "I'll negotiate with you about the scope of my interview," I choke out. "But only if you don't walk through that door right now. If you walk out of here, you'll get absolutely nothing from me but a fluffy, bullshit interview that's barely suitable for *Rock 'n' Roll.*"

She turns around slowly, and the minute I see her face, I know every cell in her body is sighing with relief. Obviously, she had no desire to walk out that door. Indeed, she was counting on me stopping her, exactly the way I did.

I'm expecting her to head back to the couch, but she doesn't. Instead, she takes a slow step toward the armchair—toward *me*—her hazel eyes on fire. "Here's an idea, Reed: How about you let me shadow you this whole week to see what your life is really like? If I can't tour with RCR, then I'll 'tour' your life. I'll observe you and interview you along the way, about whatever topics you're comfortable talking about." She's closing in on me, making my dick come alive with each step.

Without consciously telling my body to do it, I rise from my chair, my body drawn to Georgina's like steel to a magnet.

"You won't have to answer any question you don't want to," she purrs. "So, really, what's the risk to you in saying yes to this idea? I'll shadow you for a week, and then I'll write my piece, whatever it turns out to be, and take my chances as to whether CeeCee decides to publish it in *Rock 'n' Roll* or the other magazine. Either way, you're required to do an interview. Let's spend a week together and see what comes of it."

Georgina has reached me now. We're standing mere inches apart, our body heat mingling. I swallow hard. I have no desire to let anyone see how the sausage gets made in my world. On the other hand, though, Georgina is right. I can pick and choose the questions I answer. Control the narrative. And it certainly wouldn't be the worst thing in the world to have this woman tied to my hip for an entire week. By day two, at the latest, she'll surely be naked and spread eagle in my bed.

She looks up at me, her full lips wet and her hazel eyes sparkling. "I won't take no for an answer," she whispers. And for the first time in my life, the phrase doesn't make me want to scream "No, motherfucker!" It makes me want to whisper, "Yes, baby, yes. Whatever you want."

I extend my hand. "You've got yourself a deal. Well played."

Her face lights up with surprise. Joy. *Relief.* And, suddenly, she looks every bit the twenty-one-year-old newbie she is. "Seriously?"

I nod. "One week. You'll be my shadow. I'll be your interview subject. And we'll see what happens."

"Will you still get me a hotel room, so I won't have to commute from the Valley?"

I force myself not to smirk. If I get my way, Georgina won't be sleeping in a hotel room this coming week. She'll be lying next to me, naked, every fucking night. "Of course," I say, extending my hand again. "Do we have a deal, Madame Reporter? Can we finally agree to put this Penny Lane bullshit to rest?"

She stares at my extended hand without moving. And I can practically see the gears in her head turning. I lower my hand. Oh, for the love of fuck. *What now?*

She looks up and grimaces at me. "Sorry, I just realized there are two more things I have to ask for—"

"Georgie!"

"Before shaking on it."

"No."

"Two teeny-tiny things."

"No."

"And, then, I swear, we'll absolutely be able to put this deal"—she smiles adorably—"to bed."

Chapter 24
Georgina

R eed lowers his hand and plops onto the couch, looking highly annoyed with me. "Whatever else you're going to ask for, the answer is no. I'm done negotiating with you."

"But you haven't even heard what I—"

"It doesn't matter. Amateur hour at the poker table is over. Scoop up your chips and walk away while you still can, Miss Ricci. The deal we just negotiated is my final and best offer."

I sit in the armchair across from Reed, my heart racing. "Just listen to me."

He puts up his palm. "Tread carefully. Whatever you're going to ask for, make sure it's worth risking what I've already put on the table. Maybe, in response to whatever new things you demand, I'll demand something new, too. Something you don't want to give. Or, maybe, I'll start taking things *off* the table. Stuff you thought was already settled and done. Do you really want to risk that?"

Shit, he's intimidating. Confident and sexy and formidable beyond belief when he flips into his "music mogul businessman mode." But it can't be helped. Just before I shook Reed's hand, I realized I'd never forgive myself if I didn't get two more items sneaked into our deal. "Yeah, both things are worth it to me," I say confidently, even though I'm shitting a brick.

Reed scoffs, leans back on the couch, and motions like he's giving me the floor. "Let's hear it, then."

My stomach somersaults. I take a deep breath. "Okay. First off, about that party tonight—"

"*No.*"

"*Listen.* I want *you* to take me there, Reed, in my official capacity as a writer for *Rock 'n' Roll,* solely to—"

"No."

"Listen! I want to observe how RCR lets off steam after a show. And I also want to break the ice with them for my future *group* interview of them and my solo stir-fried interview with Dean. Reed, come on. Readers would want to read about a star-struck fan getting to party with rock royalty, and you know it. It'd be a huge missed opportunity for me to not go. In fact, I'd even say it'd be a gross dereliction of duty if I *didn't* go, which *might* get me fired."

Reed's dark eyes are unmistakably *unimpressed.* Well, damn. I thought I was being pretty persuasive. But, okay, I'll try another tack.

"Reed, like I said, I had a RCR poster on my wall as a teenager. 'Shaynee' is one of my all-time favorite songs. My fourteen-year-old self would never forgive me if I missed this party. I know you party with rock stars all the freaking time. For you, it's as ho-hum as eating a bag of chips. But it'd be a once in a lifetime experience for me, and, selfishly, I *reallllly* don't want to miss out."

Reed exhales like he's painfully bored. "Are you finished? Have you now exhausted all your less than persuasive arguments regarding item number one?"

"Only if you're going to say yes. If not, I've got another ten minutes all cued up."

He can't resist smiling at that. "Okay, so, if I'm understanding this correctly, Little Miss Georgina Ricci is dying to party like a rock star, huh?"

"She is. But for professional purposes only."

Reed can't help chuckling. "All right, sweetheart. I tell you what I'll do. Actually, I was already contemplating doing this exact thing. I talked to Owen about this yesterday, as a matter of fact. A week from today, next Saturday, I'm going to throw a party at my house—a fucking awesome rager, celebrating the special issue. And you and the other writers assigned to the project will be my guests of honor."

I leap up from the armchair and squeal and jump around with glee.

"Every artist on my label who isn't on tour will be there, so they can meet you and the other writers. It'll be a chance to break the ice and brainstorm. And, of course, you'll have the chance to party like a rock star, exactly as your fourteen-year-old self would have wanted."

I can't stop jumping around, laughing and hooting like a maniac, and Reed can't stop laughing at my silly display.

"Are you drunk?" he asks, laughing.

"I feel like it!" I say, giggling. "Thank you!"

"I take it we've reached agreement on your item number one?"

"Yes!" I shriek, doing a stupid little twirl. "Thank you so much!" When I come out of my spin, I have the impulse to hug him, *again,* but jerk back sharply at the last second, same as last time, as if I'm saving myself from a burning pyre. For the love of fuck. I can't hug this sexy man. If I do, then I'll kiss him. And if I kiss him, then I'll fuck him—maybe even in this room. And if I fuck him, especially here, then I'll lose all my bargaining power on item number two—which, frankly, is the far more critical item for me to secure.

I stand stock still in front of Reed, my chest heaving from my little dance, to discover Reed's cheeks blazing red and a massive erection bulging behind his pants. Oh, God, that hard-on is making my mouth water. I want to rub myself against it... and then pull it out of its bondage and ride it like a pony.

But, no.

I have to remain strong.

I have to get through my second demand without folding like a beach chair, or I'll never again have a shred of bargaining power with him. That much is clear.

Out of nowhere, Reed clears his throat and abruptly strides across the room. "You want a beer, party animal?"

I plop onto the couch, my heart racing. "Sure. Thanks."

Reed's gorgeous body is poetry in motion as he glides across the room. His ass divine. He grabs two bottles from a mini-fridge, pops their caps, crosses the room again, and hands a cold bottle to me. To my surprise, he sits next to me on the couch this time, foregoing his armchair. And, as he settles into his seat, I can't help noticing his boner is gone.

Reed takes a long swig of his beer. "Just a heads up about the party," he says. "Red Card Riot won't be there. They'll still be on tour. But that's for the best, because I want to introduce you to 22 Goats, and they won't come if RCR is invited."

I tilt my head. "The 22 Goats guys don't like the RCR guys?"

"Wow. You don't follow celebrity gossip at all, do you?"

I shake my head.

"C-Bomb and Dax had a pretty big falling out. The other guys don't give a shit about any of it, but nobody in either band is willing to cross the picket line. They've gotta support their guy. It's how it works in a band."

I open my mouth to say, "I bet my stepsister, Alessandra, would know all about the beef between C-Bomb and Dax. She follows celebrity gossip religiously, especially when it comes to musicians." But, instantly, I shut my mouth, realizing I now need to add "item one-and-a-half" to my list of demands. Crap! I can't attend Reed's rock-star-studded party without bringing Alessandra as my plus-one. And not even as a ploy to get her signed to River Records. No, that's what my second item will address. But because Alessandra, the girl who attends a renowned music school and is obsessed with music and musicians, and always has been, deserves more than anyone I know—and far more than me—to party like a rock star with Reed's roster of world-renowned rock stars. "Hey, uh, before we leave item one for good... " I begin.

"Oh, for the love of fuck!" Reed blurts, throwing up his hand. "What now, Georgie?"

I press my palms together in prayer. "Can I *please* bring someone to the party, as my plus-one? I mean, not as a date or anything. Someone—"

"Your stepsister?"

I nod sheepishly. "Not as a ploy to get her signed. She could stand in a corner and people-watch the entire night and never talk to you or anyone, and it would still be the best night of her life."

Reed swigs his beer, rolling his eyes. "She's a student at Berklee in Boston, you said?"

I nod effusively. "She just finished her second year last week. She's in LA for my graduation. Please, *please,* don't make that poor girl sit at her mother's house watching Netflix on a Saturday night while I'm at your house, partying like a rock star with 22 Goats."

Reed pauses. And then shocks me by saying, "Okay."

"Okay?"

"She can come."

Without meaning to do it, I leap onto his lap and straddle him. "Thank you!" I throw my arms around his neck and kiss his cheek. "Thank you, thank you, thank you!"

Instantly, Reed's erection hardens deliciously underneath me. "*On one condition,*" he adds.

I freeze on top of him, panting... and wait.

"Neither of you will try, even once, to get me to listen to her music that night."

"I promise."

"I'll be off the clock, Georgie."

I nod enthusiastically. "I promise I'll control myself. And, don't worry, Alessandra would never try to sell herself

Lauren Rowe

to you, anyway. Not that night, or ever. She's painfully shy and the worst at tooting her own horn. Plus, I'm sure she'll be too star-struck that night to say two words to anyone but me."

Reed tilts his head back and exhales, annoyed with me. "Georgina, come on!"

"*What?*"

He lifts his head, still keeping his arms firmly planted at his sides. "Why would you tell me that about her? Think, sweetheart." He puts a palm on my cheek. "Use that amazing bean of yours, baby. At some point, you *are* going to try to sell me on her music, right? In fact, I'm guessing that's your item number two. And do you really think telling me she's 'painfully shy' is a good selling point for an artist you're trying to sell to me?"

My stomach drops. "Fuck." I slide off him and slink back to the armchair and curl my legs underneath me.

"Well, shit. I didn't mean to make you run away," he mutters.

"She comes alive onstage, Reed. She's only painfully shy whenever she doesn't have a guitar in her hands." I bite my lip. My nipples are rock hard and my clit throbbing from our unexpected contact a moment ago, and I'm finding it hard to think straight. "Actually, yeah, can we just move on to item number two now?"

"Sure. Did I guess right?"

I nod. "Did you happen to check out Alessandra's Instagram page, like I asked you to do the other night?"

Reed chuckles. "You didn't 'ask' me to check it out. You shrieked her handle at me, right before speeding off in an Uber, both middle fingers raised in the air. And, no, I didn't check her out. In fact, I forgot her handle two seconds after you screamed it at me. Call me crazy, but I don't tend to do favors for shrieking people who've passionately told me to fuck off and die." He subtly adjusts his hard dick in his pants, and the gesture zings me straight in the clit. *I want that.*

206

"Fair enough," I say. "But that's water under the bridge now, right? Now that we've both agreed we could have handled things better that night. Surely, now that we're friends again, you're feeling inclined to listen to her music now... to put our deal to *bed*?"

"Nope. I have zero desire whatsoever to listen to your stepsister's music. Especially not now that I know she's 'painfully shy.'" He shifts in his seat again, relieving his hard-on, and shoots me a smile that doesn't reach his eyes. "So, are you ready to shake on a deal now or what?"

"*No*. Reed, it would take mere minutes for you to listen to Alessandra's demo, and I'd be eternally grateful to you."

"You should already be eternally grateful to me. I'm letting you follow me around for a week, throwing a party for you, and letting you bring Alessandra as your guest to the party. Actually, you know what? Thanks to your lack of eternal gratitude for everything I've already agreed to give you, I'm thinking maybe I should start taking things *off* the table. Maybe we don't need a full week for our interview. Maybe we can get it done in five days. Yeah, that sounds good. Five days, it is."

"Reed, no."

"Hey, I warned you. Think hard before throwing in new, last-minute demands that might fuck up what you've already secured. You're about to learn an important, but basic, lesson in negotiations the hard way, Georgie. *Know when to cash in your chips and run like hell*. Actually, the more I think about it, I think we can do our interview in *four* days."

Fuck! I feel like I'm going to pass out. But I can't fail Alessandra now. If one of us is going to swerve, it's going to have to be Reed. "The three songs on her demo are about three minutes each," I sputter. "I'm asking for less than ten minutes of your time."

"We're down to three days now. Tick tock. Cash in your chips, baby."

I grit my teeth. "River Records would be lucky to sign Alessandra. Don't agree to listen to her demo for *me*. Listen for *you*."

"Two days." Reed shakes his head and taps his watch. "You're blowing it, Georgie."

What the fuck is wrong with him? One minute he's charming and sweet, and throwing me a party, and grinding his dick into me as I'm kissing his cheeks like crazy, and the next he's—

Oh.

I suddenly get it.

I know what Reed is doing. What he wants.

He wants me to bribe him.

To figure out his price.

Everyone's got one, right?

Well, then, I guess I'll just have to pull out the big guns, and figure out Reed's.

Chapter 25
Reed

Georgina's entire demeanor shifts on a dime. Right before my eyes, she transforms from a panicked possum in a trap to a sultry *femme fatale*. She gets up from the armchair and straddles me on the couch, batting her eyelashes at me. She rubs her nose against mine. "All right, Mr. Rivers. Let's cut the crap. I'm ready to close this deal, sweetheart. You said everyone's got a price." She runs her finger across my cheekbone. "So, what's yours, honey?"

Hallelujah. "I don't have a price, Georgina."

She shoots me a snarky look, fully aware I'm throwing her own naïve words back at her. "How about this?" she purrs, her fingertip making its way to my ear. "You agree to listen to Alessandra's full demo—all three songs—and, in exchange, I'll give you a lap dance that lasts the same amount of time as you give Alessandra's music."

My cock is hard underneath her, my breathing shallow. But I force myself to keep a straight face and my hands on the couch cushions. I've come this far. I'm not going to cave until I get exactly what I want. I say, "Wasn't it you who told me to fuck off and die when I suggested this very sort of bargained-for exchange was your agenda from the start? And now, here you are, mere days later, surrendering your righteousness like an expired passport?"

She grinds herself into my steely bulge. "I've learned a few things about negotiation tactics since then. I've got a very good teacher."

209

Oh, fuck. I'm on the bitter cusp of throwing my arms around her and kissing the hell out of her sultry mouth. Which I absolutely can't let myself do, or else I'll surely cave and give the girl anything she wants.

"Lemme guess," I say, my chest heaving. "Has a certain hothead spent the entire past week regretting the way she flew off the handle the other night?"

"Maybe I've realized bribing you with something I want to give, anyway, would, in fact, be a win-win."

My cock is straining. Aching. More likely than not, dripping with my need for her. "Would this lap dance be performed in the nude?" I ask.

She looks shocked. "*No.* I'd perform it in this. Right here and now." She motions to her outfit—a short skirt and low-cut blouse. "After shaking on the deal, I'd give you a little show... " She nuzzles her nose against mine. "And then you'd listen to all three songs, right here and now, as well."

I shake my head. "For a *clothed* lap dance, I'd be willing to listen to *ten seconds* of the *first* song. But that's it." My tone is businesslike. Flat. Like we're two farmers negotiating the price of grain. But, inside, I'm a hurricane of pent-up sexual arousal. On the bitter edge of folding like bad poker hand.

"Ten seconds?" Georgina purrs, skimming her lips across my cheekbone. "That's an insult to lap dancers everywhere, Mr. Rivers. Or, at least, to this one."

I can barely breathe. "You saw me listen to Bryce's sister's music. Ten seconds is all I need—to assess a demo, to be clear. I need much, much longer than ten seconds to do something else."

She giggles. "Come on. A sexy lap dance ought to get me *at least* a full-song listen."

"Okay, time out for a second." I put both palms on her gorgeous face and her pouty lips part in surprise, begging me to kiss them. "Think, sweetheart. Why would you even want me to listen to a full song, even if you could get me to agree to that?"

She furrows her brow like she doesn't follow my logic.

"Imagine you get me to agree to a full-song listen. And then, imagine that, ten seconds in, I have the same reaction I had to Bryce's sister. Hard pass. If I know I'm not impressed after ten seconds of a song, would it really benefit Alessandra if I'm then obligated by the terms of our agreement to keep listening to the same fucking song that doesn't impress me for another three minutes?"

A light bulb goes off on Georgie's beautiful face. She gets it. "Ah."

I drop my hands and grip the couch cushion again, forcing myself not to interact. Not to grab her ass. Not to give in. Not to cave. "See?" I say. "You gotta think a couple moves ahead. Be careful what you ask for in a negotiation, because you don't want to screw yourself by unexpectedly getting exactly what you've asked for."

She slides her arms around my neck and my cock jolts. "But what if the song *isn't* a hard pass? What if you think an artist has potential? You wouldn't turn off a song after ten seconds in that case, would you?"

"No," I concede, barely able to breathe through my arousal.

"You'd continue listening to the entire song, right?"

I take a deep breath and collect myself. "Not necessarily. Sometimes, if I like someone's voice and style, but hate the song, I'll listen for about thirty seconds and then flip to another song, hoping the next one will click better for me."

She processes that. "Okay, so... " She skims her lips across my jawline. "How about I give you one *clothed* lap dance in exchange for you listening to the first thirty seconds of each of her three songs."

Georgina looks proud of herself for that suggestion. Hopeful. Fucking adorable. But I shake my head. "You gotta sweeten the pot more than that, Ricci. A clothed lap dance ain't nearly enough for three songs. What else you got to offer me?"

She twists her mouth. "Two lap dances? A clothed one... plus, a second one in my bra and undies."

Now, we're cooking with gas. "You're getting warmer." I can't help touching my palms to her back, and she shudders exquisitely at my touch. I say, "Would you do both lap dances here, in this room?"

Her breathing is labored. She's begun grinding herself into my hard-on, causing my cock to throb and strain. "No," she says. She skims her lips across my jawline. "I think we should do the bra-and-undies lap dance in my hotel room. Don't you? And I'll throw in a striptease, down to my bra and undies, too." She's panting now. Grinding herself enthusiastically into my cock. Getting herself off. And I'm loving it.

"We'll do the striptease and lap dances at my house tonight," I say, skimming my lips across her soft cheek. Inhaling her scent. Craving her like I've never craved anyone in my life. "Not your hotel."

She nods effusively, her body grinding against mine, her lips a breath away from mine, begging to be kissed.

"*And,*" I whisper, on the cusp of pressing my lips against hers, "you'll stay at my house this week, while you're 'shadowing' and 'interviewing' me. In one of my guestrooms, if you want. Or in my room, with me. Either way, you'll stay at my house this week."

She lets out the softest of moans as she continues rubbing herself against me. "I suppose it *would* be easier to follow you around, if I'm staying at your house."

I'm trembling with arousal. I whisper, "Say yes, Georgina."

"*Yes.*"

I skim my lips against hers, desperate to breach her

borders and claim her. "We've got a deal?" I say softly. "What do you say, baby?"

She grinds herself hard against me. Grabs either side of my head and grips my hair. She's breathing hard. Dry humping me like her life depends on it. "What do I say?" she murmurs breathlessly, her eyes half-mast. "I say 'Yes,' Mr. Rivers." She smiles. "Actually, no." Her eyes ignite. "I say, 'Yes... yes... *yesss.*'"

Chapter 26
Georgina

With a low growl, Reed smashes his lips into mine. And, I swear, I almost come as his tongue slides inside my mouth. In short order, we're passionately kissing, both of us on fire. I clutch at him feverishly as I kiss him, grind myself against his steely hard-on beneath me, desperate for him.

"Consider this my first lap dance," I gasp into Reed's hungry lips. And in reply, he slides his strong hands down my back, straight to my ass cheeks, and grips me *hard*. Like I'm a life preserver and he's a drowning man. Like I'm a drug and he's the junkie. All of it, making my body jolt and writhe on top of him with pleasure.

I thought I remembered what it felt like to kiss this scorching hot, formidable, sexy asshole of a man. But I was wrong. Before this moment, I rated kisses in my head as good, great, and fire. But, now, I'm being forced to recalibrate as I realize the top rating possible for any kiss, for the rest of my days, won't be fire any longer. Forevermore, it will always be: *Reed Rivers.*

I can't get enough. And, clearly, Reed feels the same way. As he kisses me, he touches me voraciously. My cheeks. Neck. Hair. Ass. And with every touch of his fingertips, palms, lips, and tongue, every grind of his hard-on against my throbbing center, his body confesses the truth: he was never, ever going to let me walk out that door to hook up with Caleb. No fucking way. My body is his, until this thing, whatever it is, has run its course. Exactly like he said.

As our kiss intensifies, Reed lifts my skirt, and I spread my thighs, giving him the access my body so forcefully craves.

I'm vaguely aware the crowd in the arena is roaring as RCR finishes playing a song. But then, the band launches into their next song—their huge smash hit, "Shaynee"—one of my all-time favorites—and I can't help gasping with added excitement.

"I'll take you to see the show another night," Reed growls hoarsely into my lips, apparently reading my body language. "You can pick the city, baby. I'll fly us wherever you want to go and we'll sit front-row center. But right now, you're staying right here. Right now, you're all mine, baby." With that, Reed's fingers breach the crotch of my cotton panties and slide deliciously inside me, making me moan. "You're so wet," he growls.

He begins stroking my aching clit with his slick fingers while simultaneously, with his other hand, lifting my shirt and pushing my bra off and away. When my breasts are freed from their entrapment... Reed leans back from kissing me to look at them. And what he sees, clearly, he likes a lot. With an animalistic growl, he leans in and devours me. Sucking. Licking. Reveling. Holy shit, he's freaking motorboating me! And all the while, he's continuing to finger-fuck me with zealous expertise.

A sound of pure pleasure lurches out of me. A sound no human has ever manufactured unless they're dying or coming hard. My eyes roll back into my head... my insides clench and warp in slow motion... my clit zings and aches with a tingling, zinging warning... and then... *Bam!* A rocket of bliss envelops me as my center and everything connected to it, including the deepest muscles of my core, begin clenching so hard, I'm seeing little white stars.

"Oh, God, Georgina," Reed says, his breathing labored. "You're so fucking incredible." He tilts his lap sharply, sliding me off him, sending me onto my back on the couch. His eyes on fire and his body quaking with lust, Reed yanks up my skirt, and begins peeling off my moistened undies. "I've wanted to taste you since the minute I saw you."

"Reed," I breathe, feeling swept away by my arousal.

"You want me to eat your pussy, baby?"

I nod profusely.

"Say it."

"Yes." I lick my lips, coming down from my orgasm. "Yes, yes, yes."

He tosses my undies behind him on the couch. "I'm going to eat your pussy better than it's ever been done, beautiful girl. You're going to come harder than you've ever come in your life."

I gasp, simply because, um, I just did. Does he mean he's going to make me come even harder than *that*? Holy shit.

With obvious enthusiasm, Reed grabs my thighs with his large hands, spreads me out before him, grabs my ass from underneath, and pulls my center into his waiting lips... where he then proceeds to eat and lick and nibble and suck and finger the living fuck out of me until I'm moaning like I've never moaned before.

It's a shocking whirlwind of pleasure. An overwhelming avalanche of stimulation. Nobody's ever performed oral on me quite like this before. With so much... expertise. Confidence. Enthusiasm. *Passion*. The pleasure, right out of the gate, is so extreme, so full-throttle, I'm not sure I can withstand it without losing control of myself, either physically, emotionally, or both...

I clutch at the couch cushion underneath me, feeling like I'm grasping at the last shreds of my self-control. Maybe even my sanity. And soon, the way Reed's licking and stroking, hitting all the right magical spots, over and over again, methodically, without reprieve or apology, is too much to bear.

"Oh, God," I choke out, coming like a wrecking ball.

Wave after wave of glorious pleasure slams into me. It's making my eyes roll back into my head and my entire body seize. Just like Reed promised, it's the best orgasm of my life. Holy crap.

Finally, when the pleasure subsides, I wipe at my face and realize, to my surprise, I'm more than dripping with sweat. *I'm crying.* Tears of euphoria. It's a first for me—bursting into tears at the moment of release. But, then, I've never in my life had an orgasm this powerful. This all-encompassing. This heavenly.

When Reed raises his head from my thighs, he looks drugged. Feral. His lips and chin are slathered in me. His dark eyes are burning with desire. At the sight of my sweaty, tear-stained face, a wicked smile spreads across his stunning face. "Good?"

"The best, ever." I wipe at my face. "Don't freak out I'm crying. I just lost control—"

"Georgie, it's totally natural. Believe me, it's the best feeling in the world for me to take you that high."

His understanding makes me relax and smile. "Oh, God, Reed, that was so fucking *good.* I've never felt anything that good in my life."

Reed runs his warm palms over my bare thighs, hiking my dress up even higher onto my belly. "There's a lot more where that came from, beautiful," he says. "When I fuck you, I'm gonna make you—"

Without warning, the door to the small room swings open, and a production assistant pokes her head in, making me jump like a cat on a hot tin roof and scramble feverishly to cover my bare breasts and thighs and crotch and—

"Oh my God!" the P.A. blurts, saying the words along with me. She turns her face away. "Caleb sent me to look for someone."

"I think you found her," Reed says calmly. "Wait in the hallway for a minute. I want to talk to you."

"No, I'll go and—"

"*Wait in the hallway for my signal*," Reed commands sharply. "I want to talk to you."

"Reed, no!" I whisper-shout. "Let her go. Please. Oh my fucking God."

For some reason, Reed's not freaking out like I am. In fact, he's as cool as a cucumber. He calmly hands me my underpants, and when I snatch them from him, shooting him daggers, he says, "She's already seen me camped between your naked legs with your pussy and tits hanging out. Pretending she didn't see won't make her un-see it."

"Fuck."

I get my undies on and pull myself together, trembling with embarrassment. Holy fuck! This is worst-case scenario for me. Getting caught with the big boss between my naked thighs with my wahoo and tits hanging out on the first day of my employment. I can't believe I let this happen. It's nothing short of a disaster for me.

At Reed's signal, the young woman sheepishly re-enters the room, her head pointedly turned away. "Sorry to bother you, Mr. Rivers."

"And Miss Ricci," Reed supplies, making me throw my palms over my face. "You can look at me. We're just sitting here, having a conversation."

She slowly turns her head to look at Reed. "Uh. Caleb sent me to find Miss Ricci, and get her phone number for... him. He said Miss Ricci is, uh, coming to tonight's after-party in his suite... as his... personal guest, and that I should, um, arrange a hotel room for Miss Ricci... at the Ritz... on the same floor as... Caleb's room?"

To my shock, Reed flashes me a beaming smile. A triumphant, elated one, like he's the heavy weight champ who just scored a knockout punch in a title fight. And, all of a sudden, I get why Reed called this poor girl back into the room and supplied my name and orchestrated this horrifically humiliating moment. *So he could spike the ball in the middle of Caleb's end zone.*

"Change of plans," Reed says coolly to the PA. "Tell Caleb I've decided Miss Ricci isn't attending his party tonight, after all. Not as his personal guest, or in her official capacity. And she's not joining the tour this coming week, either, or interviewing him individually. You can tell him I've nixed all of it for business reasons. But assure him, please, that Miss Ricci is working on a fresh, new angle for a full-band interview, which we'll lock down next month after they're back. This week, however, Miss Ricci will be working on a piece about me, as required by my arrangement with the head of *Rock 'n' Roll.*"

The poor woman looks like she's going to keel over from stress. "Um," she says. "Yeah, I really don't think I can say all that to Caleb."

"Sure, you can," Reed says. "Tell him everything I just said, using my exact words. However, do not, under any circumstances, talk to anyone, including Caleb, about what you think you might have seen in this room when you first walked in. Whatever you thought you saw happening between Miss Ricci and me, you were mistaken. We were simply having a conversation."

The girl grimaces with discomfort. "I'd never say a word about anything. Because I didn't see anything besides two people talking. But, um, Mr. Rivers, would it be okay if *you* tell Caleb everything you said?" Her face is pleading. Vulnerable. Panicked. "Please? Because I don't think I can remember it all. And, also because... " She takes a deep, shuddering breath. "I think Caleb is going to get really pissed off when he hears all of that, and I really don't—"

"What's your name?"

"Amy O'Brien."

"Nice to meet you, Amy," Reed says. "You're traveling with the tour?"

She nods. "I'm assigned as Caleb's PA. Whatever he needs... " She looks at me and blushes. "I mean, as his gofer. You know. Not for... "

She clamps her lips shut, and again, I bury my face in my palms. Holy crap, this is a nightmare.

"Let me explain something to you, Amy," Reed says, his tone brimming with condescension. "I'm the reason you get a paycheck every two weeks. Not Caleb. I'm actually Caleb's boss. Did you know that?"

"Yes, sir."

"Which means, if you think about it, I'm *your* boss. And *that* means when I tell you to do something, then you're gonna fucking do it, unless, of course, there are extenuating circumstances. For instance, if you're feeling scared for your physical safety, you need only tell me that and all bets will be off. Are you feeling scared for your physical safety to go tell Caleb what I said, Amy?"

"Uh... " She sighs and shakes her head, obviously wishing she were feeling scared for her physical safety right about now.

"Is that a no?" Reed asks.

"That's a no." She grimaces, again telegraphing her fervent wish to feel physically threatened rather than have to traipse back to Caleb and tell him what Reed said.

"Do you have any *religious* objections to telling Caleb everything I just said?" Reed asks.

"No, sir."

"Is there any reason whatsoever you can't tell Caleb what I just said, other than the fact that you hate confrontation and conflict and maybe don't want to watch him have a tantrum?"

"Well, also, I can't really remember what you said. My brain is kind of freaking out right now, to be honest, Mr. Rivers."

"I understand. Listen carefully, Amy. I'll repeat it all for you." Slowly, Reed repeats everything he said earlier, and the poor girl nods and holds back tears the whole time. "Repeat it back to me, Amy O'Brien."

She does. Not well, but she manages.

"Good. And that's all you're going to say. If Caleb asks *why* Miss Ricci isn't going to the party, or *why* I've decided the tour and individual interview aren't happening, you'll say he can talk to me about it, if he wants clarification."

"Yes, sir."

"Amy, do you remember signing an NDA when you accepted this job?"

"Yes, sir."

"Do you understand what an NDA is?"

"It's a non-disclosure agreement."

"That's right. It means if you tell anyone about the private things you witness while on tour, you could not only get fired, but also sued for the money set forth in the liquidation clause of the contract. You understand that, right?"

She turns green. "Yes, sir. I won't say a word about anything to anyone, but what you told me to say."

"Good. Because if I hear so much as one word of gossip about Miss Ricci and me, I'll blame you. And I won't go easy on you, Amy. I'll not only fire you, but also sic my lawyer on you to get the full extent of our legal remedies."

Amy nods. She's physically trembling.

"You can go now, Amy. Good talk."

"Yes, sir. Thank you. Sorry."

And off she goes, looking like she's dragging herself to her own execution.

When she's gone, Reed turns to me, looking triumphant. Turned on. And ready to finish what we started before that poor, poor girl interrupted us.

But we're most definitely not on the same page. I feel sick. Panicky. Disgusted at what Reed just now put that poor girl through, even though I'm also selfishly grateful to him for protecting our secret with such relentlessness. But most of all,

I feel angry with myself for putting myself in a position where it was so easy for me to get caught with my tits hanging out and my panties off and my thighs spread for Reed... on the first freaking night of my job! If I was going to fuck the big boss, why'd I do it *here*, where anyone could stumble upon us? Why didn't I at least lock the freaking door? When word gets out I'm fucking Reed, which it will, who's going to respect me? Absolutely nobody, that's who.

"Now, where were we?" Reed mutters, reaching for me like the past few minutes of torture didn't happen.

But he's delusional if he thinks I'm going to fuck him now. In this room. Or at all. In a flash, I feel gripped by the instinct to flee and never look back. My heart exploding, I stumble off the couch, muttering curses under my breath when I bang my knee, and then sprint, like a bug-eyed bat out of hell, straight out the door.

Chapter 27
Reed

I chase Georgina down the hallway and grab her arm, but she rips herself from my grasp. "I can't do this."

"Do *what*?"

She whirls around, her eyes panicked. "*Fuck the big boss.*"

I hear footsteps nearby. People talking and laughing. So, I pull Georgina through a nearby door marked "Janitorial." And suddenly, we're standing mere inches apart in a large closet. I pull a cord to turn on a bulb, and then back Georgina into a shelf with my arms on either side of her. "I'm not your boss. We've already established that."

"You think that PA who saw you eating my pussy knows that?" she whispers frantically, looking near-hysterical. "Right now, that girl thinks I fucked you to get my job!" She rubs her forehead. "Oh, God. Everyone is going to think that same thing, Reed—the same thing everyone always thinks about me—that I get whatever jobs or opportunities, not based on merit or hard work, but thanks to nothing but my tits and ass—because some asshole in charge wants to fuck me!"

My stomach drops. *Shit.* "Okay, calm down," I say soothingly. "Nobody is going to find out anything, because that PA isn't going to say a word. You saw how I put the fear of God into her. Do you think I get off on bullying little PAs like that? No, of course, not. I did that for you. Because I knew you'd freak out, exactly like this."

"It's really important to me that everyone knows I got this job because CeeCee believes in me, Reed. Because she thinks I'm a good writer. And not because Reed Rivers wants to fuck me!"

Fuck, fuck, fuck. "Of course, sweetheart," I say soothingly. "All anyone has to do is talk to you for half a second to realize you're smart as hell and a total badass and absolutely deserve to be here."

"Oh, God." She palms her forehead. "*Caleb.* Once he finds out you've nixed the party and tour, he'll assume we're fucking. What else could he possibly conclude? And then he'll tell the rest of the RCR guys about us, and then my interview with the band, and with Dean individually, will be awkward and stilted and embarrassing, and everything I've dreamed about achieving in my life will be shot to hell—"

"Okay, stop. You're spiraling, Ricci. Pull your shit together." I put my palm on her cheek. "Nobody will ever know I've gotten into your cute little cotton panties. Will they *assume* that's what I *want* to do? Yes. But they would have assumed that, anyway, whether that PA walked in on us or not. Because, news flash, Georgie, I'm *me*—a guy who likes sex with beautiful women. And, news flash, baby, you're not only beautiful but sexy as fuck, too. So, *of course*, people are going to think there's a strong chance I want to fuck your brains out. But so does every other man who sees you, Georgie, not just me. It'd be weird if I *didn't* want to fuck you."

Georgie looks moderately appeased by that logic.

"Frankly, if guys on my roster, especially Caleb, think I'm aiming to fuck you, then that's fantastic. In fact, that's precisely what I want them to think."

"What? *Why?*"

My cock feels like it's going to explode from the excitement of Georgina's two incredible orgasms and the closeness of her heaving body in this cramped space. I take a deep breath. "If they think I'm hot for you, then they'll stay the fuck away. The guys on my roster know not to cross me. They've seen what happens when they do. I've got them well trained."

"What does that mean?"

"It means I've made it clear in the past I don't play nice when someone on my roster fucks a woman I'm already fucking or have set my sights on fucking."

Her eyebrows rise. "How have you made it clear? What happened?"

"It doesn't matter. All that matters is them knowing I want to fuck you, whether I've been successful in doing that or not. That's enough to make you off-limits to them."

I scowl. "I'm not your property, Reed. You can't call dibs on me like the front seat of a Chevy. I'm a professional journalist. Here to do a job and do it well. If I happen to be fucking you on the side, then that has nothing to do with my job. The two things are completely separate."

Holy shit. She's so fucking sexy when she's angry, I can't contain myself. I press myself into her so she can feel how hard she makes me. How badly I want to get inside her. "Of course, you're here to do a job. That's indisputable. And, of course, you're going to do your job well. Now, tell your brain to shut the fuck up, would you? You're overthinking this. *Nothing's changed.* The PA will say nothing but what I told her to say. Our deal is still in full force and effect—we're gonna have a fun week together at my house, during which you're gonna try to use sex as a weapon to pull more out of me for my interview than I ever thought possible, and I'm gonna let you think it's working like gangbusters so I can keep fucking you and eating your sweet pussy all week long. It'll be a great time had by all." I skim my nose along her jawline while pressing my cock into her center, and she rubs herself against my hard-on in reply. "Come on, baby. Use me for a good time. Use me to try to get yourself a job with *Dig a Little Deeper.* Use me to make all your dreams come true." I press myself even harder into her and bite her earlobe. "Use me however you want, Georgie, just as long as you let me use your body this entire week, starting right now. Baby, I've never been so turned on by anyone in my life, I swear to God, and I don't think I can survive the night if I don't get inside you right fucking now."

A little moan of arousal escapes her throat as she continues riding my straining bulge—until, finally, she throws her arms around me, turns her head, and smashes her mouth against mine.

Instantly, the second my lips meet Georgie's, a dam breaks inside me. A tsunami of arousal slams into me. Panting, I frantically unzip my pants as Georgina furiously pulls down her undies, whimpering with arousal as she does.

"I'm on the pill," she gasps out. It's a comment that only makes me realize I hadn't even thought about protection—which is so unlike me, so utterly out of character, I don't even know who I am right now. What spell has this sexy girl cast on me?

She pulls my hard cock out of my briefs, its head already dripping with the evidence of my blossoming addiction to her. Breathing hard, I grab her ass, pick her up roughly, slam her into a shelf, and impale her, thrusting hard into her until I'm balls-deep and growling with relief. Oh, God, she's perfect. Wet. Tight. Warm. *Bliss.* Just this fast, I'm losing my fucking mind.

Georgina moans my name as I growl hers and begin thrusting like an animal against the shelf. As I get into a groove, she digs her fingernails into my shoulders, making me jerk and moan. She bites my neck and begs me not to stop, making me feel like I'm going to pass out.

Her excitement is obviously mounting as I plow into her, over and over again. I'm spiraling. On the brink of exploding.

"Yes," she growls with each powerful thrust. "*Yes, yes, yes.*"

I'm delirious. On the cusp of complete ecstasy. But I hang on, not wanting to release before her. Thankfully, just when I think I can't hang on a second longer, just when I think I might not be able to stay *conscious* a second longer,

Georgie comes, *hard*, throwing her head back into the shelf behind her and stiffening exquisitely in my arms as her muscles ripple and clench around my cock. Oh, for the love of all things holy. If there's a more sublime sensation in human existence, than the sensation of Georgina Ricci coming hard around my cock, I can't fathom it. It's a pleasure so intense, so all-consuming and addicting, I can't help coming, too. Which I do, so fucking hard, I'm momentarily paralyzed by the ecstasy shooting through my body, all of it culminating in flashes of blinding white and yellow light.

As I come down from my incredible orgasm, my heart is crashing seismically. My back is soaked in sweat. I place Georgina's feet on the ground, and she immediately tilts her glorious face up to mine for a kiss. Of course, I oblige her, devouring her mouth while raking my hands over her cheeks, neck, and hair. I can't get enough of this woman. This siren. She's my new drug. An addiction I couldn't possibly resist, even if my life depended on it.

When our mouths disengage, Georgina sighs happily. "That was fucking incredible."

I take a deep, shuddering breath, trying to calm my racing heart. "When you came, that was as close to God as I've ever gotten in this lifetime. Holy shit, Georgie. That was fucking insane."

"I've never had an orgasm during intercourse before. It felt incredible."

I run my thumb over her plump lower lip. "Sweetheart, this is only the beginning. This week, oh my fucking God. I'm gonna show you what your body can do—things you didn't even realize were possible."

She bites her lip. "We're gonna have fun this week, aren't we?"

"Oh, Little Miss Georgina Ricci, you have no fucking idea."

After another deep kiss, we pull our disheveled clothes together, smooth out our frayed hair, and quickly agree to slip out of the closet separately, just in case—with Georgie leaving first.

"I'll meet you in Greenroom B in five," I say.

"See you there," she says flirtatiously. But as she grabs the doorknob, she turns to me, her beaming, wide smile snatching the air out of my lungs. "Thank you for everything, Reed."

My heart stops as paranoia flashes through me. Does she somehow know I'm the source of the cancer charity's grant? Has she figured me out? "I haven't done anything," I say lamely.

"Of course, you have. You've agreed to throw a party and let Alessandra come. You've agreed to listen to Alessandra's demo later tonight at your house. And you've agreed to keep an open mind about your interview—to let me at least *try* to get something suitable for *Dig a Little Deeper* out of you. I'd say you've already done a whole helluva lot."

Sighing with relief, I return her smile. "I only said that last thing so I could get into your pants. Don't get too excited."

Her smile widens. "Careful what you agree to in a negotiation, Mr. Rivers. After a full week of getting into my pants, I predict you're going to open up to me more than you ever thought possible."

I chuckle. "That's what I want you to think, sweetheart. Don't hold your breath on that."

"We'll see."

"I'm not one of the fraternity boys you're used to wrapping around your little finger for tips. As gorgeous as you are, I'm sure I'll be able to withstand your attempts to 'unpeel my onion' just fine."

"Challenge accepted." With that, she turns the knob, and off she goes... leaving me alone in a janitorial closet, with a body that's alive and pulsing in a way it's never been before, and a mind that's racing. How the hell am I going to spend an entire week fucking that gorgeous woman without breaking down and giving her every last thing her devious little heart desires?

TO BE CONTINUED…

Reed and Georgina's scorching-hot love story continues with the second book of The Reed Rivers Trilogy: BEAUTIFUL LIAR. You don't want to miss what happens next in this fiery, sexy romance!

Want to read about Reed's best friend, Josh Faraday? Read Josh and Kat's explosive and sexy trilogy, beginning with INFATUATION.

If you want to read about sexy Dax Morgan of 22 Goats, read ROCKSTAR.

Be sure to sign up to receive news of releases or giveaways, by email or text:

NEWSLETTER – http://eepurl.com/ba_ODX

WEBSITE - http://www.laurenrowebooks.com/

US ONLY: Text the word "ROWE" to 474747

UK ONLY: Text the word "LAURENROWE" to 82228

Find Lauren on social media by clicking the links below!

FACEBOOK – https://www.facebook.com/laurenrowebooks/

INSTAGRAM   –
https://www.instagram.com/laurenrowebooks/

TWITTER - http://www.twitter.com/laurenrowebooks

FACEBOOK GROUP –
https://www.facebook.com/groups/760337070730959/

BOOK+MAIN   -
https://bookandmainbites.com/laurenrowebooks

A brief list of books by Lauren Rowe is located at the front of this book. Further details below.

Books by Lauren Rowe

The Reed Rivers Trilogy

Reed Rivers has met his match in the most unlikely of women—aspiring journalist and spitfire, Georgina Ricci. She's much younger than the women Reed normally pursues, but he can't resist her fiery personality and drop-dead gorgeous looks. But in this game of cat and mouse, who's chasing whom? With each passing day of this wild ride, Reed's not so sure. The books of this trilogy are to be read in order:

1. *Bad Liar*
2. *Beautiful Liar*
3. *Beloved Liar*

The Club Trilogy

Romantic. Scorching hot. Suspenseful. Witty. The Club is your new addiction—a sexy and suspenseful thriller about two wealthy brothers and the sassy women who bring them to their knees... all while the foursome bands together to protect one of their own. *The Club Trilogy* is to be read in order, as follows:

1. *The Club: Obsession*
2. *The Club: Reclamation*
3. *The Club: Redemption*

The Club: Culmination

The fourth book for Jonas and Sarah is a full-length epilogue with incredible heart-stopping twists and turns and feels. Read *The Club: Culmination (A Full-Length Epilogue Novel)* after finishing *The Club Trilogy* or, if you prefer, after reading *The Josh and Kat Trilogy*.

The Josh and Kat Trilogy

It's a war of wills between stubborn and sexy Josh Faraday and Kat Morgan. A fight to the bed. Arrogant, wealthy playboy Josh is used to getting what he wants. *And what he wants is Kat Morgan.* The books are to be read in order:

- *Infatuation*
- *Revelation*
- *Consummation*

The Morgan Brothers

Read these **standalones** in any order about the brothers of Kat Morgan. Chronological reading order is below, but they are all complete stories. Note: you do *not* need to read any other books or series before jumping straight into reading about the Morgan boys.

- *Hero.* The story of heroic firefighter, **Colby Morgan**. When catastrophe strikes Colby Morgan, will physical therapist Lydia save him... or will he save her?

- *Captain.* The insta-love-to-enemies-to-lovers story of tattooed sex god, **Ryan Morgan**, and the woman he'd move heaven and earth to claim.

- *Ball Peen Hammer.* A steamy, hilarious, friends-to-lovers romantic comedy about cocky-as-hell male stripper, **Keane Morgan**, and the sassy, smart young woman who brings him to his knees during a road trip.

- *Mister Bodyguard.* The Morgans' beloved honorary brother, **Zander Shaw**, meets his match in the feisty pop star he's assigned to protect on tour.

- *ROCKSTAR.* When the youngest Morgan brother, **Dax Morgan,** meets a mysterious woman who rocks his world, he must decide if pursuing her is worth risking it all. Be sure to check out four of Dax's original songs from *ROCKSTAR*, written and produced by Lauren, along with full music videos for the songs, on her website (www.laurenrowebooks.com) under the tap MUSIC FROM ROCKSTAR.

Misadventures

Lauren's *Misadventures* titles are page-turning, steamy, swoony standalones, to be read in any order.

- *Misadventures on the Night Shift*—A hotel night shift clerk encounters her teenage fantasy: rock star Lucas Ford. And combustion ensues.

- *Misadventures of a College Girl*—A spunky, virginal theater major meets a cocky football player at her first college party... and absolutely nothing goes according to plan for either of them.

- *Misadventures on the Rebound*—A spunky woman on the rebound meets a hot, mysterious stranger in a bar

Lauren Rowe

on her way to her five-year high school reunion in Las Vegas and what follows is a misadventure neither of them ever imagined.

Standalone Psychological Thriller/Dark Comedy

Countdown to Killing Kurtis—A young woman with big dreams and skeletons in her closet decides her porno-king husband must die in exactly a year. This is *not* a traditional romance, but it *will* most definitely keep you turning the pages and saying "WTF?"

All books by Lauren Rowe are available in ebook, paperback, and audiobook formats. Be sure to sign up for Lauren's newsletter to find out about upcoming releases!

Author Biography

USA Today and internationally bestselling author Lauren Rowe lives in San Diego, California, where, in addition to writing books, she performs with her dance/party band at events all over Southern California, writes songs, takes embarrassing snapshots of her ever- patient Boston terrier, Buster, spends time with her family, and narrates audiobooks. Much to Lauren's thrill, her books have been translated all over the world in multiple languages and hit multiple domestic and international bestseller lists. To find out about Lauren's upcoming releases and giveaways, sign up for Lauren's emails at www.LaurenRoweBooks.com. Lauren loves to hear from readers! Send Lauren an email from her website, say hi on Twitter, Instagram, or Facebook.